PRAISE FOR MARK OF THE LEAST

"A wildly original and magical twist on the Robin Hood narrative, Kendra Merritt's *By Wingéd Chair* is packed to the spokes with complex characters, wry humor, and flawless world building."

-Darby Karchut, best-selling author of DEL TORO MOON and FINN FINNEGAN

"With a wonderfully crafted blend of swords and sorcery and characters based on Robin Hood, Merritt tops this story off with the lead character readers need nowadays; a strong, independent, powerful female mage who also happens to be in a wheelchair. Readers will be constantly turning pages to see what happens next to this fun group of characters through the twists and turns they won't see coming."

-The Booklife Prize

"Kendra Merritt's prose is fresh, with one-line descriptions that crack like a whip, and she doesn't miss an opportunity to surprise the reader. From the first line to the last, I was enchanted with *By Wingéd Chair*."

-Todd Fahnestock, best-selling author of FAIRMIST and THE WISHING WORLD

ALSO BY KM MERRITT

<u>Mishap's Heroes Series</u>

Magic and Misrule

Death and Devotion

Trust and Treason

Illusions and Infamy

Sparks and Scales

Wastelands and War

<u>Mark of the Least Series</u>

By Wingéd Chair

Skin Deep

Catching Cinders

Shroud for a Bride

A Matter of Blood

Unmasked

After the Darkness

The King in the Tower Collection

<u>Daybreak Colony Duology</u>

Surviving Daybreak

Daybreak Sentinel

<u>Eldros Legacy</u>

The Pain Bearer

The Truth Stealer

The Death Bringer

MISHAP'S HEROES

3
Trust *and* Treason

KM MERRITT

BLUE FYRE PRESS

For Andrew, Kyle, Mary, Clark, Tim, and Greg (and Amy). Thanks for the adventure.

ONE

Vola eyed the murky water passing under the edge of their flat-bottomed barge, one dark eyebrow arched in distrust.

"You don't have to glare at it like it's going to leap up and eat you. It's just water," a voice to her left said.

Vola glanced at the speaker, a tall slim woman with dark skin, light brown eyes, and a wide halo of black curls around her head. Rilla. Princess Allellarilla to be exact. Guardian of the Dagger Throne.

And their new employer. She'd named them Mishap's Heroes—though Vola secretly hoped the name wouldn't stick—before she'd loaded them onto a ship headed for the capitol. It only took them three days to sail up the coastline this time, and then they'd traded the sleek ocean-faring vessel for this poor excuse for a boat in order to crawl up the meandering river. With wide logs rough-cut into a flat-ish surface and lashed together with some dubiously frayed rope, the barge looked a little like a child's school project.

"Believe me," Vola told the princess, stepping back from the edge. "We've been in some places where the water tries to kill you any way it can."

Rilla raised her eyebrows. "Sounds like a good story."

"Be fair, Vola," another voice said, this one more melodious, like it was born to accompany a lute. "There were plenty of other things that wanted to kill us as well. Each more dangerous than the water. I don't see any carnivorous flora, here."

A blonde half-elf, built short and round, and strikingly beautiful, gestured at the broad plain where, true enough, there were no giant pink flowers waiting to eat them. Only waves and waves of green and gold grasses that marched all the way to the water's edge.

"And look," Lillie said with an indulgent smile. "Talon is enjoying it well enough."

Vola turned to find their ranger lounging on the edge of the barge, trousers rolled up to her knees so she could paddle her feet in the river. The rest of her was swathed in a dark cloak, her hood pulled low over her face.

The party as a whole had only seen Talon's face a couple of times. But even with her hood up, this was the most relaxed the ranger had seemed since they'd left the wilds for more civilized lands, and Vola wasn't about to ruin it by complaining about the murky water. Even Gruff, the big black wolf lazed beside her, panting like a lap dog.

"Sorry I didn't pick a more scenic route," Rilla said, but not like she was actually sorry. "I didn't want to announce our entry into the city."

Vola cocked her head. "Is this level of secrecy necessary? Or does it just come with being the spymaster for an entire kingdom?"

Rilla blinked. "I don't understand the question."

Lillie stood on tiptoe to whisper to Vola. "I think it's normal for the Guardian of the Dagger Throne."

Rilla turned back toward the front of the barge. "We'll be there soon. You can almost see the tiers."

"Good," a voice groaned at their feet. "I'm done with boats. No more boats. I beg you."

Vola bit her lip to hide her smile and tried to appear sympathetic as she peered down at Sorrel, a slim halfling who lay on the rough boards of the barge. Green tinged her normally nut-brown skin and errant curls of her reddish brown hair stuck to her sweaty forehead.

Lillie gasped. "I see it. Sorrel, if you stand up, you can see the city. We're almost there."

"No, thank you," Sorrel groaned. "I trust you not to give me false hope. And down here I'm closer to the edge in case I barf again."

Ahead of them, the mid-afternoon air shimmered, glints and flashes of light obscuring anything beyond.

"It's the city's defenses," Rilla said. "Half the Shield Throne's time and energy is spent just keeping the wards up and running. It's a good precaution, but it does interfere something awful with the air currents sometimes."

A yelp sounded followed by a large splash behind the barge.

Vola turned to catch the poleman gaping at the frothing water inches from his pole. She sighed.

A scaly green head topped with a filmy crest, surfaced about half a barge-length back and snorted. Water plumed from its nostrils and its yellow eyes narrowed before the head turned and started industriously down the river the way they'd come.

Vola sighed again, gustily, and glanced at her party members.

"Don't look at me," Lillie said. "I did it last time. I had to use a complicated spell for it, too."

Vola cocked her head at Talon.

"I'm only half-dressed," the ranger said. Gruff didn't even raise his head.

"Wouldn't it be better to jump in a river half-dressed?" Vola said. "Then your boots wouldn't get wet."

"Nice try," Talon said, and Vola could almost hear the smirk in her voice. "But it's your turn."

"Sorrel?" Vola asked desperately.

"Nnnuueergh."

"Fine." Vola pulled her scabbard and the round, scarred shield from her back. "Hold these," she told Rilla.

The princess took them with a frown as Vola bent for her boots. "I'm not sure why you keep going after it. No one likes it, it's ill-tempered as hell, and it clearly doesn't want to stick around."

"Believe me, I'd let it go if I wasn't worried it would destroy the local ecology." She tossed her boots aside.

"If we let it go, it'll just turn into some river monster we have to fight later on when it starts eating the locals," Talon said as Vola grimaced and slid off the back of the barge. The water only came up to her chest.

"I suppose as one of the leaders of those locals, I should insist you retrieve it," Rilla said. "I'm not sure I want to, but I should."

"Aren't you some kind of animal handler?" Vola called to Talon as she waded after the swamp beast. It wasn't really trying to get away. Just trying to piss her off.

If Talon responded, it was lost in all the splashing as Vola chased the swamp beast down. She reached for the muddy lead rope still hanging from its neck, but it waited until her fingers closed around it, then pulled the slippery line out of her hand. She scowled and tried again before the foul beast could swim away. The thing looked like a cross between a donkey and a crocodile with the personality of a serial killer thrown in.

The swamp beast's eyes narrowed, and suddenly it yanked, diving underwater and dragging Vola with it. Its webbed claws pulled in strong strokes, hauling Vola through the water.

She planted her feet in the muck at the bottom of the river and pushed up so her head broke the surface. She sucked in a noisy breath and surged back against its pull. Luckily, she outweighed the thing—just barely—and she managed to yank it off balance. By the time it had floundered upright in the water, she'd hauled it back to the barge.

Vola climbed up beside the pole-man, who eyed her warily.

When they'd boarded back at the harbor, he hadn't been particularly happy to have a half-orc on board. But then he'd seen the swamp monster and decided Vola was the least of his problems.

Vola tugged on the swamp monster's lead, trying to get it to jump back onto the barge. It tugged back, treading water easily. It hissed at her.

"Fine," she snapped at it. "If you won't come up, you can just swim behind us the rest of the way." It wasn't like that would be a hardship. The thing was born for murky water ways.

She tied the lead off and left the swamp monster swimming behind. There was a chance it might try towing them backwards, but she didn't think it was *that* strong.

By the time she straightened, her party lined the front edge of the barge. Even Sorrel had finally stood and stared with wide eyes.

Vola raised her gaze and caught her first glimpse of Glenhaven, capitol of Southglen. A solid wall of cliffs rose out of the plains ahead of them; tier upon tier of the city had been carved out of the white rock. A waterfall cascaded down over the terraces, which were wreathed in colorful strips of greenery and flowers. It was all white marble and glistening water, with little sparks and flashes of magic framing the image.

"Holy Cleavah," Vola said, coming up behind Lillie and Talon. They didn't even mention that she still dripped all over. They just kept staring. "That has to be at least five times the size of Brisbene."

"Six, if you count the farms around the base," Lillie said, then she flushed and shuffled her feet. "I mean, I think. I must have read that somewhere."

"I don't think this place even has an Underground. It's too clean," Sorrel said. "The whole thing is an Aboveground if you ask me."

That only seemed to hold truer as they approached. As the waterfall reached the lower levels of the city, it branched into five different streams meeting the rivers that meandered across the plains. Even their murky waterway cleared into a sparkling green by the time it wandered up to the dock set into the base of the cliff.

By the time they docked, the swamp beast seemed a little more cooperative, and it climbed up onto dry land with only a half-hearted snort.

Vola had assumed the lower levels of the city would be slums or lower income housing for those lesser races who had immigrated. Southglen's population was predominantly human, with elves coming in at a close second. But the area around the docks boasted large open-air markets surrounded by colonnades, marble banks, and restaurants with patio seating on the terraces. Humans and elves passed them in the streets, yes, but so did gnomes with their creased faces, dwarves in clusters with bristling beards, and a couple tall figures with bright scales and elongated snouts. They wore flowing trousers and skirts but looked tough enough to put Vola on her ass if they wanted to.

Rilla led them down streets paved in smooth flagstones to wide shallow stairs that marked the passages between each tier. And as far as Vola could tell, each tier was as prosperous as the next. She felt a little grubby in her travel-stained tunic and breeches, which were now soaked through with muddy water, and she wished she'd stopped to put on her shiny new breastplate instead of slinging the bag over the swamp beast's back.

Sorrel's face had regained its normal color, and she gazed

around with wide eyes. "Is it always this…shiny?" she asked Rilla.

Rilla surveyed the city, her lips pursed. "It is. I'm originally from Brisbene. You saw it there. Pretty normal. But Glenhaven is the home of the Fifteen Thrones. All the princesses live here, at least part of the time."

"Glenhaven profits from the direct oversight of its ruling body," Lillie said.

Rilla cocked her head. "Or meddling."

Vola craned her head back, but the lower tiers blocked the upper ones and only a sliver of the palace was visible far above them.

"Fifteen princesses seems like a lot," she said, well aware she was talking to one of them right now.

Rilla shrugged. "It's been that way for centuries now. The Thrones themselves choose the princesses. No one's really sure how it works; we've got wizards researching the process. But the magic seeks someone with the intelligence and skill to manage one small piece of Southglen's government. The Thrones imbue each princess with a specific type of magic dealing with their personal demesne."

Lillie nodded like this was old news. Vola tried to look like she knew what Rilla was talking about. Sorrel and Talon exchanged a glance, but it was Sorrel who finally said, "I have no idea what a demesne is."

Rilla blinked. "Think territory. Each Throne rules a certain territory of the government. There's war, justice, religion, health. Things like that."

Rilla, they knew, was the kingdom's spymaster. The Dagger Throne kept Southglen safe from treason and espionage and sabotage.

"How do you know who's in charge?" Talon said. "A wolf pack works in concert, but there is always an alpha."

Rilla shook her head. "We rule our territories equally. And if there is something that requires everyone's input, then we come together for a vote."

"You really don't have any kind of ranks?" Sorrel said. She wended her way down the street backwards so she could face them as she talked.

"No," Rilla said, then looked thoughtful. "Well, not officially. There are definitely princesses who are more popular with the public. The people love to throw parades for Justice and War." Rilla winced. "But the princesses of Public Works and Sewage Management don't get out much."

Vola hid a snort behind her hand.

Lillie did a double take as a tall, slender elf in a green dress sauntered by. Vola was close enough to notice the way she went stiff, and her limp grew more pronounced.

Vola's brow drew down, and she shifted closer to Lillie. The half-elf had admitted weeks ago that she'd originally fled from Southglen. And then, just in Brisbene, a man named Virvalim had sent a bounty hunter to collect her. He was nothing but a dark ashy smear on a wall now, but Vola still watched the crowd around them warily. She had no idea what to watch for except the name, and that was only helpful if the creep walked around with a label, but no one would be snatching Lillie if Vola had anything to say about it.

Out of habit, she checked Sorrel and Talon, too. Sorrel was Sorrel, moving through the crowd with a grin and enthusiastic grace. The quarterstaff slung over her back didn't seem to weigh her down at all, even if it was half of a god's weapon.

Talon stalked beside the big black wolf named Gruff as usual. While it was hard to tell her moods under the swathing hood and cloak, Vola thought the ranger moved with a stronger stride and looser shoulders. While in Brisbene, she'd been wound tight and miserable. Either Talon was getting used to cities or she was more relaxed after her decision to live as herself.

About halfway up the city, Rilla stopped outside a large inn. It hadn't been built with marble like a lot of the buildings so far, but the mahogany siding shone clean and smooth and the door didn't squeal when Rilla pushed it open.

The princess exchanged a nod with the proprietor standing behind the bar on the ground floor. He jerked his chin in response and raised two fingers with a questioning look.

Rilla nodded and led them to the stairs. Vola was impressed. Every place they'd been to so far demanded your cash upfront.

"I don't want you to think I'm stiffing you," Rilla said, heading down the second-floor corridor. "Your fee includes room and board. But I don't want to lead you right up to the palace. I'd rather keep you a secret for a little while longer."

Vola nodded. "So the whole city doesn't know you have us on retainer. Makes sense."

Rilla pushed a door open. "This is where I stay when I'm not at the palace. I've got a single next door. You can live here while you hunt down Myron Vidal's boss."

Sorrel bounded into the room. "Whoa, there's a bed for each of us. And look. A second entrance. In case you want to skip out on the bill?" The halfling trotted over to a door that led out to some stairs. The inn had been built around a central courtyard, complete with decorative benches on one side and straw-stuffed practice dummies on the other. "This place is swank."

"Lots better than The Snuggly Bunny," Talon said, stepping into the room. Gruff slunk toward the fireplace and didn't hesitate to curl up on the hearth.

"The Snuggly Bunny?" Rilla said with a raised eyebrow.

Vola winced. "Long story."

There was a polite tap on the doorframe, and Vola turned to see a boy of about nine shifting from foot to foot on the threshold.

He was clean and neat, and Vola guessed he was the innkeeper's son.

"I've been watching for your return, Mistress Rilla," he said breathlessly. "You have messages."

"Thanks, Pellor." She took the stack of envelopes from the boy. "Have my bag dumped in my room, and there's a…mount tied up outside the inn. See that it's stabled. Away from the horses. It bites."

The boy ran off as Rilla sorted through the messages quickly and efficiently, honing in on one toward the back. She broke the seal and read, her eyes scanning the text.

Vola hated to pry, but they were working for the princess, now. "News?"

Rilla's lips twitched in an aborted grin. "Your first assignment, seems like."

Vola straightened, and the others perked up from their places around the room.

"I've been tracking the man who hired Myron." Rilla waved the paper at them. "The same person who was buying people from your Lord Arthorel. Even though slavery is against the law. One of my operatives has been trackng his correspondence. Seems Myron was right. He's up to something in Glenhaven."

Vola cracked her knuckles, remembering Henri's face behind bars. It made her growl. "What would you like us to do?"

"Find his messenger. Track down who he's contacting and what he wants. See if you can learn where he is. I'm going to work the problem from the other end."

"What do you mean?"

"Like finding the middle of the rope by following both ends. I'm going to pull on ropes and see which one yelps."

TWO

ONE OF THE other perks of working for a spymaster was that they already had a place to start. Rilla gave them the name and location of her operative who had already done the legwork and could tell them exactly where and when they could find their target.

"So, what?" Sorrel asked the next morning as they trotted down a pristine street lined with little shops displaying dishes and knick-knacks. "We're going to follow our bad guy's messenger, and then what? Beat the information out of him?"

"We're not going to beat anything out of anyone," Lillie cried. And then she bit her lip and looked at Vola. "Are we?"

"No," Vola said. "Of course not."

"We could poke it out of him," Talon said, drawing a dagger that glinted in the sunlight.

Vola reached out and pushed her arm down. "We're not poking it out of him, either. We're just going to follow him. As long as he doesn't know we're there, he'll lead us straight to whoever our bad guy is corresponding with."

"You know, with an employer who's a princess, I kind of

expected quests that were a little more, I don't know, grand," Sorrel said.

"She did hire us to do the more nitty-gritty and dangerous tasks that her rank wouldn't allow her," Lillie said. "She was pretty clear."

"So, we'll start with the nitty-gritty and work our way to dangerous," Vola said. "At least we're getting paid this time." She tapped her belt purse. She'd hidden the hefty fee they'd received from rescuing Rilla under the mattress in their new hotel room, but Rilla herself had provided them with a signing bonus which Vola had kept as spending money.

Sorrel perked up. "That is something special." None of them were used to actually having money. They'd met because they'd each needed a job, and their first employer turned out to be the bad guy. Which made it hard to collect your pay. Not to mention he'd been dead broke, so looting hadn't been very lucrative either.

They passed through a market with stalls set between the large pillars of a decorative colonnade. The babble of a hundred different conversations made Vola's head spin, but Talon slowed just beside a vendor hawking colorful scarves and patchwork skirts. Lillie eyed a stall full of old books.

"Later," Vola told them and dragged on their arms.

"Let them look, paladin," the next vendor down said, catching Vola's attention. "I have fine weapons. Shields. Greaves. You look like you could use some greaves. And your boots are only leather. How can you fight battles in leather?"

Vola sighed. "Pretty well, actually. Thank you for your concern."

The vendor, a middle-aged man with a scraggly beard, followed them behind his stall as they started to move on. An apprentice worked beside him, the bright ring of his hammer against metal emphasizing the vendor's words. "Paladin, I can engrave any piece of armor with the symbol of your god. No extra charge. Who do you serve?"

His eyes traveled down to Vola's chest, where her emblem hung from a tarnished chain. A curved fish knife.

His eyes narrowed, then he leaned his elbows among his stock and smirked. "Cleavah," he said. "You serve Cleavah? Goddess of vengeful housewives?" He snickered. "What do you do? Go after cheating husbands?"

Vola planted her boots in the street and crossed her arms over her gleaming breastplate. She was glad she'd worn it. It was so much more fun to swell with indignation when the metal caught the sunlight just right.

"Why?" she said. "Are you worried?"

The man's eyes traveled up all six-and-a-half feet of her and widened until she could see the whites by the time they got to her unsmiling face.

Vola tilted her head. "You know She's also called the mother of sharp implements. Would you like me to show you some?"

The man made a "hurgh" noise and slid out of sight behind his stall.

Lillie craned her neck to see. "He fainted. Do you suppose we should call for help?"

Vola sighed. "Come on. It's getting late. We don't want to miss the messenger."

Rilla's operative worked at the Southtown docks, which managed to be even fancier than where they'd docked yesterday. They checked in with him at his desk beside the wharf and then found a bench in front of the customs building to loiter on. The building itself had been carved into the white marble wall of the terrace so the facade didn't provide much of a place to hide, but there were enough people bustling back and forth that Vola was fairly confident they could blend into the crowd.

A half-orc nearly seven feet tall in plate armor couldn't

normally say that, but then she'd never been in a city that was quite so diverse.

Vola kept her eye on the clerk, and less than an hour later, he met her gaze nonchalantly as he handed a packet of envelopes over to a gangly boy of about fourteen. His head tilted almost imperceptibly toward the boy.

Vola gave him a little nod in return and turned her shoulder so it wasn't as obvious that her eyes never left the messenger. She nudged Sorrel and Talon, and Lillie sat up.

"Show time," she said under her breath.

The messenger, easily distinguishable by his bright carrot-colored hair and spray of freckles, slipped out of the dock's holding area, and up the streets, moving like a fish upriver.

Vola and the others followed.

The boy moved through the city as if he'd been born walking the streets. Vola had a hard time keeping sight of him. He was tall for a human, but skinny, and wove his way through the crowds and ducked between buildings, using little passages between the tiers that Vola wouldn't even have noticed.

Lillie limped along, trying to keep up, and Vola was torn trying to keep the boy in sight and not outdistance Lillie. The wizard's face pulled, and Vola knew her leg pained her but she was trying not to complain.

Lillie caught one of the concerned looks Vola sent her and grimaced. "Go," she said. "I'll catch up. I know the city better than you."

Vola exchanged a glance with Sorrel, who nodded. "I'll stay with her. We'll watch each other's backs."

"Good, Talon with me. Can Gruff flank him and keep him in sight without alerting him to our presence?"

Talon just gave her a wordless snort. The black wolf slipped away through the crowd, and Vola and Talon kept on, following the boy between buildings.

He ducked between a bakery and a scribe's shop, and Vola sped to keep him in sight. She popped out the other end of the narrow alley and ran smack into a broad woman trailing six children.

"Shit—I mean, damn—I mean…bother." Too late. A little lightning bolt zapped the flagstones at Vola's feet, and the family jumped back with squeals of surprise.

"I'm so sorry," Vola said. "I have a goddess who doesn't like it when I swear." She pointed to the cloudless sky, blaming the lightning bolt on Cleavah.

The woman humphed and gathered her progeny around her to stalk off down the street.

Ahead, the boy had stopped in his tracks and stared back at them.

"Fudge buckets," Vola said. "Do you think he saw us?"

Talon's hood turned toward her, and Vola could imagine the grim look.

When Vola met the boy's eyes, he blinked, then took off running.

She sighed. "Yeah, I thought so. Run for it. Maybe we can still catch up."

They raced to follow the boy, but he was faster than a lumbering paladin in full armor. And he had a head start.

"Gruff says he's cut through a temple up ahead," Talon said.

They ducked around a man with a tray selling sausages and darted up the stairs to the next level, the scent of fried fat following them.

Talon pointed to the soaring facade of a house of worship with tall, deep alcoves for the effigies of the Greater Virtues outside.

"He's in there?" Vola said. "Is there another exit?"

"Gruff is checking the back now."

Vola put her shoulder to the bronze door, cast with images of the triumphs of the gods, and pushed.

The door creaked open easily enough, and Vola and Talon stepped through into an open, echoing chamber. A dome stretched across the space above them, painted with murals, and huge statues carved from the finest blue-veined marble lined the round room.

Vola's eyes narrowed as she stepped across the intricately patterned floor. There wasn't anywhere the boy could have gone. Unless he'd ducked through the little door in the back that was clearly meant for the priests' personal quarters.

"Now!" an unfamiliar voice called.

"Oh, of course," Vola said as figures boiled out from around the statues to attack. "It's an ambush."

Talon reached for her bow, but three small figures jumped her and pulled her down. Vola met one of the attackers with a lowered shoulder and bowled them out of the way before she drew her sword and shield. She charged the figures swarming Talon.

She bashed them aside and pulled Talon to her feet. The ranger drew the daggers from her belt and bared her teeth. Her hood had fallen back when she'd gone down.

Vola put her back to Talon's and surveyed the temple. They were surrounded by nearly twenty…children? Goddess, none of them could be over fifteen, all of them ragged and rough around the edges. Vola caught sight of the messenger with his bright head of hair hovering off to the right.

"Don't do this," she told the kids in a low, calm voice. "We're professionals. We don't want to kill you."

"Speak for yourself," Talon said and flipped her dagger around.

There was some shuffling and most of the kids glanced at a tall girl directly in front of Vola. The girl's eyes flicked over their weapons and armor before she finally snorted. "Come on. There's only two of them."

"Four actually," Lillie's voice said from the doorway.

"Five if you count the wolf." Sorrel unslung her staff from her back and spun it so it blurred.

The girl's eyes went wide, and she called, "Now!"

Vola shook her head as the girl launched herself at the paladin. "You ruined your element of surprise." She caught the girl's attack against her shield, a makeshift knife leaving a scar across the rough metal. She heaved and sent the leader of the urchins flying.

Sorrel leaped from the door, joining Talon in the fray, while Lillie whispered, light gathering around her hands.

A door banged in the back of the church and a priest stumbled into the main sanctuary. "What is going on here?"

"Don't worry, Father," Sorrel called. "We'll clean the blood off the floor later."

Lillie released her spell and a blanket of sparkling light settled over the children attacking them. It stuck to several of them, making them pause to shake their arms and brush at the shining threads. Lillie frowned and closed her fists, and the ones covered in light slumped to the floor, eyes closed in deep slumber. That left only five of the bigger kids.

Vola turned her sword in her hand and concentrated on blunt force rather than impaling anyone. She wasn't in the habit of spearing children, and as a protector of orphans, Cleavah would have plenty of objections as well.

With a yell and a surge, she caught the leader by surprise. She ducked, shifted, and launched the girl back, so she slid across the polished floor and fetched up against a pillar.

The girl climbed to her feet and glared at the messenger, who shifted from foot to foot off to the side.

"Come on, gang. He's not worth all this." She jerked her head and the other urchins wasted no time scattering.

The messenger moved to follow, but the ragged leader turned

on him. "Don't you dare. We're done protecting you. Don't bother coming back."

The gang flowed out of the temple, leaving behind their sleeping comrades and the messenger, whose gaze flicked frantically between Vola and the door.

"You'll never get through," Vola growled. Lillie blocked the way, her hands glowing.

But the boy tried anyway. He darted for the open air.

Vola leaped for the red-head, and they went down with a scuffle of elbows and feet. Vola would have thought her greater weight and her armor would have crushed him, but he got in a few solid blows around her breastplate and landed an elbow in her face that nearly broke her nose. She growled and yanked the leather message pouch from his waist even as he grasped the chain around her neck and pulled.

Her emblem came free with a snap, and she jerked back, her hand going to her throat. "Hey!"

The boy scrambled back, and his foot shot out to catch the hand that was propping her up so she fell on her face. He popped to his feet.

"Vola!" Lillie stepped forward, leaving just enough space for the boy to zip past her and out the door.

Lillie turned with a yell, shooting a firebolt at him. It splashed the cobbles at his heels as he disappeared around the corner.

Vola groaned and shook out her hand before standing. That would bruise by morning.

Sorrel and Talon stood over the remaining assailants who slept in the middle of the temple.

Lillie limped to Vola. "Are you all right?"

"I think my ego hurts more than anything," Vola said with a wince. "Did you hit him?"

"No," Lillie said with a blush. "But I wasn't really trying. I didn't want to hurt him."

"Thank you for not killing in my house of worship," the priest said, moving around the sanctuary to examine the losing party.

"No problem," Sorrel said, leaning on her staff. "They call us Mishap's Heroes, not Children Slayers."

"No one calls us Mishap's Heroes, either," Talon grumbled. "Just Rilla."

The priest rubbed his bald head, then did a double take, catching sight of Sorrel. He climbed to his feet. "You carry the weapon of a god."

Sorrel's eyes narrowed, and she lowered the staff. "How can you tell?" The staff had morphed into its incognito form. A plain quarterstaff with only a leather wrapped handle.

"It's aura. I can't...I can't tell who it belongs to exactly, but it is a weapon of divine strength." He frowned. "And you've been waving it around like a glorified stick."

Sorrel's mouth fell open, and she flushed. "Well, I-I mean...yeah."

"Young woman, divine power is so much more than a blunt instrument."

Talon moved back toward Lillie and Vola. She'd replaced her hood. "Did he get away?"

"Yeah," Vola said, touching her chest where Cleavah's symbol should have been hanging.

"And he took your emblem," Lillie said, biting her lip.

Vola forced herself to drop her hand. It was only a trick that made it feel like she was missing a protective weight around her shoulders. The emblem was just a symbol for Cleavah's favor. It was not the favor itself. It wasn't like Cleavah would forget her just because some urchin had stolen it in a fight.

"Yeah," she said again and took a deep breath. "But I got something even better off him." She raised the messenger's bag. "Should we see who our bad guy is consorting with?"

THREE

They rescued Sorrel from the opinionated priest who continued to harangue her about her use of a god's weapon by the simple expedient of dragging her outside into the sunlight.

Vola leafed through the papers that had been tucked in the messenger's satchel. The words swam under her gaze, reminding her that orc histories were usually oral for a reason. With some work, she sorted through the stack of bills, complaints, taxes. Until she got to the last one. She squeezed her eyes shut and tried again, but even concentrating, she still couldn't make the letters mean anything.

"Uh, is it just me or is there something wrong with this letter?" Sorrel said.

"It's not just you; it's in code," Talon said.

Vola blew out her breath. "Oh, thank the goddess," she mumbled.

The three of them looked at Lillie.

Lillie blinked. "What? Why are you all looking at me like that?"

Sorrel waved her hands vaguely over her head. "Well, I mean. Of the four of us…when presented with a code…"

"Can you break it?" Talon said.

"Oh, for heaven's sake, are we really that clich—"

"Yes, we are," Vola said and thrust the envelopes at Lillie.

Lillie rolled her eyes and stepped out from under the church's portico so the light fell across the envelope. "Hmm. That's…strange."

Vola followed her, being sure to stay out of her light. "What's strange? Was the code really that easy?"

"Not easy exactly," Lillie said. "Just…one I already knew. Nobles use it for a lot of their correspondence. It makes them feel special." Lillie flushed, and Vola deliberately didn't ask any further.

"What's special about this letter?" Sorrel said.

"That's just it. It's kind of boring for being encoded. It's just an address and a couple lines of text. 'Hi, how are you?' That sort of thing, except no thought logically follows another. It's…scrambled. Like the rest of the message is missing."

"Or it's in more code," Sorrel said, eyes wide as she stood on tiptoe to eye the paper in Lillie's hands. "A code within a code, how cool would that be?"

"Or it's a red herring to throw us off the scent," Talon said.

Sorrel made a face. "If they already know we're after them, then we're going to be in a lot of trouble with Rilla."

Vola tapped the paper. "Message or not, we should find this guy. If he's the one the slaver is contacting in the city, he's our next lead. And Rilla wanted to know who the slaver was contacting."

Lillie hesitated, then straightened her shoulders. "It doesn't list a name. Just an address. But I know the area. Several tiers up from us."

Lillie led the way. They could move at her pace now they

weren't following anyone, and Vola deliberately slowed them even more any time they came to more steps.

As they'd noticed before, the whole city was built with artistry in mind. But the tier Lillie finally led them to was a step above all the rest. One of the topmost tiers, it overflowed with pink and purple trumpet flowers which climbed the pillars alongside the sidewalk and cascaded over the edges of the terrace.

Vola glanced over the side to take in the view and froze. The plain stretched out, an endless sea of green and gold split with several gleaming waterways. A couple were clearly man-made or man-helped, and they crisscrossed the grasslands, cutting it into intricate patterns. The magic of the wards didn't seem to warp or distort anything from up here.

"Holy cow," she said under her breath.

Lillie shrugged at the view.

Talon shuddered. "Could we please not stand so close?" she said. She retreated to the other side of the street where the buildings were set into the cliff. Gruff went with her and pressed his large body against her legs.

"Pff, this isn't that high," Sorrel said and jumped up the stone railing. She trotted along the edge, hopping over the trailing flowers in her way.

Vola craned her neck. "I beg to differ. There're only two tiers above us. And then the palace."

"Yeah, but I grew up in mountains."

Talon choked as Sorrel hopped again and spread her arms out for balance.

"I'm with Talon on this one," Vola said, her fists clenching at her sides so she wouldn't lunge to pull the halfling from the ledge. "Could you get down now, please?"

"Oh, come on. I could do this drunk."

"Yes, we believe you. You don't have to prove it."

"It is perhaps unwise to draw attention to ourselves when we are tracking down our enemies," Lillie said.

Sorrel sighed gustily. "Fine. Jodin Battle-called said, 'give no advantage to the enemy you would give to yourself.'" She hopped down.

"How close is the enemy, anyway?" Vola asked.

"Just ahead," Lillie said. "I doubt anyone is home in the middle of the day like this. Nobles tend to visit with friends in the afternoon and head out to parties in the evening. But we should be cautious, anyway."

"Right, so no kicking down the door?"

Lillie's eyes widened. "What? No! Don't do that."

Vola leveled a glance at her.

Lillie flushed. "Oh, you were joking."

Talon remained as close to the building facades as she could get, and the rest of the party joined her.

"This is the one," Lillie whispered as they approached a walled villa pressed against the cliff above them. White walls barred them from the front courtyard and the actual residence behind and a wrought-iron gate kept the rabble out. "This is—"

Lillie choked as her eyes passed over a plaque placed in a prominent position just outside the gate.

"What?" Vola said, reaching for her weapons. "What is it?"

"It's...it's a death plaque. Commemorating a family member who recently passed away."

Vola chewed her lip, looking from Lillie to the plaque. She stepped up to the newish looking bronze plate and ran her finger along the words so they wouldn't swim around so much.

In loving memory of Otis Virvalim, brutally slain in the third month of this year. You will be remembered. You will be avenged.

"Virvalim." Vola chewed her lip. "Virvalim, wait. Wasn't that the name of the guy who hired the bounty hunter to kidnap you in Brisbene?"

"Yes," Lillie squeaked, and she spun on her heel. "We have to go."

"Wait," Vola said, but Lillie was already halfway to the stairs leading down to the next tier, moving faster than Vola had thought she could.

Vola called, "Wait, he's dead."

Lillie didn't slow.

Relief warred with concern as Vola exchanged a look with Talon and Sorrel. They hurried to catch up.

"Lillie, wait."

"No," the wizard said, sounding a little winded. "We have what we came for. I know who lives there, I know enough that we can take the next step. Any more than that can wait."

"Lillie, you're clearly spooked." A woman carrying a basket brimming with flowers stepped in Vola's way. Vola growled, took the woman by the shoulders, lifted her, and set her down a few feet away, looking dazed. "I need to know what we're running from if we're going to protect you."

Lillie stopped so abruptly Vola nearly ran into her back. She met Vola's eyes. "I know," she said quietly. "I know, and I will tell you. But not here."

Vola clamped her mouth shut on any more questions and followed quietly as Lillie led them back to the inn on the third tier. She waited all the way till the moment they entered their room and shut the door behind them.

"I don't understand," Vola said to the door. "Virvalim is dead. This is good news. You don't have to worry about him anymore."

Vola turned to find Lillie standing beside the window wringing her hands. The wizard's normally fair skin was mottled red and white.

"It's not Otis Virvalim we need to look out for," she said. "It's his father." She hugged herself. "Because I killed his son."

The bottom dropped out of Vola's stomach.

"Uh, you what?" Sorrel said.

Lillie closed her eyes. "I killed Otis Virvalim. He was a pig and an abuser and a rapist, and I executed him." She covered her face with her hands.

Vola took a couple of steps so she could sink onto the sofa by the fireplace. Sorrel stepped onto a cushion and perched on the arm.

"I thought I was supposed to be the scary one," Talon said, crossing her arms and leaning on the wall.

Lillie gave a wet chuckle and pulled her hands from her face.

"Okay," Vola said slowly. "Okay, let's take this from the beginning. It can't be that..." Well, she couldn't say bad. It was bad. It looked very, very bad. But they knew Lillie. She was the quiet one. The level-headed thinker.

But then Vola had also seen her lose her temper over injustice and a man who'd touched her without permission. It had taken them a long time to see it, but Lillie was as dangerous as any of them.

"How did you know him?" she asked.

Lillie stepped forward and sat on the very edge of the opposite couch, her hands clenched in her lap.

"I didn't. Not well at least. We were nearly the same age and both...both children of prominent noblemen. I knew of him from others. But we weren't friends. I didn't...I didn't have any friends. Just my father and brothers. I was on a break from the university and Papa asked me to go to a party. As a favor to him. I found Otis pressing his suit on a girl, a servant who clearly did not want his attentions."

"Pressing his suit..." Talon said. "Dammit, you can't say raping?"

Lillie's eyes flashed to Talon, who had draped herself over the back of the third couch. "He didn't get that far. I provoked him with his pants around his ankles so he would turn his attention on me."

Vola raised her eyebrows. "Oh?"

"So I could kill him in self-defense," Lillie said. A little gentler this time.

Sorrel tapped her teeth. "What I want to know is…was he really called Otis? Who would name their kid Otis?"

"Otis the Odious, I heard him called," Lillie said. "Before…"

"Before you straight up murdered him."

Lillie looked stricken. "You have to understand. Murder—execution—is not illegal between nobles. Especially not if it's self-defense. However, the victim's family can always challenge the execution, and you have to defend your actions in trial by combat. The victor is obviously innocent. And the loser…well, they clearly aren't and the gods chose to punish them."

Vola's mind raced along the possibilities. She remembered Lillie as she was when they'd met in Water's Edge. Quiet, uncertain, and very, very alone.

"You left because you didn't think you'd be able to defend yourself against his family."

Lillie's lip trembled. "If they'd challenged me and I'd died, my family would have been beyond disgraced. They would have been dishonored by the murderer in their midst." She looked down at her fists wrapped around each other in her lap. "I couldn't do that to them. I wouldn't."

"But you came back," Vola said.

Lillie looked up and met her eyes. "Because I am not a criminal. I did what I had to do. That girl is well because of my actions. Otis Virvalim is not alive to hurt anyone else, and I will not live in fear because of the choices I've made."

Vola sank back into the sofa and picked at the armrest. It

wasn't the type of hotel to have frayed upholstery, but if she was handed any more surprises like this, she'd end up fraying it herself. "Fair enough. What happens if his father finds out you're here?"

"He will challenge my execution, and I will have to defend myself. Worst case, he will beat me."

"Do you have to defend yourself alone? Don't nobles have champions that fight for them all the time?"

Lillie looked thoughtful. "Champions are allowed. It is unlikely that Gregor Virvalim fights his own battles."

Vola gestured between herself and Talon and Sorrel. "Then worst case, Gregor Virvalim loses his trial and drops his case. Because we wouldn't let you defend yourself alone. You know that, right?"

Lillie's eyes shone and her jaw clenched. "I did know that," she said quietly. "But I did not want to count on it without asking."

"Stupid," Sorrel scoffed. "But I guess I get it. Do we tell Rilla?"

Lillie winced. "It shouldn't have any bearing on the investigation. I admit, I didn't think about the consequences of being hired by a princess of Southglen. She might not wish to associated with someone like me."

"Sounds like there's nothing legally wrong," Vola said. "I don't want to blindside her with this, though. I think our best bet is to keep you out of Virvalim's way so it never comes down to a fight."

"Operation Keep Lillie Incognito," Sorrel said, pumping her fist in the air.

"And catch the bad guy," Talon added.

Sorrel pumped her fist again. "And Catch the Bad Guy!"

FOUR

"SHOPPING?" Sorrel said. "Our next step in the investigation is shopping? Lillie, I think you might be trying to get away with something here."

Lillie glared at Sorrel from beside the entrance to the market. Columns supported a wide piece of marble over their heads, shielding the stalls below from the sun and possible rain, though Vola hadn't seen any inclement weather since they'd arrived. The stalls all faced an open square where shoppers milled and street musicians played for a couple dancers with colorful scarves and tambourines.

"I'm not in the mood for browsing, if that's what you're implying," Lillie said with a huff. "Lord Virvalim is the head of his family's trade empire. Most of his fortune is a result of his business deals with foreign lands and the caravans that travel between them. All of which end up here, in the city. This is as good a place as any to look for leads. The letter didn't get us anywhere."

Vola nodded, eyes on the stalls. "Maybe we can find a reason he'd be consorting with a slaver and a…magic stealer…person."

Talon snorted. "Is that the technical term?"

"You know what I mean." Vola moved toward the stalls. "And while we're at it, we can look for some hair dye for Lillie."

"What?" Lillie's hand flew to her hair. "What's wrong with my hair?"

"Nothing," Vola said. "But it's pretty recognizable. If you don't want Virvalim to recognize you or know you're back in the city, we should color it or cover it."

"Cover it, please," Lillie said, dropping her hand, though from the way it fluttered she was still thinking about it. "I'd rather not do anything too drastic. My mother gave it to me, after all."

That was the first Vola had ever heard that Lillie even had a mother. She had to have one. Presumably even nobles came about the normal way. But why was there a little melancholy in Lillie's eyes when she said that?

They wandered through the stalls, trying to look like they belonged. They fit in a little better on the far side of the square where a series of weapon merchants and armorers had set up, and Vola leaned against a stall featuring a variety of blunt weapons.

Sorrel fingered the weapons as if comparing them with her own staff, while Lillie and Talon migrated toward a stall with bright scarves.

"Can I help you find a new weapon today?" the vendor asked Vola. "Er, ma'am?" His eyes searched for an emblem or some indication of her rank.

Vola's fingers crept to her empty neck and tried not to feel bereft without Cleavah's symbol. "Paladin," she said. "I'm just browsing. But these are nice."

"All the way from Ganchin. Fine quality. And rare, since it's so dangerous to cross the sea."

Vola pursed her lips. "I'll bet. Few are brave enough to make the trip. Who does the traveling for your business?"

"My brother. He's always had itchy feet."

"There's probably a cream for that," Sorrel said, absently.

The man's brow dipped in a frown.

"Don't mind her," Vola said. "These are more expensive than the fellow down at the end. Why should I buy from you?"

The vendor drew himself up, his green mantle straining across his broad chest. "My prices are higher because I didn't sell out to that bastard Virvalim."

Vola's gaze sharpened, but she just cocked an eyebrow nonchalantly. "Oh?"

"I own my own business. I have to meet all the costs of travel and customs and licensing myself. But that just means you're supporting a common family man. Instead of putting more money in that noble's coffers."

Vola raised her eyebrows at his tirade. "And it's not like he needs anymore, clearly," she said, leaning in.

"Exactly. But nobles are all the same, greedy, self-centered. Virvalim's after the princesses to get more trade back into the hands of the nobles."

Sorrel gasped. "How does he think he can get away with that?"

The vendor shrugged his massive shoulders. "He can't. Thank the gods the princesses were chosen for their smarts, not for their blood. They know limiting trade to the nobles will only hurt the city."

"So what would his next move be? Buy up all his competitors?" Vola said.

"He could try. I doubt the princesses would let him. And they're not going to pass any of his fool laws. He'd have to get rid of the Law Throne to even get close."

Vola's eyes widened a fraction. "Wouldn't it be treason to try?"

"Of course." The vendor's florid face paled a little in the bright sunlight. "This is just gossip. Just marketplace moaning. I don't think the lord really has it in for any of the princesses."

"'Course not," Vola said, pushing up off the stall. "Listen, I'm more of an edged weapons kind of girl. She's the one who's into blunt instruments." Vola cocked a thumb at Sorrel, who gave the vendor a little wave. "But thanks for the gossip."

Vola slid a silver piece across the stall and gave the vendor a wink.

She sauntered away as nonchalantly as she could manage with Sorrel trotting at her heels.

"Okay, so Virvalim might be working against the princesses because he wants more money and power?" Sorrel said. "Boring."

"It's always about money, power, or sex," Vola said. "That's all people care about."

"Yeah, well, one day I'd like to meet a villain who wants to turn the world upside down just because he wants to see people stand on their heads."

"All right, we'll put Sorrel down for one psychopath," Vola said as they approached Lillie and Talon.

"What?" Lillie said, turning. She'd purchased a blue scarf with a green fringe that matched her eyes and draped it over her head as if to keep the sun off.

"Nothing," Vola said. "Have you got anything besides Virvalim wanting to keep his trade empire?"

"Not much," Lillie said. "The market gossip seems to all deal with the nobility and the princesses, though. Apparently there are quite a few nobles who aren't happy with all the reforms the princesses have been pushing through."

"Ugh, politics. Is this all going to turn out to be about politics?" Vola said, watching Talon shift along the stall in front of them.

"What's wrong with politics?" Lillie said.

Vola sighed. "It's just not my thing."

Talon reached out to touch the edge of a frilly dress covered in lace. Then she snatched her hand back.

"I'm with Vola," Sorrel said. "You can't hit politics on the head and tell it to behave."

Lillie's expression went thoughtfully amused. "Actually, you can. You just need different weapons."

Vola stepped up beside Talon. "Are you looking for something specific?" she said under her breath.

Talon jumped back from the stall. "No," she said too quickly.

Vola reached out to lay a hand on Talon's arm, gentling her. "You're allowed to look."

Talon's hood swung back toward the stall.

Vola let her hand drop and deliberately looked at the sky. "Back in Brisbene, you said you didn't want to hide who you were anymore, and we told you we'd help. We said you could try anything you want. Do you want to try something new?"

Talon mumbled something that sounded like, "I don't know."

"It's all right if you don't," Lillie said, stepping closer. "How can we help?"

"Do you want us to go away?" Sorrel said. "Or do you want us to watch?"

"I want us to stop talking about it," Talon said with a groan.

Lillie brightened. "What if we all bought something?"

"I knew you were angling for a shopping trip," Sorrel said.

"This isn't for me," Lillie said. "This is for Talon. To help her feel more comfortable. None of us is particularly feminine, so what if we each picked something that we've never tried before? That way it will be new for everyone."

Vola thought Lillie was plenty feminine compared to the rest of them, but it was a good idea. Vola reached out for a piece of green silk sliding over the edge of the stall. It did feel soft and supple between her fingers.

"Oh," Sorrel said, glancing around, eyes shining. "Oh, okay. I see how shopping could be fun. What about..." She darted to the next stall over. "This?" She placed a headdress covered in paste jewels and feathers over her hair. One fell down and obscured face. "Or, wait. What about this?" She ditched the headdress and grabbed up a wide strip of stiff fabric with lacing down the middle. "What is it?"

"That's a corset, Sorrel," Lillie said.

"Huh. Underwear. Okay, underwear could be cool."

Lillie stepped up to a stall displaying little colored pots and brushes. "All the girls my age wore makeup to parties, but my brother always said rouge was for harlots." She studied the pots for a moment before selecting several. "I think we'll see if he was right or not."

"Talon, you're not even looking," Sorrel called.

Talon's hood swung back and forth between everything on offer, and Vola could tell she was getting overwhelmed. She put a hand on her shoulder.

"Do you like this?" Sorrel held up the frilly lace thing the ranger had been eying before. Sorrel was so short it pooled on the flagstones, but it was clearly supposed to be a dress with puffed up sleeves and a lacy overskirt.

"Er, should I like it?" Talon said.

Sorrel tilted her head. "I mean, I don't." She looked down at her plain gray tunic, tied at the front with string. "But then maybe you shouldn't trust my judgment on this."

"It's not about shouldn't or should," Lillie said, coming over to them with her hands full of pots. "It's about finding something you like. It's not going to be the same for everyone. For instance, I don't like the way I look in red." She freed a hand to tuck back a strand of her hair. "It clashes. But Vola would look amazing in jewel tones."

"Oh, really?" Vola stammered. "I was thinking the green. It would blend in more."

Lillie gave her a pained look, and Vola felt like she'd failed some sort of test. "You can choose the green if that's what you really like," Lillie said. "But I think you should try the red."

"Talon, what do you want to try?" Vola said, hastily. "A dress? A skirt? Maybe makeup like Lillie."

A vendor with a tray of candy around his neck passed between them shouting, "Ten pieces, one gold. Richest chocolate in Glenhaven. Ten pieces, one gold."

Talon jumped and then growled. "This is ridiculous. I feel ridiculous."

"Yes," Lillie said gently. "It's natural to feel that way when you try something new. But look at it this way. You are nowhere near as ridiculous as Sorrel right now."

They all looked over to find Sorrel dressed in the feathered headdress and a corset that was as long as she was tall, examining a beaded fan, trying to figure out how to open it.

"True," Talon said. She heaved a giant sigh and shifted close enough to the clothing stall to sort through the piles.

Vola eyed the green silk, but after Lillie's comment, didn't have the heart to actually pick it up and hold it up to herself.

Instead, she sidled toward the next stall which was piled high with books. She'd never been a big reader. Words were more frustrating than anything when they refused to stay still. But these had bold pictures painted across the front featuring women in low-cut gowns and men with long hair blowing across their armored shoulders. The nearest title she could make out was *Love's Peril*.

The others were going for clothes or makeup, but Lillie had said they should pick something they'd never tried before. Orcs had a rich oral history, stories of triumph and valor they told over the campfire. But they weren't exactly known for their romances.

Before she could overthink it, she grabbed the copy of *Love's Peril* and plunked her money down on the counter.

"Wow, really?" Sorrel said, making her jump. The halfling had ditched the headdress and the corset and carried two scraps of black fabric. "Not what I was expecting you to go for."

"Hey, the whole point of this is to not judge each other."

"I'm not judging, just observing."

"What did you choose?" Vola asked.

Sorrel held up the black fabric scraps. "Underwear."

Vola raised her eyebrows. "Bold move. You've always wanted to try it?"

"Always as in ever since I saw it about five minutes ago. Do people really wear stuff like this all the time?"

"I don't know. Mine doesn't really look like that, but your options are limited when you're almost seven feet tall."

"Yeah, two feet tall, too. But I figure I can cut it down. The monks who raised us had me convinced underwear had to be ugly to be functional."

Lillie was still trying to help Talon. "What about underwear? Sorrel picked underwear."

"Wouldn't fit right," Talon mumbled.

"Oh." Lillie blushed crimson. "Oh, I hadn't thought about that. What about a skirt? Something simple," she said. "It doesn't have to have frills if you don't like frills."

"It's not that I don't like frills," Talon said, her voice cracking. Vola knew that tone of near-panic. "I'd still have to wear it. I can buy any of these things, but I'd still have to make the decision to wear them. That's the hard part."

"One step at a time," Vola said. "You're not just going to go home and change your clothes and suddenly feel completely new. Just take the next step."

"Work," Sorrel said. "It's going to take work to learn how to be a girl."

"And to be comfortable with it," Lillie said. She tapped her lip. "I have an idea." She dove into the pile of clothes and came back with something that looked like a short dress in a light blue with lace around the hem.

"Pretty," Vola said.

"It's a nightgown," Lillie said. "Attractive and feminine, but without the commitment of wearing it where everyone can see."

Talon stared at the proffered garment, then rubbed her face once really hard. "Next step," she growled. Then snatched the nightgown.

FIVE

THEY MADE their way back through the streets with their purchases wrapped in pink tissue paper and tucked under Vola's arm. For a brief moment, she wished they'd brought the swamp beast to serve as a pack mule, since that was its original purpose. But she still had teeth marks from all the others times it had objected to hauling their stuff, so the impulse didn't last long.

As they passed the mouth of an alleyway, a finger of breeze stroked Vola's cheek and she stumbled a bit. She knew that touch. She frowned and glanced down the alley. Then up to the sky.

"Are you sure, lady?"

"Am I ever not sure?" Cleavah's voice came back to her.

"No." Vola sighed. "Guys, I think we need to go this way."

Sorrel trotted back to peek around the corner. It looked like a normal alley, high windowless walls on either side with the back opening up behind the shops. Except that in a city built against a cliff face there was no guarantee they wouldn't be trapped at the other end.

Sorrel looked up, brow furrowed. "Why?"

"Just trust me on this," Vola said with another sigh.

"Oh. Okay," Sorrel said, and she headed down the alley, taking point. She pulled her staff from her shoulder and swung it jauntily like she was just out for a stroll. Looking at her, you wouldn't necessarily realize she held a god's weapon ready in her hand.

"What are we doing?" Lillie said as she passed into the alley.

"I'm not sure," Vola said, following her. She signaled Talon to guard their rear. "An errand of Cleavah's. She pointed me this way."

Sorrel reached the end of the building and peeked around the corner both ways. She hissed and waved Vola forward. "You were right. Trouble."

Vola craned over her to see. Behind the buildings, the alley opened into a shadowed, squalid space pressed up against the cliff of the city. Several boys scuffled against the dirty cobbles.

Vola recognized the carrot-haired boy they'd taken the message from the day before. The one who'd made off with her emblem. He seemed to be bearing the brunt of the beating. At least he was on the bottom with his lip split already. Though he used his long, bony knees to great effect.

The other three boys wore fine tunics, and their hair had been washed sometime this century. But nice clothes didn't make you a gentleman when you ganged up on someone smaller than you.

"Get off me," the carrot-haired messenger said.

"Not till you say it," one of the boys said. He stood back a bit from the others as his friends held the messenger down. "Say you're trash."

"No!"

"My father says you're a thief. You're good for nothing else." He looked down his long nose, nearly crossing his eyes.

"I didn't steal nothing from you."

Vola's stomach clenched tight, and it didn't take another sign from Cleavah to urge her forward. "All right, I've seen enough."

She stomped up to the group of boys, making sure she clanked. "Let him up."

The boy with the big mouth straightened and glared at her. "Who are you?"

"Does it matter? Or are you just going to sneer at me, anyway?"

"Probably. You're interrupting. I demand to know your name before you turn around and mind your own business, greenie."

Vola let the insult slide right off with a subtle shift of her shoulders. Then she folded her arms across her chest to make herself look bigger. "Volagra Lightbringer. Now what's your name, stripling?"

"Rexum," the kid said, as if that should mean something.

"Nice to meet you, now get off of him."

"Don't you know who I am?"

"Nope, don't care."

The boy spluttered, going very red.

Vola lowered her chin, ready for a fight. "If you don't move, I'm going to make you."

"You lay a hand on me and you'll be subject to law!"

Vola reached over and hauled the big, snub-nosed boy off the messenger. She set him aside like an empty laundry basket.

Then she cocked her head at the little lordling.

"You'll pay for that," he cried.

"I did ask nicely first."

There was a whistle from above, and Vola glanced up to see Sorrel had climbed to the roof and now perched on the shingles. "Three bodyguards," she said and pointed to the next alley. "On their way."

Three armed figures sauntered into the alley and took stock of the standoff. The one in the lead wore a red livery and his eyes traveled from the three scrawny teenagers to the nearly seven-foot-tall half-orc.

Vola just shook her head.

"Guards, attack her," the boy in the lead said, pointing. "She dared to trod on Rexum's honor."

"Your honor is beating up other boys?" Sorrel said from the roof. "How noble. Also, you should know before you start that you're outnumbered."

"What?" the boy cried. "Can't you count, halfling?"

"Oh, I wasn't including you."

The boy screamed, face going a magnificent shade of purple. Spit flew from his mouth as he cried, "Get them!"

The bodyguards rolled their eyes but they reached for their weapons as if they were used to this.

"Wait," Lillie called, limping up behind Vola. "Wait, this is not how things are done in Glenhaven. Is it, gentlemen?"

Her words made the bodyguards pause.

Lillie turned to the boys. "Shame on you, using your superior rank and status to terrorize someone below you. Your duty is to protect and succor those beneath you."

"Are you serious?" the boy said. "No one believes that anymore."

Lillie's face went hard and uncompromising. "I assure you I take it very seriously. You have no excuse, absolutely none, to hold your power over another being. You are better than that." Lillie shook her head, expression showing just how disappointed she was.

Wonder of wonders, the boys shuffled their feet.

"Listen," Lillie told the nearest bodyguard, who was plump enough he'd probably never had to defend his charge seriously. "If you take your charges home and forget about this little incident, we won't tell the constables that you nearly drew steel against a paladin under divine orders."

The lead bodyguard sucked in his fat cheeks and took a step back, eyeballing Vola.

"What's this now?" Vola said out of the corner of her mouth.

Lillie gave her a placid little smile. "It's illegal to attack a paladin on a holy quest from one of the Virtues."

The lead bodyguard glared at the boy, Rexum. "She's a paladin?"

The boy's mouth fell open. "I didn't know!"

"Because you weren't paying attention," Lillie said. "There were several clues. Lightbringer? That's a paladin name if I've ever heard one. And who else would traipse into an alleyway to save a thief?"

"She has a point," the bodyguard said. He speared his charge with a glance. "You want to explain this to your father? Or should I?"

He herded the boy out of the alley, closely followed by the other two and their guards.

"Do better next time, gentlemen," Lillie called and three sets of scrawny shoulders flinched.

"Is it really illegal to attack a paladin?" Vola asked, cocking her head at Lillie as the group of whiny nobles disappeared around the corner.

Lillie looked aghast. "Do you think I would lie?"

"No, of course not. It's just, no one else seems to mind drawing steel against me."

"Hmm," Lillie said, pursing her lips and glancing down at the messenger, who smeared the blood across his chin with the back of his hand. "In the city at least, we are supposed to be respectful of our religious figures. The princess of the Faith Throne has done so much for tolerance and freedom to worship within the city. Of course, your rank would be more evident if you had your emblem."

Vola's eyes narrowed. "Speaking of..." She reached down to haul the messenger to his feet.

He blinked owlishly up at Vola.

Sorrel hopped down from the roof, landing easily on her feet. Talon stepped out of the shadows, Gruff at her side.

"You saved me." The messenger's voice cracked on the last word. He couldn't have been more than fourteen, already as tall as Talon with skinny limbs and a long nose. Human probably. At least, there didn't seem to be anything strange about his ears except for the amount of dirt in them.

Vola snorted. "It was nothing," she said. "Scaring off a couple of bullies."

"A couple of nobles," he said. "They could have drug me before the constables. Would have been just as easy as cornering me in a back alley. They could've killed me and nobody would have said nothing."

"A noble has a duty to protect those below him or her," Lillie said with a sniff. "They just haven't learned that yet."

The boy snorted. "Where're you from, lady?"

Lillie's mouth dropped open, but before she could answer, Vola held the boy's shoulder with one hand and riffled through his pockets with the other.

"Nobles can do whatever they want," he said. "They call me a thief and suddenly I'm a thief, no matter what anyone else says."

Vola pulled her emblem out of his pocket and let it dangle before his nose for a second.

He grinned and shrugged. "No hard feelings. I didn't actually mean to take that one. But the delivery job only pays so much. This would have made up the difference if I'd gotten to sell it. Nothing personal."

"Steal from another paladin, and I'll make it personal." Vola turned to leave the alley.

"Yeah, that's easy to say." The boy trotted along as the others trailed her. "But threats don't feed no one."

Vola stopped abruptly, struck by his words. She surveyed his threadbare clothes, his bare feet, his split lip. And it occurred to her that maybe Cleavah hadn't led her in here just to retrieve her emblem. Her lips thinned as she dug in her purse for three silver. She tossed them to the boy, who caught them, his mouth falling open.

She raised the emblem in her fingers. "I'm not taking this back because you stole it. I'm buying it from you. Understand?"

He gaped, showing off a gap between his back teeth. "Buying…"

"And look. Next time someone tries to knock you off your feet, try this." She took the boy's fist in her hand, turned his arm, and showed him how to ram his elbow into her solar plexus. "It knocks the wind out of them. And if you stay forward on your toes, keep your weight balanced, then it's them that will go over instead."

"You…you're teaching me."

"Just something very basic. To protect you against more bullies."

"Even basic lessons cost money."

"Not to me," she said quietly and turned to herd her party from the alley.

"Wait," the boy said.

She stopped.

"The message. The one for Virvalim. It didn't make sense, did it?"

She exchanged a look with the others. "How did you know?"

"It wasn't all there."

"There was another part?" Lillie said. "A missing piece of the code?"

"Don't know about a code, but there was something I was supposed to say. I was supposed to say, 'he's ready. He's waiting for them to move on the Thrones.'"

Vola straightened.

Lillie let out her breath. "Moving on the Thrones."

"Them," Sorrel said. "Who is them?"

The messenger shrugged. "Don't know. I just run the messages to Virvalim. If there's anything more, he spread it out somewhere else."

"In case the messenger is caught by an enterprising paladin and her posse," Sorrel said.

"Why are you telling us this?" Talon said.

The boy shrugged. "That emblem ain't worth a whole three silver. Figure that evens it out."

Vola's chest swelled with indignation, but Lillie reached out to place a calming hand on her forearm.

"What's your name?" she asked.

"Finn."

"Thank you, Finn."

Vola turned to her team. "A coup," she said. "Is that what moving on the thrones means?"

"What else would it mean?" Sorrel said.

Lillie shook her head, lips pursed.

"We have to tell Rilla," Talon said.

SIX

T HEY LOOKED for Rilla at the inn, but all they found of her was a note.

"Meet me at the Justice Hall the first chance you get. I have another piece to the puzzle."

They all exchanged a look and dropped their packages in their room.

"Do you think she learned someone's plotting against her and the Thrones?" Sorrel said as they left the inn only a few minutes after they'd arrived.

"She's a princess and a spy," Vola said. "She probably spends most of her time assuming someone is plotting against them."

"I meant like imminently," Sorrel said. "Where is the Justice Hall, anyway?"

Lillie pointed up. "All the way at the top."

They tilted their heads back and blinked at the marble walls silhouetted against the afternoon sun. Tiers upon tiers rose ahead of them, covered in flowers and climbing greenery until the last terrace loomed over all the rest.

"What, the palace?" Sorrel said.

"It's a part of the complex but not in the palace proper."

"I thought Rilla didn't want anyone to know she'd hired us," Sorrel said. "Why would she have us come directly to the palace?"

Lillie shook her head. "Anyone can come and go from the Justice Hall. To observe trials and executions, plead cases, or post bail. It's only a short walk from the prison, so there's a lot of foot traffic."

The last tier of the city rose taller than the others, with the palace perched directly in the center. Even Vola was winded by the time they reached the three wide staircases which cut through the cliff to the palace complex above them. Lillie led them to the left.

The palace itself rose in gleaming towers of white and gold, with staircases spiraling up to arching bridges supported by fine latices. Sprawling colonnades spread on either side, anchoring the palace to the top of the cliff as if it would float away in the breeze. Or topple over onto the city it protected.

Lillie led them along the nearest line of columns as scudding clouds passed overhead, leaving a patchwork of sunlight against the marble.

A steady stream of foot traffic moved under the colonnade, some heading deeper in to wide courtyards, and some heading back toward the staircases and the rest of the city.

Each courtyard strung along under the shadow of the palace housed different functions of the city's justice system. In one courtyard, benches and several desks all set up in a row were for appeals and petitions; in another, people scanned bulletin boards posted with lists of names and bail amounts. Further back, trials and public punishments were being held in the open air.

Rilla didn't seem to be involved in any of these. Vola searched each crowd for a glimpse of the dark princess in her usual green and gold coat. As they grew closer to the end of the colonnade, the press of people lessened until they were the only ones headed for the last courtyard on the right.

There, finally, Vola caught sight of Rilla leaning on a waist-high railing, one boot propped up on the lowest rung. They came out from under the columns, into the full sun. In the center of the courtyard stood a gallows, an empty noose hanging from the crossbeam. Guards stood around the edge of the space, dressed in gleaming armor washed in gold.

Vola stepped up beside Rilla and leaned on the railing. Lillie joined her as Sorrel and Talon came up on Rilla's other side.

The princess's light eyes remained fixed on the gallows, her mouth pulled into a frown.

"Kind of a creepy place for a meet and greet," Sorrel said, climbing up to sit on the railing. "What's up?"

Rilla smiled grimly as another cloud covered the sun, sending the whole courtyard into shadow. "I found a rope that yelped. We'll see people hang for treason today."

"Ah," Vola said, folding her hands together along the railing. "Is his name Virvalim? Cause that's the news we came to tell you."

Rilla straightened. "What? No." She ran her hand along her hairline. "Shit, he's in on it, too?"

"He was the one at the other end of the message from our bad guy. Coded and verbal. The messenger gave us the help."

"Wonderful. I'll add him to my shit list. But I can't move against him without more. Verbal messages don't hold up in front of the Justice Throne, no matter who they're given to. Still, maybe he'll jump after we execute his boss, Ephyra, here."

Lillie shot straight up. "What?"

Across the courtyard, a gate banged open and two more guards dragged a figure through the columns. The sun chose that moment to burn through the clouds and spear down into the yard, illuminating the man. He wore a rich brocade tunic in a pale blue, obviously expensive though rumpled as if he'd spent the night in it, and he blinked like he needed a pair of spectacles.

Lillie sucked in a breath.

"String him up," Rilla said.

"No!" Lillie flung herself at the fence and tumbled over. "No, don't!"

The man's head snapped up, his graying hair falling into his eyes. "Lillie?"

Lillie's hands blazed, fire spreading to her fingertips, and the two guards holding the man dropped his arms to snatch their weapons.

Vola's heart leaped to her throat. "Oh, shit." She ignored the mini lightning bolt that struck the ground at her feet as she vaulted the fence. "Wait," she called to the guards. "Lillie, what the hell?"

Lillie had reached the man, and she spun to put herself between him and the guards. "Vola, please," she cried. "He's my father."

Vola held up her hands, glancing back at Rilla. The princess stood behind the railing, one hand raised to stay the guards while she watched silently.

"Vola, trust me," Lillie cried.

"You know I do," Vola said with a deep breath. "But be very, very sure of what you're asking us to do." Her fingers itched for her sword but it was so illegal to draw steel in the presence of royalty Vola didn't want to risk it. Even if said royalty was their boss.

Talon's bow was in her hand, empty and pointed at the ground, but ready. Sorrel crouched in the dirt, eyes darting between Vola, Lillie, and the guards surrounding them.

Vola held Lillie's gaze deliberately. The wizard wasn't the impulsive one. But she'd admitted she'd murdered a man who'd broken her personal code of honor. And if her honor called her to defend her father here against a princess and her entire country, Vola had no doubt she would do it.

The only thing Vola didn't know was what she herself would do if Lillie called for her aid. She'd only known her a few weeks, but she trusted Lillie. More than she trusted most paladins. She'd made a choice that had hurt the wizard before, and she'd vowed never to do it again, but could she really protect Lillie if the wizard forced them into a fight with one of the rulers of this land? And what about Talon and Sorrel? They deserved her protection, too.

Lillie stood frozen at the older man's side, flames flickering around her fingertips. Her chest heaved as her eyes darted between her father, the guards, and the princess. Ephyra, for his part, didn't even glance at the opening the guards had left. He stared at Lillie, bottom lip between his teeth. The familiar expression hit Vola in the gut.

Lillie finally closed her eyes. Then, after an interminable moment, she dropped her hands, the flames guttering out. She took a deep breath and stalked forward, gaze locked on Rilla.

Six feet from the railing, she stopped, shoulders squared. "What—" She had to stop and clear her throat. "May I ask what this man's crime is?"

Rilla remained serene, sharp eyes on Lillie's face. Her hand was still raised, keeping the guards from making a move.

"He is guilty of treason. His seal was on sensitive information sent to the enemy. His defense did not hold up in trial, and he is sentenced to execution for conspiring against the Thrones."

A shudder went through Lillie's body, and she glanced back at her father, who sagged at the edge of the gallows, looking lost and small.

She faced Rilla again and dropped to her knees with a wince. Vola just kept herself from lunging to catch her.

"Guardian of the Dagger Throne," Lillie said. "I come to you humbly and officially begging for mercy. Grant this man a stay of execution. Allow me to plead his case before you and before the gods." The words sounded rehearsed, like she'd had to memorize them in some long-ago school room.

Then she glanced up and met Rilla's gaze, blue eyes blazing. "Five minutes, Rilla. Give me five minutes to convince you this man doesn't deserve to die today."

Rilla finally dropped her hand, and the guards fell into parade rest. "You can have ten, Lilliara Ephyra."

Lillie's eyes widened, and Vola sucked in a breath.

The guards took the man's arms to lead him back toward the door. He craned his neck to look over his shoulder at them. Lillie climbed to her feet, face lined with pain, and Vola stepped forward. But Lillie gestured her back and hurried after the man.

"You knew who she was," Talon growled as Lillie sped out of earshot.

Vola turned, arms crossed. She was interested in Rilla's answer as well.

"Of course," the princess said. "I'd be a pretty bad spymaster if I hired a group of adventurers without doing a little research."

Sorrel tapped her chin. "So you know all about us, huh?"

"Why didn't you tell her?" Vola said and jerked her head at Lillie, who was whispering fiercely to her father as the guards took him back through the gate. "If you knew who he is to her, why didn't you warn her?"

"I wanted to see what would happen," Rilla replied, completely at ease.

"So this was a test?" Sorrel said.

Rilla's mouth hardened. "It's only a test if there's a right answer. There's no right answer for something like this."

Rilla led them through a back way into the palace and an interior receiving room decorated in dark browns and reds. It was mostly just a fireplace and a couple of sofas, but there were two doors and it made the back of Vola's neck itch not to know what was behind the other door.

"Your ten minutes starts now," Rilla said after they'd all filed into the room.

Lillie whirled. Vola would have wasted time with accusations, wondering what Rilla had intended by letting things play out in the courtyard. Had she really thought Lillie would attack? Would she have let her?

Lillie didn't bother with any of that. "What evidence do you have?" she said. "What led you to my father?"

"I followed our lead from the other end and found correspondence leaving the country that shouldn't be leaving the country. A detailed analysis of the magic on the Thrones of Southglen. Their strengths and weaknesses and as much as anyone knows about how they work."

Lillie's mouth went pinched and white. "And my father was the one studying the Thrones. Or at least he was before I left."

"More than that," Rilla said. "The information was under his seal."

Lillie sucked in a breath.

"I take it that's important," Vola said, cocking a hip against the nearest couch.

"It's like someone giving their word," Lillie said. "Only more official. If my father put his seal on something, he's staking his honor on it. And his life." Lillie glanced at Rilla. "Could it have been stolen?"

"The seal itself was still in his possession, and he never reported it stolen for any amount of time. He was the one with the most recent research regarding the Thrones, and he claims not to have given it to anyone else. His only defense is that he says he didn't do it. Swears it. But everything I have points to him. I have enough to arrest the entire family and see them hang for treason."

"The entire…" Lillie whispered.

"The only reason you're here is because I can confirm you were in Brisbene at the time, with no contact between you and your kin."

"Could he have been framed?" Vola asked. "We know Virvalim is conspiring against the Thrones. He could have planted the evidence to take the attention off himself."

"It's the only thing that makes sense," Lillie said. "Please, Rilla. I know my father would never do this. He would never commit treason. He would never conspire against the Thrones."

"And what evidence do you have?" Rilla asked quietly.

Lillie threw back her shoulders. "Only myself. My father was the one who taught me honor. He taught me my duty as an Ephyra. He taught me what it meant to serve the Thrones faithfully. He studies them yes, but only so he can better serve." She paused, breathing heavily. "Has he ever shown you any disloyalty?"

Rilla folded her arms and kicked the back of a sofa. "No," she admitted. "There are plenty who complain about everything the princesses are doing. There are even some who openly oppose our programs and work. But your father has never been one of them. Virvalim doesn't surprise me. Ephyra did."

"Unless it's all a clever ruse," Sorrel said, tapping her teeth.

"Sorrel!" Lillie cried.

"Not helping," Vola said.

"It did occur to me," Rilla said. "Your father seems quiet, but no one will deny that he's quite clever. I assumed he must be the head. The leader. The thinker behind the plot. I hoped that by getting rid of him quickly, it would leave the rest scattered with no one to lead them."

Lillie winced and glanced at the elegant clock on the mantle.

"You hired us to find the truth, so let us do so." She gestured to the clock. "Stall the execution. Give us time to prove my father is innocent."

Rilla hesitated.

"Would you rather kill someone now and have the real culprits go free? Or would you rather wait and catch the entire guilty party?"

Rilla sighed. "Obviously the latter. You have a week. And keep your heads down. I don't want them to know we're coming for them. Not until we know who they all are." She turned to the door. "I have to leave this for now. The anniversary for the Elven Exile is in less than three days, and I can't wiggle out of the ball this time. Even for something like this. I'll send word to the prison that you're free to question Ephyra. You're on your own from there, unless you find something earth shattering."

She closed the door behind her.

Sorrel collapsed on the rug with a groan. "Oh my gods, for a minute there in the courtyard, I thought we were all gonna die."

"I'm sorry," Lillie said, flushing.

Sorrel raised her head. "Oh, don't get me wrong, it would have been fun as hell, but we'd have been *dead* dead at the end of it."

"As opposed to only dead," Talon said.

"Did you see those guards? I believe the correct term is beefcake."

Lillie reached up to take the clock in her hands. "A week. I have a week to exonerate my family and prove they didn't do this."

"We," Vola said. "We have a week."

Lillie tried to smile at her, but she went back to staring at the clock. "I know they didn't do this. I know it. And to think that anyone would accuse them of it…" The clock in her hands burst into flames before crumbling into a pile of ash.

They stared at the pile on the rug.

"Oops," Lillie said.

"What do you mean, oops?" Vola said.

"What do you mean, what do I mean? I mean, oops! I didn't intend to do that." She stared at the rug. "I hope it doesn't stain."

"Damn, Lillie. You're scary," Sorrel said.

"I am not. I didn't mean to."

"That's what makes it worse."

"It just happens sometimes," Lillie said.

"Is that the last thing Otis Virvalim heard before he died?" Talon said.

"Shut up!"

"Are we allowed to joke about that?" Sorrel asked.

"No!"

"I just hope you're not holding anything of mine the next time you get angry," Talon said.

SEVEN

THE PRISON WAS ATTACHED to the palace at the back of the Justice Hall. It seemed more like something to reside at the bottom of the city, but it was carved into the last little bit of cliff face before you got to the wide open plain above the city. Maybe prisoners who were found guilty were chucked over the side to save time and money.

This close to the top, Vola expected something a little brighter, with more sunshine and grates to let in fresh air, but the passage a royal guard led them down burrowed deep into the cliff face, cutting off everything from the outside world. The tunnel was clearly built for humans and elves, and Vola had to duck to keep from bashing her head on the roof. She'd never thought of herself as claustrophobic before, but she couldn't help feeling like the whole place was ready to come down on her.

She shuddered as the guard led them from one passage, down some steps into another. Finally, at the end of the hallway another cross passage opened up and here were the cells. Each gate opened onto a space lit with sunlight but only about six feet by six feet wide. Vola had thought they were deep into the cliff but apparently they were close enough to the top that the cells them-selves were just pits dug into the plateau above and left open to the air and to the elements. If it rained, the inmates would be drenched, if the sun never stopped shining, they'd be broiled.

At the end of the row stood a figure in full plate armor, arms crossed as he guarded the last cell. Vola glanced up and down the empty passage.

"I guess Rilla doesn't want anyone to know they've arrested a noble," she said.

"It's not the nobility that's the problem," Lillie said. "It's the treason. It would cause a stir. Some would be calling for my father's head. Some would be indignant that she dared arrest him without a public proclamation. It would be a mess."

Lillie stepped up to the plated guard and tipped her head back to meet the guard's eyes.

"We're here to speak with the prisoner," she said.

The full helm tilted, barely acknowledging her. "No one talks to the prisoner." The voice was thin and tinny, as if traveling a very long way through a very narrow tube. Definitely not what Vola had been imagining.

"They have full access," their escort said. He only wore chain mail and a surcoat of green. "They have permission from the princess herself to investigate his crimes and find the truth."

The helm tilted back up. "No one talks to the prisoner without proper authorization."

The royal guard's hand smacked his forehead. "I'm the proper authorization. I'm here specifically to say they have the proper authorization."

"Code not recognized."

"What do you mean, code not—There is no code. The code is let them in."

"Code not recognized. Proper authorization needed."

The guard made a frustrated noise. "Just give me a sec. We're still working out the kinks in the new system." He pulled a stone out of his pocket covered in spell markings and he swiped his thumb over it.

"What?" a voice came from the stone, sounding remarkably like a pissed off Princess Rilla. "Did you bring them to Ephyra yet?"

"Er, sorry to bother you, Princess. We're having trouble with the prison guard?"

Rilla made a noise, and Vola could well imagine the look on her face. "Oh my gods, these things are more trouble than they're worth, I swear…Let them in." Her voice snapped out, but the plate armored figure remained motionless.

"They have the proper authorization. I give them the proper authorization."

"Code not recognized."

"Dammit, what code? There's a code? Just a minute. Let me find the damn manual…"

There was a shuffling noise from the stone.

Sorrel tilted her head. "Do you suppose it has a switch or something?"

Vola glanced at the figure. It seemed perfectly normal if you ignored the fact that it didn't have eyes behind the slit in its visor. Just a yawning darkness.

"What happens if you touch it?" Sorrel asked. "Could I just climb up and open the back of its head?"

"Better not," Vola said.

"These things are usually triggered by anything they see as an act of aggression," Lillie said.

"I imagine removing its head would be seen as an act of aggression," Talon said.

"But then we could fight it. Earn our entry."

"Ah," Rilla's voice came again. "Wonderful. The wizard that spelled this one had a sense of humor. I really love that in a man. Try this one." She cleared her throat. "Get out of the way!"

The figure snapped to attention and finally lumbered to the side with a series of clanks.

"It's moved now," the royal guard said. "Thank you, Princess."

"Gah, finally," Rilla grumbled. "Try golems, the wizards all said. They're steadfast and reliable, and no one can get through them. They failed to mention no one can get through *to* them, either. Dumb as the material they're made of. Stupid stacks of metal—"

The message spell cut off, leaving them standing in the hallway alone except for the guard and the golem.

"I'll uh, I'll stay here while you question the prisoner," the guard said. "In case this thing doesn't want to let you out again."

"I still want to open up the back of its head," Sorrel muttered as the guard stepped forward to unlock the gate. "What do you suppose is in there?"

"Magic," Talon said.

"Well, duh."

As soon as the gate was open, Lillie rushed through into the bright sunlight beyond. "Father?"

"Lilliara." The man on the other side opened his arms as Lillie collided with him.

From this close, Vola could see the resemblance in the shape of their eyes and noses. The man was full human, with graying dark hair and brown eyes. But Lillie was still clearly his daughter. He was as short and round as she was.

"Are you all right?" Lillie pulled away far enough to scan him up and down. "Did they hurt you?"

"No, no, of course not. It isn't like I put up a fight. Wasn't even sure what was happening at first." His voice was low and sonorous. It reminded Vola of one of her favorite knights at the paladin academy.

He mopped at the sweat standing out across his brow, darkening the edge of his hair, and Lillie tugged him over to the side of the cell where the afternoon sun was just beginning to leave a sliver of shade.

"What are you doing here?" Ephyra asked. He probably had a first name, but since everyone else seemed to refer to nobles by their family name, Vola hadn't heard it yet. "Where did you go? I thought you'd run away. To find your mother or some other such fantasy."

Lillie flushed. "I—I did run away, Father. I'm sorry. I'm so sorry I didn't tell you. I got into some trouble, and I desperately didn't want it to affect you. Turns out you got into more trouble than me."

Ephyra blushed as red as Lillie. So that's where she got it from. "I don't understand what's happened," he said, touching his brow. "No, I do understand. I just don't believe it."

"We're here to help you, sir," Vola said. She straightened and tried to appear competent and in charge. "Your daughter's convinced the princess to stay your execution for a week while we find the truth."

"Who—?" Ephyra stared up at her. "Who are you?"

"Father, this is Volagra Lightbringer, paladin of Cleavah," Lillie said, gesturing to her. "And Sorrel Thornbough, and Talon."

Talon nodded, her hood casting most of her face in shadow, while Sorrel examined the walls of the cell.

"I've been traveling with them," Lillie said. "They are my friends and companions, and I trust them completely."

"Then I suppose I must place my fate in your worthy hands." Ephyra held out a hand to Vola. Vola took it and shook. He glanced down and turned her hand over, studying it. "Orc hands. No, half-orc hands. And a paladin." His gaze traveled over Talon and Sorrel, too, and Vola imagined he was making an assessment of them as well.

Sorrel stepped close to the opposite wall and craned her neck to see the top. Then she reached out a hand to stroke its surface.

"It's an interesting combination," Ephyra was saying. "Perhaps you'd allow me to take some notes later."

"Father! That's very rude."

"Don't pretend you haven't been taking notes," Vola said with an indulgent grin at Lillie.

She spluttered.

"You can borrow hers when we're through with this," Vola told Ephyra.

"What happened, father?" Lillie asked, taking his hands in hers.

Sorrel took a running jump at the wall, but her fingers slid against the smooth stone.

"I don't know. I mean, they said I was arrested for treason. That I'd been sending information on the Thrones out of the country. To an enemy."

"Were you studying the Thrones?" Vola asked.

Sorrel took another running leap. Talon's hood tracked her as she slid back to the ground.

"Yes," Ephyra said. "I'm always interested in the role their magic plays in each princess that is chosen. The process is fascinating. Did you know that each god imbued a throne with—"

"Father."

"Oh, right. Yes, I study the Thrones. I probably have the most up-to-date knowledge about them in the city. But I would never share that knowledge without the express permission of the princesses. I know how that information could hurt them."

Vola figured it was like getting the schematics of a siege engine and being able to identify the weak points before a battle. If their enemy was planning to move against the Thrones, they would want every little advantage they could get.

"Do you know anyone who could have stolen the information? Or your seal?" Vola said.

"They're both kept under lock and key at the manor. In my office. They've been confiscated now by the Dagger Throne."

"And how do you feel about that?" Talon asked as Sorrel tried pushing off from one wall with her foot and launching across to the other. She bounced off and rolled back to the ground.

"You're going to set off some kind of alarm," Vola told her.

"How do I feel about the Dagger Throne confiscating my research?" Ephyra said, brow scrunched. "It was theirs in the first place, so it's not really confiscating, is it? I would have sent all my findings to the princesses when I was done. At least to the Magic Throne. I'm more upset that I can't continue my studies. I was getting to a point where I actually felt like I understood how the Thrones imbued the qualities they wanted on the princesses they chose."

"And of course, you're upset they might execute you for treason."

Ephyra glanced at Lillie, who bit her lip. "I have left behind several legacies I am very proud of. I would rather not be falsely accused or die for something I have not done. But if I cannot die with honor, I have at least taught my children to carry my honor with them."

"Your children," Vola said as Lillie scrubbed at her cheeks. "How many do you have?"

He cocked his head, like he was surprised she didn't know already. "Lilliara is my youngest, and she has three older brothers. A gift from her mother."

"Would they know someone who might want to frame you?" Vola said. They didn't have a lot to go on here, but Ephyra certainly didn't seem like a treasonous man out to usurp the Thrones. He seemed genuinely more interested in his research and the effect it would have on the world.

Ephyra blinked. "Perhaps they would know more. Xavier is a knight of the realm. He is much better about paying attention to the outside world while I lose myself in books. Innis is his shadow. And Kellan is more like me. He was helping me with my research."

"Where are they now?"

Ephyra shook his head. "I have no idea. They fled when I was arrested. In order to remain free."

"That doesn't sound like Xavier," Lillie said.

"It doesn't sound very knightly, either," Talon said.

Sorrel took another crack at the walls, launching herself from one to the other, climbing between the two as if they were a ladder.

Ephyra's eyes narrowed. "I told them to hide. I did not want my entire family beside me on the gallows. Not when they are even more innocent than me. And there are still some ways Xavier listens to me."

"He doesn't usually?" Vola asked.

Ephyra spread his hands. "He is an adult. Many children grow up to think they are smarter than their parents."

"We'll find them," Lillie said. "We'll make sure they're safe."

"Lillie." Ephyra stopped the wizard with a hand on her arm, and he pulled her closer. "I do not want you caught up in this mess as well."

"And I don't want to see you hanging from a noose," Lillie said, lowering her chin and meeting her father's eyes. "I know your mind, and I know your honor. This is the legacy you have given me. And I will see you free before the end of the week. I promise."

They embraced.

Vola cleared her throat and glanced up at Sorrel, who sat triumphantly on the edge of the wall.

"Don't worry," she called down. "They have all sorts of magic and alarms up here. But they're easy to avoid. You can see the lines all over the place."

"Would you get down before that golem comes in here and decides we're trying to escape."

"We're not the prisoners," she said.

"Do you want to try explaining that to it?"

Sorrel grimaced. "All right, all right. I'm coming."

She jumped down, rolling at the bottom to break her fall, before she sprang to her feet again. She cracked her neck.

"You were right, Vola," she said. "Missing persons cases to treason and treachery. We're moving up in the world."

EIGHT

OUTSIDE THE PRISON, they stepped into the scattered sunlight. Clouds still scudded across the sky, but they seemed wispier than before, letting more light shine through. Lillie's face was set with determination and the others followed her through the columned courtyards without argument.

Vola's mind turned around and around. How were they going to prove Ephyra's innocence? They had an entire conspiracy to unearth and the weight of a princess's expectations to manage, not to mention Lillie's own stakes in this. They passed out of the Justice Hall's open-air courts, onto the ledge above the city and Vola paused near the edge.

The others started down the staircase, but Vola let out a breath as she stared at the tiers layered below them. The city itself was enormous. And woven through it all was corruption and dissent, hidden in the shadows, poking its nose out only to yank back when the light passed over it. She glanced at Lillie's retreating back and chewed her lip between her tusks. This whole thing was only going to bring pain. She knew it. No matter what they found.

She hurried to catch up with her party as they stepped down onto the next level.

A hand caught her elbow. She yelped and whirled, drawing her sword.

The others all sprang into action, drawing weapons, and Lillie's hands gathered fire from wherever she kept it.

A gangly youth with red hair and a spray of freckles grinned at them uncertainly.

"Finn?" Vola said, trying to control her beating heart.

"Hi," the messenger said with a little wave.

Vola shook her head and sheathed her sword. "What are you doing here? How did you find us?"

The boy shrugged. "Wasn't that hard. I just followed you."

"'Cause that's not creepy," Sorrel muttered.

Vola rubbed her forehead. "Why did you follow us? Did you need something?"

"Just…just wanted to give you this." He thrust out a wilted bouquet of lavender blooms, his fair skin going deep red under his freckles.

"Er," Vola said. Her eyes darted to her friends, who looked on in open amusement.

"I've never really seen Vola as the flower type before," Sorrel said, head cocked. "More like the blade and ax type."

"I think it's sweet," Lillie said.

"You don't…you don't like them." The boy's face fell and his shoulders drooped a little.

"I didn't say that," Vola said quickly. "They're, er, lovely. But, um, why are you giving them to me?"

Finn kicked the dirt under his feet. "'Cause you saved me. Just wanted to say thank you."

"You did that already."

"Well, thank you again." He thrust the bouquet out again, and Vola didn't have the heart to not take it.

"You're welcome, I guess." Her eyes narrowed as her fingers closed around the sticky stalks. "Where did you get these?"

His brow drew down in affront. "I didn't steal them, if that's what you're asking. Not unless you count climbing a wall and cutting them from some nob's branches."

"Oh yeah, totally not stolen," Sorrel said.

With a sigh, Vola thrust the bouquet into her belt. At least she'd smell nice.

Lillie sneezed, then glanced at Vola apologetically. "Sorry, I'm allergic."

"You might be allergic to everything," Sorrel said.

It was a good thing Lillie was the only person Vola knew who could look good blowing her nose. Since she did it so much.

Lillie put Sorrel and Talon between herself and Vola.

Vola eyed the messenger who'd originally had the correspondence that led them to the conspirators. "Finn, when you were running messages, did you ever take any to the Ephyra household?"

He shrugged. "Nah. But I wasn't the only one who ran those kinds of messages."

"Who else?"

"I don't know them personally. I just know he had us all spread out. Didn't want us to be able to identify each other."

"Yeah, that would be too easy."

"We should still search the Ephyra manor," Lillie said. "To see if Rilla might have missed anything. Or if there's any evidence of where my brothers might have gone. We need to find them before they do anything drastic in response to father's arrest."

Since that was what Vola was going to suggest, she gestured for Lillie to lead the way. Finn fell behind, chattering in Vola's ear as they descended two more tiers.

Lillie's steps grew more comfortable as they approached a villa perched on the edge of the terrace. A wall surrounded the sprawling manor covered in climbing trumpet flowers. Lillie rubbed her nose and smiled.

"You're not allergic to these?" Sorrel said.

"Father always made sure the flowers in the garden weren't the ones I had trouble with," she said with a sad smile.

Two royal guards stood outside the gate to the residence. These wore plate armor as well, but they'd left off the helms. Perfectly normal faces peered at them, one human with ruffled brown hair. One elven with a long blond braid.

As Vola opened her mouth to greet them, Sorrel stepped up and rapped her knuckles on the elf's plated thigh.

"Er, yes, hello?" the elf said, brow furrowed as he stared down at Sorrel.

"Not golems," Sorrel announced. "Aren't you supposed to say something like 'do not trespass, citizen?'"

The human guard gave her a sidelong look, then focused on Vola. "Mishap's Heroes?"

"Oh," Vola said, shoulders drooping. "Yes, I guess that's us."

"We have orders to let you into the accused's house. You may proceed."

"Thank you." Vola turned and glared at Finn, then pointed at the ground. "Stay here," she said. "And behave."

He thrust his hands in the pockets of his thin trousers and grinned at her. "Sure."

Lillie already pushed through the gate, her hands trembling a little. Inside, a garden paved with patterned stones and lined with an eight-foot-high wall spread from them to the front door of the pristine marble villa. To their left, the wall dipped to waist height so as not to obstruct the view of the rest of the city and the plains below.

Lillie stepped across the paving stones and placed her fingers on the front door. It opened without pause, as if it recognized her touch.

The rest of them exchanged a glance, then followed Lillie as she stepped into her home for the first time since she'd left in disgrace.

A plush rug softened the marble stones under their feet and Lillie drifted from archway to archway down a long hall, peering into each room as if she walked through a dream.

Vola stepped up beside her as she paused outside of what was clearly her father's study. A large desk dominated the space, and bookcases lined the walls with glass fronts.

"I need a minute," Lillie told her quietly.

"We can search the rest of the house," Vola said. "While you take your time."

"Thank you."

Vola stepped back and hand signaled the other two to follow her deeper into the manor. A set of steps carried them to the next floor where bedrooms and pretty little salons opened onto the main hallway.

Vola raised her eyebrows as she surveyed the display of wealth. It wasn't overly ostentatious. The Ephyra's obviously didn't go in for ornate, gilt-encrusted clocks and frilly lace upholstery that cost more than the thread it was made of. But the furniture was sleek, well-built and polished to a high shine despite having sat abandoned for however long since Ephyra had been arrested.

Vola signaled Sorrel to take the nearest bedroom and Talon the next in line while Vola went for the furthest along the hallway.

This bedroom had obviously belonged to Lillie. Unless one of her brothers had been into pink horse decor. Vola pursed her lips, sifting through the signs of a doting father and an unlimited bank account. Vola's estimation of Ephyra went up in the time it took to look over Lillie's room and decide little had changed since she'd left it. It took a strong will to raise a daughter in such wealth without turning her into a spoiled brat. And Lillie could be called many things—naïve, idealistic, a little soft—but spoiled was not one of them. She took her responsibilities seriously and was always willing to learn the things she didn't know from people who could teach her.

There wasn't any dust, but there was still a depression in the bedspread where someone had sat. Little bottles of lotion and perfume scattered on the vanity top hadn't been righted, and a stuffed horse had fallen beside the bed as if dropped and forgotten. The bookcases were mostly organized, but there were several tomes on magic scattered on the floor in front of it as if they'd been sorted through.

It looked like a bedroom someone had left in a hurry, and Vola guessed no one had been in here to disturb anything except to clean. Ephyra must have been waiting for his daughter to return, as if she'd just stepped out to pick up something from the market.

Vola closed the door behind her and searched the other room on the end. Ephyra's himself if she was any judge of the books scattered across the half-made bed. Not that knights couldn't read, but this felt more like a scholar's sanctum.

There wasn't a lot in here that seemed out of place, either. No confessions of guilt lying around, nothing that indicated his research at all. Rilla's people must have cleared the place of anything related to the Thrones before they'd gotten here.

There was a step in the hall that Vola recognized as Lillie, and she left to join the wizard. She stood in the doorway to her room, staring.

"Is anything different?" Vola asked.

"Just me." She stepped inside and ran a hand along the vanity's edge. "It's exactly as I left it. He didn't even pick up my books."

Vola could only imagine what that might mean to a man like Ephyra and a daughter like Lillie.

Lillie checked under the bed, in the drawers of the vanity, behind the books, doing a much more thorough job than Vola, but finally she shook her head.

"Nothing," she said. "But I don't imagine anyone would have hidden anything in here. If they even had anything to hide." She trailed off with a frown and went to double-check the other rooms that Vola, Sorrel, and Talon had searched.

She paused in the last bedroom. There were as many books in here as there'd been in Lillie and Ephyra's rooms.

"Kellan," Lillie said while the rest of them crowded behind her. "He was helping my father with his research on the Thrones while I was away at school."

"Do you have any idea where he and your brothers would hide?"

Lillie raised her hands helplessly. "Not really. I didn't really know Xavier and Innis all that well. They were quite a bit older than me. I think...I think they blamed me when Mother left. Since they grew up with her. They never said as much out loud, though. Father wouldn't have stood for it."

"What about Kellan?" Vola said. "He was closer to you in age."

"A little. We shared a lot more interests. We should double check the books. In case Rilla and her people missed anything."

"What are we looking for?" Vola asked as she moved toward the shelves.

"Journals. Anything handwritten about the Thrones. You'll know it when you see it."

That was easy for Lillie to say. Vola had a hard enough time with printed words. She couldn't imagine actually being able to scan a page and learn anything without having to scrutinize it forever first.

She picked up some books anyway while Sorrel and Talon joined her. But if they were printed instead of handwritten, she put them down again. The ones that could be journals she handed off to Talon and Sorrel.

"Was your brother really into eclectic art featuring half-naked dudes?" Sorrel asked.

"What?" Lillie cried. "No."

"Really? Cause it's right here in the middle of the shelf."

Talon glanced over Sorrel's shoulder. "I think there's a word for that. It starts with a P."

"My brother would not keep po—" Lillie snatched the book from Sorrel and stared at the page. "Oh. Oh my."

"Did you know he was into men?" Talon asked.

"This is not a thing we would have talked about. Although he did seem to have a fascination with the sports at school. To watch, not to play. Oh dear."

Vola whistled.

"Look, he's allowed to ogle whoever he wants," Lillie snapped. "I just don't need to be touching his…Oh, ew."

She snapped the book shut and stuffed it back on the shelf.

"That's not where it goes," Sorrel pointed out helpfully. "He had it right here. In the middle out in front."

Lillie's brow furrowed. "What?" She double-checked the cover. "That's not right. It's not like him to misfile a book."

"Even one like this?" Vola said.

Lillie frowned and snatched the book up again. She flipped through the pages, her cheeks blazing red, until a loose sheet of paper fell out on the ground.

She picked it up, absently returning the book to the shelf.

"It's a note," she said with a gasp. "Lillie, if you've found this, you must leave. We'll be safe under the water, but you can still get out of the city. You've not been implicated, yet. Please, stay safe."

"Under the water?" Sorrel said. "What's that mean?"

"Not sure." Vola kept her eyes on Lillie's face. The wizard was tearing up.

"He left this for me," she said, voice choked. "They were waiting for me to come home. Even after all these months."

Her fingers crumpled the edges of the page as she squeezed her eyes shut. Talon reached out to clasp her shoulder, and Sorrel wrapped her arms around the wizard's waist.

"Let's figure out where they are," Vola said, gently. "Then you can talk to them again."

Lillie nodded, lips pressed thin and tight.

"Maybe Rilla would have an idea," Sorrel said as they left the house and waved to the guards at the gate. "As the city's spymaster, she's got to have like all the maps."

"Yeah, but there's water everywhere," Talon said.

"Under the water." Sorrel tapped her teeth. "Do you think they're in the harbor? In like some kind of bubble? Is that possible?" She glanced at Lillie, their resident magical expert.

"Um," Lillie said, brow furrowed.

"Under the water?" a voice chirped near Vola's elbow. "Are you looking for the nobs's hideout?"

Vola jumped and stared down into a freckled face. "Finn?"

"That's still my name," he said.

"You know it's not polite to eavesdrop." Lillie's lips pursed.

Finn shrugged. "I know. But it's hard not to when people stand on the street talking about their business." He gestured to the sunny pathway, and indeed, several people walked along chatting.

Finn turned to Vola. "I got this for you." He held out a short scabbard. "Maybe you'll like it better than flowers."

It looked like a short sword. Which would be little more than a dagger in Vola's hand. "Where did you get this?" she said suspiciously.

He gave her a hurt look. "It's not like anybody was using it."

She growled and rubbed her forehead. "You *are* a thief, then. Take it back, Finn. Right now. You can't just pick up anything you like. It doesn't belong to you."

"I can't take it back," he cried. "I don't know who I nicked it from."

"You steal so much that you can't be bothered to remember who your victims are?"

"You make it sound like I stabbed them."

Talon cleared her throat. "You mentioned the nobs's hideout."

"Yeah, underwater," Sorrel said.

"Care to elaborate?" Lillie said.

Finn crossed his arms and pouted. "There're some nobs hiding out under the lower waterfall. People go there when they don't want the guards to find them."

One of the upper waterfalls fell nearby, providing a pleasant background rush and a light spray of mist in the sunlight.

"But you just happen to know about it," Vola said, raising an eyebrow.

"I know about lots of hiding places. You said underwater. This one's underwater."

"If you know about it, how come the guards can't get to it?"

"Not everyone knows about it. And it's protected. You have to be a really strong swimmer to get in. Most guards sink."

Vola rolled her lip between her tusks. She was as strong a swimmer as she was in everything else. The paladin academy had put them through all sorts of training. It was really bad press when a fully armored knight fell in a pond and drowned.

Her companions, on the other hand… She glanced at Lillie and Sorrel and Talon. She wouldn't be surprised if Sorrel could swim, but the halfling was light enough she wouldn't really be able to fight the current. Talon would actually have to take her cloak off long enough to jump in, and Vola wasn't going to make any assumptions about Lillie's abilities, magical or otherwise.

"All right, raise your hand if you can swim."

Sorrel's hand shot up, and Lillie raised hers tentatively, but Talon crossed her arms and huffed. "There wasn't a lot of water where I grew up."

Vola could probably get Talon through as long as the ranger didn't mind holding her breath. But she doubted Sorrel could drag Lillie to wherever they were going all by herself.

Her breath huffed in a little laugh. "Luckily, I know a strong swimmer."

She turned on Finn, who twitched under the full force of her glare. "You're going to take us to this hideout. At least close enough to point it out. But first…" She held up the scabbard.

Vola led them to one of the many temples in the city. There were plenty dedicated to individual gods, both the Virtues and the Obstacles, Lesser and Greater. But there were even more that served as a generic space to welcome any worshipers who didn't want to make the trek down through the city to their specific temple.

Vola found one easily and dragged Finn inside by the collar of his thin shirt. He grumbled, but Vola got the impression it was more for the show of it than anything else.

"Offering for Cleavah," she said to the attendant and laid the scabbard on the altar. "Now say you're sorry."

"Sorry," Finn muttered.

"Right. Now you can take us to the nobles' hideout. With one stop along the way."

Nearly an hour later, they stood on the lowest tier of the city opposite the docks where one great branch of the waterfall crashed into the river. Vola held the collar of Finn's shirt in one hand and the lead rope of the swamp beast in the other.

It had tried to take a piece out of Vola when she'd fetched it from the stables, but she'd bashed it on the nose once and now it chewed something half rotten it had snatched off the edge of the wharf, glaring at each of them in turn.

"All right, Finn," Vola said.

The boy pointed to the waterfall. "It's past there. You have to go under the rock, but the waterfall makes it all frothy and dangerous. But once you're past, it's supposed to open up onto a cavern on the inside. Never been there myself."

"And you're not going in today. I can't tow five of you. Now go, and stay out of trouble."

"Like telling a starving man to avoid the cake," Lillie said.

She wasn't wrong. Vola dug in her belt pouch and produced a couple coins, which she handed to an incredulous Finn.

"Payment for your time. So you shouldn't have to steal anything today, right?"

Finn shrugged and ducked his gaze, kicking at the little trickle of water making its way over the edge of the wharf. "I guess. It's not really about that."

"Then what's it about?"

"Everyone already thinks I'm a thief. They think it without proof. So…I might as well steal stuff, right?"

Vola's breath hissed through her teeth, his argument striking deeper than bone and sinew. Deep enough to hit memory and history.

"You know, you don't have to be the things that everyone calls you," she said, keeping her voice quiet. "You can be something better. If you let them tell you what you are, then they're winning. They're controlling you. Being something else is harder, yes, but then you get to win."

He stared at her, mouth set in a sullen line. "That's easy for a paladin to say. You guys are strong and noble. Everyone loves you."

Vola tilted her head. "Did you know that most people think orcs are evil?"

He shifted his feet on the wet flagstones. "Well, yeah, but *you're* not."

Her eyebrows twitched. "See, even you think it a little bit. They think we're evil because they're not paying attention. So, I decided to prove them wrong."

She met his eyes before turning to the harbor to survey the swift current. On to the next problem. Finn would sort himself out, or he wouldn't. She'd done what she could.

She'd left her breastplate back at the inn when they'd picked up the swamp beast, but a sword and shield were heavy enough.

"All right, then." There was nothing for it except to go.

She hopped into the river from the wharf, expecting the swamp beast to come along. It liked swimming well enough when they didn't it want to.

But instead of hopping in after her, the beast raised its head so her arm was nearly wrenched out of its socket.

Vola growled and wiped the water from her face with her free hand. "Come on, you. Bath time. You like water. Get in."

The thing pulled against the lead so she bobbed in the current. She kicked and then planted her feet against the slippery stones of the wharf and tugged. "Come on."

Talon slapped the monster on the rump, and it squealed and dove into the river, plunging Vola underwater. She came up, spluttering. The swamp monster glared at her from a few feet away, treading water.

"Let's go, before it realizes it's on its home turf and decides to eat me. There's no metal between me and its teeth right now."

Sorrel jumped, grabbing both knees for maximum splash. Lillie sat on the edge and lowered herself into the water, scraping down the edge of the wharf. Talon pulled her cloak off and tied it around her waist, her pale face set in a worried scowl. Her sandy-colored hair was already damp from either the spray or sweat.

"Just keep hold of the swamp beast," Vola said as Talon awkwardly plopped into the water. "I'll keep it moving in the right direction, and Sorrel will keep it from eating anyone."

She made sure the three of them had wrapped their hands around the swamp beast's harness, a rough rope they'd tied around its chest and withers. Then she set off toward the falls, dragging the beast with her.

As the spray made it hard to keep her eyes open and the current pulled against her, she dove, pulling on the lead rope. Powerful strokes kept her moving steadily forward, and she glanced back over her shoulder. In the fuzzy murk of the water, Lillie and Talon gamely kicked and held onto the swamp beast while Sorrel kept it in line following Vola.

The swamp monster's crest rose and bubbles streamed from slits in its neck. Vola shook her head. The thing could breathe water as well as air. Wonderful. Because it really needed that advantage.

She turned back, cheeks puffed out while she held her breath. The rock face plunged into the water ahead of them and she kicked forward to get down far enough to dip under the barrier.

Her chest ached as she swam under the rock, eyes squinting for any sign of a cavern. Nothing. And it was much darker here, under the falls and all the rock.

A light sprang into being just ahead and darted away, illuminating the surface of the rock above them until suddenly it found an opening and flickered as if calling to her.

Vola cast a grateful glance back at Lillie and swam for the opening as fast as she could manage. The current receded the further from the falls they got, and Vola used the edge of the opening to propel herself toward the surface. The swamp monster tugged against her, but she hauled on the rope and burst from the water with a gasp.

She reached back even before her vision cleared and grabbed for Lillie and Talon. Sorrel was already at the surface, shaking the water from her eyes. Lillie gasped and Talon coughed, rubbing at her long face.

Vola glanced around, taking stock. Lillie's light had gone out, leaving them in murky twilight. Some pale glow came from moss growing along the walls, giving Vola just enough light to see a shelf of rock extending into the water in front of them.

Vola dragged Talon to the rock and shoved until the ranger rolled up onto it and out of the water. It took Lillie two tries to follow. Sorrel hopped up with ease and began squeezing water from her hair and tunic.

Vola looked back at the swamp beast and tugged on the lead. "You want up or are you going to paddle around in here."

It glared at her and tugged back.

Vola shrugged and wedged the rope in a gap in the rock before hauling herself out of the water.

"I wonder if Rilla knows about this place?" Sorrel said, hands on hips as she gazed around the cavern. Rock walls arched over them nearly three stories up, and the shelf they stood on sloped up out of the water to a broad passage in the stone ahead. Light flickered against the walls of the passage like the flames of a torch.

"If she did, wouldn't she have looked for Lillie's brothers here?" Talon said.

There was a splash as the swamp beast put both front legs up on the rock shelf and hauled itself out of the water.

"Seriously?" Vola said. "You know I offered to help."

"We should proceed," Lillie said. "There appears to be someone down that—"

A fierce yell made them jump, and Vola drew her sword and

pulled her shield from her back. Sorrel went to pull her weapon around, but the staff got caught in the edges of her wet tunic and she fumbled it. It clattered against the stone, and she scrambled to catch it before it rolled into the water. Lillie spun to help her and slipped on the wet rock, landing on her face with an oof.

Three figures boiled out of the passageway, two in full plate armor, and suddenly Vola wished she'd risked swimming with hers.

She met the first figure, planting her feet and raising her shield to deflect the blow with a clang. She followed it with a good shove and knocked the armored knight on his ass. He splashed into the two inches of water lapping the rock shelf.

The second armored figure rushed her.

"Wait!" Lillie cried, climbing to her feet, dripping. "Wait, don't attack."

The knight rushing Vola staggered, and Vola easily stepped out of the way. The one on the ground raised his visor and squinted at them. "Lillie?"

"Xavier," Lillie said, her voice coming out in a breath of relief.

The third figure, a young man who could only be a couple years older than Lillie, stepped forward. "You came back."

"Kellan," Lillie said.

The young man stepped forward to wrap her in his arms, not caring that she was soaked.

Vola sheathed her weapon and held out a hand to the knight on the ground. "Sorry," she said. "No hard feelings."

He bared his teeth at her and clanked to his feet without taking her hand. "Nice hit," he said. "But the rest of your team needs some work."

Vola bristled but couldn't help casting a look back at Sorrel, who'd finally caught her weapon and stood staring mulishly at the staff. Talon had left her bow back at the inn but had drawn both daggers. She looked disappointed that the fight hadn't turned into anything. With her cloak tied around her waist, her patchy beard was plainly visible.

"Lillie, what are you doing here?" the last brother said. Innis, if Vola remembered right.

"I got your note," she said, pulling away from Kellan. "In Kellan's, er…room."

Kellan flushed bright red and stammered. It seemed painful blushing ran in the family.

Xavier frowned. "I didn't know you'd left a note. Anyone could have found it."

"It was, um, well-hidden," Sorrel said. "Probably only Lillie would have found it. Anyone else would have been…distracted."

"There were a lot of distractions in the book," Talon admitted.

"She was desperate to find you," Vola said. "We all were. We've been sent to help prove your father's innocence. And yours by extension."

"Do you know who might have framed you?" Lillie said. "Who would have stolen Father's seal and sent the research to Southglen's enemies?"

"Any one of the traditionalists," Xavier said. He pulled his helm from his head, letting shoulder-length hair cascade down in a torrent of flaxen waves. Vola tried not to roll her eyes. If she'd tried the same thing, bits of her braid would have been stuck to her sweaty forehead. Xavier's hair had less red in it than Lillie's, but it was still an incredible shade of honey, without any of the flyaways and sweat it should have had after being shoved in a helmet.

Xavier caught her looking and gave her a sidelong smirk. He turned and flipped his hair over his shoulder so it caught the glow from the moss around the cavern.

Vola's eyes narrowed.

"They all knew what Father was working on," Innis said. He pulled his own helm from his head, revealing a much starker face than the other two brothers. Maybe he took more after his mother, the elf. He was a lot less round with more angles and sharp edges.

"Did any of them come around asking about it, Kellan?" Lillie said.

The youngest Ephyra brother went red any time anyone looked at him. A lot like Lillie, actually. He wore his red-gold hair short, and someone had given him a leather jerkin that didn't quite fit. He kept tugging at the bottom edge. "No. I—I mean, no more than usual. Like Innis said, they all knew what we were researching. But Father would never have just given his notes to anyone."

"Did anyone hold a grudge against him?" Vola asked.

"Yeah, Virvalim," Xavier said, tucking his helm under his arm and picking up his sword. He straightened to level a sharp glance at Lillie. "He said you fled after you killed Otis. He blamed Father for not raising you right."

The blood drained from Lillie's face, leaving her pale and shaking.

"He almost challenged Father in your place, and Father would have answered him, too. You know he'd do anything for you."

"I was trying to protect him by leaving," Lillie said. "I was trying to protect all of you."

Xavier sighed and stepped forward. He ruffled Lillie's wet hair. "Never mind. What are big brothers for except to clean up their sister's messes?"

Lillie sucked in a sip of air, and Vola stepped closer to her.

"The point is, if you're looking for someone to blame, start with Virvalim and his friends," Innis said.

"Unfortunately, the evidence we have against Virvalim is too weak," Vola said. "We need something more substantial."

"We can give you a name or two," Xavier said, heading toward the back passage. "Virvalim's got plenty of traditionalists on his side. They all agree the princesses need to be taken down a notch or two. But there are a couple who he trusts more than others. You can start there. Maybe one of them will lead you to Virvalim himself. The sooner, the better. It's damp down here."

"We'll get you out of this," Lillie said to his retreating back. She reached to clutch Kellan's hand. "I promise."

NINE

KELLAN LED them back through the passage, past a couple of small chambers where bedrolls were laid out on the floor. The brothers were clearly using another larger cavern as a living area. A rickety table was pushed up against one wall with papers strewn over its surface. Someone had stuck a bunch of notes to the stone wall and attempted to connect them with some red string, but half the pages had fallen and now hung loose like a child's mobile.

The cave system ended in a rounded dead end with a design chalked onto the floor.

Lillie raised her eyebrows at Kellan. "I didn't know you did portals."

He ducked his head. "I've been practicing." He grasped Lillie's hands. "I was serious in my note. You shouldn't be here, Lillie. You don't have to get involved. It's treason we're talking about."

Lillie lifted her chin. "I'm not running away again. I'm not going to leave you three to die on a gallows next to Father."

Kellan shook his head. "It's not just that. Virvalim wants you dead. If you go toe to toe with him —"

"I'm not the same person I was when I left Glenhaven." Lillie glanced at Vola and the others with a small smile. "I have a lot more friends on my side now."

"So does Virvalim."

"He has to catch me first. And I intend to make sure he's the one strung up for treason before that happens."

"Lillie —"

The sound of plated boots clanked behind them and Xavier came up the passage. Kellan dropped Lillie's hands and stepped back.

The swamp beast, standing sullenly at the end of its lead rope, tried to take a bite of Xavier as he passed. The thing's teeth scraped along the plate armor of his arm, and he jerked back.

His eyes narrowed at Talon, who held the lead. "Keep your beast in check," he said. "This is hard enough to polish without cleaning river slime out of the gouges."

Talon glared but said nothing, her cloak still dripping from her shoulders. She'd left the hood down.

Xavier blinked at her for a moment before turning to Vola. "He doesn't say much, does he?"

"She," Vola said as Talon's lips curled back, revealing teeth.

"Oh." He glanced back, taking in Talon's patchy beard and sharp features. "If you say so."

"Xavier," Lillie said, voice snapping in the passage. Talon pulled her hood back over her head even though the damp fabric clung in odd places ,and Vola knew it had to be clammy.

He shrugged. "Start with Lord Tildon. He's Virvalim's oldest friend and right-hand man. And we have the most information on him. We can give you more names once we've done the legwork finding them. But this one shouldn't be too hard to take out. Not for you three." He wiggled his eyebrows at Vola.

She gritted her teeth. Three? Who was he excluding?

"We'll look into it," she said.

"You can go through here." Kellan gestured to the portal. "We're the only ones who can get in this way. Everyone else can only get in by swimming, but we can escape out the back if we're ever discovered."

Talon didn't wait for more of an explanation. She just dragged the swamp beast forward and stepped into the chalked diagram. A flash of light made Vola raise her arm, and when she lowered it, they were gone.

"Works for me," Sorrel said with a shrug and followed Talon.

Lillie glanced at Vola, and Vola raised her chin. "You know I'm not going through before you," Vola said quietly. "I can't protect you if I'm on the other side of the city and you're not."

Lillie sighed. "Very well." She turned to her brothers, who were watching with interest. "I'll be back soon with some good news."

"Stay safe," Kellan said, brow drawn down.

Xavier gave Lillie a mock salute as she stepped into the portal.

Vola followed. There was a bright flash which made her eyes water, but between one step and the next, the feel of the air on her skin changed. Instead of damp and cool, a fresh breeze brushed against her.

She blinked the tears from her eyes and found herself in a bower off the main thoroughfare of one of the higher tiers. Not far from the Ephyra manor. Night had fallen over the city, lights springing up along all the streets, a twinkling string of flashes climbing up the cliff.

Talon wrestled with the swamp beast in an open archway, while Lillie scribbled in her spellbook. Sorrel squinted down at herself, patting her hands up and down her torso.

"Missing anything?" Vola said.

"Nope," Sorrel said. "Just making sure."

"Lillie?"

"Sorry, just taking notes on Kellan's spell. It's clever. I actually think I could manage it without the diagram, matching it to the occasion. Although having it chalked there does make it more permanent—"

Vola let her babble as she led the way back to their inn. They made it back without incident, and as the others filed into their room, Vola knocked on Rilla's door. No one answered.

"Rilla must still be up at the palace," she said as she rejoined her party.

"Probably pulling on more ropes." Sorrel flopped down on a couch. "Treasonous ropes. Ropes that yell."

"She mentioned the annual ball," Lillie said. "I imagine the princesses want to present a strong, united front in the face of this treasonous plot. They're probably preparing for that." She grinned as she leaned her hip against the back of Sorrel's couch and scanned a list she'd started in her spellbook.

"What are you so happy about?" Vola said.

"We have a lead." She chuckled to herself. "This might not be as hopeless as it seemed this morning."

"You have any ideas about how to flush Lord Tildon out?" Sorrel said.

"Not yet. But I have his name, and from there, I can get everything else we need." Her eyes blazed, and her smile wasn't quite so nice as it had been a moment before.

"Good," Talon said. Though her tone didn't sound too happy. She'd stripped off her wet cloak.

Vola took it from her and arranged it on a peg above the mantle so it would dry.

"I'm sorry about Xavier," Lillie said quietly.

Talon shrugged, light eyes still on the flames. "It's not his fault. I don't look like a girl."

"There is never an excuse to be rude," Lillie said sharply. Then she sighed and rubbed her forehead. "He was always Mother's favorite. And she wasn't exactly known for her caring nature.

Father was always careful not to show favoritism, hoping to make up for the damage she did."

Sorrel's gaze roved over the room and settled on the packages they'd brought back and discarded earlier that day. "What if you did look like a girl?"

Talon's eyes flicked to her. "What?"

Sorrel bounded off the couch and snatched up the tissue wrapped nightgown they'd convinced Talon to buy. She held it out to Talon. "We could all use a change of clothes right about now, anyway," Sorrel said, tugging the bottom of her damp tunic.

"I don't know…" Talon started.

"We'll make it a party. A really low-key relaxing party in front of the fire."

"A party with nightgowns?" Talon said.

Sorrel's eyes widened, and she gasped. "Oh my gods, it'll be that slumber party Lillie's always wanted."

Lillie flushed. "It was an offhand comment once when we'd just met."

Sorrel rustled the paper of the package. "Look, just put it on." She gestured to the screen in the corner of the room. "You can test it out and see how you like it, and if it's awful, you don't have to show us at all."

Talon bit her lip, but it was hard to ignore Sorrel's infectious grin. "You won't laugh if I don't come out?"

"Of course not," Lillie said.

Talon's lips thinned, but she finally snatched the package and slunk toward the screen.

"Pillows," Sorrel said. "We need all the pillows."

"What? Why?" Vola pulled the scabbard and shield from her back and propped them against the wall beside the door, ready if she needed them.

"Because that's how you do a slumber party, duh," Sorrel said, pulling all the cushions from the sofa onto the floor in front of the fire.

Vola dug in her pack for a dry shirt. "If you don't change, you'll get them all wet."

"Oh, good point." The halfling scampered over the cushions to the other side of the couch. She pulled her staff from her back and tossed it across the bed she'd claimed. Then she paused. "Do you think that priest was right?"

"What priest?" Lillie had her bag open on her bed, contents scattered across the covers.

"The one in the temple. Who said I was using Maxim's Warhammer as a glorified stick."

"Well, I mean, you are," Vola said, pulling her shirt over her head. "I guess what matters is whether or not that bothers you. You doing okay, Talon?"

"I feel stupid."

"Oh, no," Lillie said, straightening.

"Oh, yes."

"What's wrong?" Vola said.

"There's…too much skin. Is there supposed to be this much skin?"

"Didn't we get the long one?" Lille said, sliding off the bed.

"Yeah, but there're no sleeves. Just these little…strap things."

"Oh, well, that's normal."

"Maybe for you!"

"All right," Vola said, holding a hand out to Lillie. "We're trying to find something Talon likes. Right? If she doesn't like it, then she doesn't like it."

"I like the-the idea of it. I just…"

Lillie brightened. "Oh, I know." She lunged across the bed to grab a long fall of silk.

"Where'd you get that?" Vola said.

"I grabbed a couple things at the manor. Mostly books. But

this was my mother's. One of the only things she left me." She tossed it over the top of the screen. "Put this on over it. It will cover your shoulders."

The silk slithered over the top of the screen and disappeared.

Finally, Talon appeared around the edge, face pinched.

Vola cocked her head as they took her in. "Not bad," she said with a breath of relief. The silk robe fell almost to the ranger's feet, covering the light blue frills of the nightgown they'd picked out.

"What do you think?" Vola said.

Talon picked at the long belt. "I like this. It's nice, and it makes me feel nice, but not…exposed."

Lillie smiled. "Then you should keep it."

Talon's eyes widened. "You said it was your mother's."

Lillie shrugged, turning her head. "That makes it sound special, but it's really not. My parents' marriage was a contract," she said. "A way to bring elven blood into the Ephyra line. My mother stuck around long enough to bear four children, and when I was born, she was done."

"She left you," Talon said, flatly.

"I don't even remember her. She left the robe, but it doesn't fit me. I think she hoped I would grow up more like her, tall and thin. I prefer it on you." The last part she added in a small voice.

Sorrel popped her head out from behind the screen. Vola hadn't even noticed her head back there. "Did any of us have a normal childhood?"

"Er. Me? Mostly." Vola raised her hand. "Weirdly supportive parents. They just happened to be an orc chieftain and a woman who likes to the throw axes when she's drunk."

Talon scratched at the sandy hair growing from her chin. There were places where the skin was raw and damaged, places where she'd tried to shave it off with a dagger or maybe a machete.

"Would you like me to help you with that?" Vola asked. She cleared her throat. "Getting rid of the beard might help you feel more like yourself."

Talon grunted something that wasn't a yes but also wasn't a no. Vola fetched the shaving kit from her pack and settled Talon in front of the fire while Lillie wobbled around on the cushions, trying to find a comfortable spot.

She held up a little pot of salve. "This will keep the hair from growing back so fast. It also softens it when it does. But it works better if you shave first."

"Why do you have all this?" Talon asked, eying the straight razor and the little bowl for cream.

Vola's cheeks went hot, and she shrugged as she lathered Talon's chin. "I, uh. I have a bristly top lip. Comes from my father's side of the family. My Aunt Urag can grow a full beard if she wants to. She's the one who taught me about the salve."

Sorrel came out from behind the screen dressed in her new black underwear. It was clearly too big, but she'd crossed the straps in the back and tied them so the triangles in the front at least stretched to look fairly normal.

"Nice," Vola said, not sure if she was supposed to say anything else.

Sorrel put her hands on her hips. "I like it. Also, it was all I had that wasn't wet."

She bounced across the cushions to the fire, deftly avoiding the shaving area.

"Try that," Vola told Talon a moment later and handed her a wet towel to wipe the froth from her chin.

The ranger sat rubbing her smooth face for a long moment afterward, and Vola pretended not to see the way her throat bobbed.

"So, what else do you do during a slumber party?" Talon said, voice rough.

Vola shrugged. "I didn't even know what one was until Lillie told us." She glanced at the half-elf.

Lillie flushed under their scrutiny. "I…uh. I've never actually been invited to one."

"You what?" Vola froze as she put away the shaving kit.

Lillie's shoulders hunched. "I never had a lot of friends growing up."

"Me neither," Sorrel said quietly. "Only Hazel."

Vola and Talon exchanged a look. She'd be willing to bet Talon had grown up mostly alone aside from Gruff. And there hadn't been many children willing to play with a little girl who was green and saw red any time she got angry.

"I'll bet its pillow fights," Sorrel said suddenly. "That's what you do for slumber parties. And telling dirty stories. Like that one Vola's been carrying around."

"What?" Vola said, stiffening.

"What?" Lillie said, perking up.

"It's what she picked out at the market," Sorrel said. "The thing she's never gotten to try. *Love's Disaster*. Or something like that."

"Peril," Vola said quickly. "*Love's Peril*. I thought it would…" She sighed. "Okay, fine. I've always wanted to try one of those books. I like…I like love stories and orcs don't have a lot of romances."

"What's been stopping you?" Lillie asked.

Vola rubbed her eyes. "The words…I can read just fine if I focus on one letter at a time, but when I see a whole bunch of words all together, they swarm together and go squiggly."

Lillie tilted her head thoughtfully. "I've…I've heard of that. There are some people who have a harder time with letters. Is it common in your family?"

"My dad's side, again," Vola said. "Most orcs don't like writing. Probably the uncivilized side coming out."

"No," Lillie said, her face brightening. "No, it makes perfect sense. Orcs have an oral history. They tell their stories, right? They don't write them down. Probably because the words won't sit still for them. They worked around it, and a whole culture grew out of it."

"Try telling that to the rest of the world," Vola muttered.

Sorrel, the little traitor, trotted back over with the book in her hands. She handed it to Lillie.

"I could read it aloud," Lillie suggested. "If you'd like."

"It's not that important," Vola said.

"I want to hear it," Sorrel said. "I want the angst and the happy ending. The whole shebang, please."

"Me too," Talon said.

Lillie, who would never say no to reading a book, especially one that was already in her hands, smiled and opened it.

"Oh." Her face cleared. "I've read this one. It's actually quite good. It has this whole subplot with the queen, and the heroine has to court the prince in order to win his heart. There's magic and mystery and a ball…" She trailed off, staring into the distance. "A ball."

"What?" Vola sat up on the cushions.

Lillie scrambled over the back of the couch to find the list she'd left in the mess on her bed. "The ball. The annual ball. The one Rilla's been worrying about. Lord Tildon will be there. He always is."

"Are you suggesting we go to a party to track down a traitor?" Sorrel said.

"I am."

"Woohoo, I'm in." She batted her eyes at Vola. "And maybe Vola can find her handsome prince there."

Vola hit her with a pillow. "There. Pillow fight. Now our night is complete."

TEN

"I THINK I'm beginning to hate this mission," Sorrel said with a frown as she and Vola watched Lillie sort through second hand stalls in the market the next day. "Weren't we just here yesterday?"

"She said we need clothes for this party the nobles are having." Vola tilted her head as Lillie held up something pale pink and stared at it before shaking her head.

In that moment of distraction, the swamp beast nipped Vola on the elbow. She yelped and leaped back as far as the lead rope would let her. She glared at the thing.

"You'd think you'd appreciate the fresh air." She crossed her arms, keeping her elbows as close to her body as possible. She was starting to regret bringing it along, but Lillie had hinted that they'd have a lot more packages today.

Talon followed Lillie, hood down in public for the first time that Vola could remember. She was trying out her new clean-shaven jaw, and with her fitted cuirass giving her more of a waist-line, the effect wasn't half bad.

"What do you think about blue?" Lillie asked her.

"I actually like the pink better," Talon said after a moment's hesitation.

Lillie blinked. "Oh. I was avoiding it because I thought it was a cliché."

"Maybe for you it is," Talon said.

Lillie's smile brightened her face. "Pink it is. And maybe black for Sorrel."

"What's wrong with what I'm wearing?" Sorrel called.

Lillie cocked an eyebrow at the plain gray tunic. "For a ball? Really, Sorrel."

Sorrel rolled her eyes.

"Think of it like equipping yourself for battle. This is our chance to armor ourselves according to the challenge."

Sorrel groaned. "There is not nearly enough fighting in this investigation," she said. "When do I get to hit something again?"

Vola gave her a sympathetic look.

Sorrel pulled her staff around and stared at it, a frown settling between her eyebrows. "I wonder if Maxim doesn't like how I'm using his weapon. I really do just hit people with it."

"I mean, he gave it to you," Vola said. "Not to Hazel, and not to Tallah. The other monks couldn't make it work for them. Just you. So he must have wanted you to have it. And to use it the way you would use it."

"Yeah, but there's so much more it should be able to do. Maybe I should try learning some of that." She looked chagrined and glanced up at Vola. "When I kept it, I was just thinking it would do more good out in the world. I didn't really think I'd have to work at figuring out how to do that good. Bash the bad guys is my normal approach."

As she spoke, Vola caught movement out of the corner of her eye. She glanced over the swamp beast's scaly back and saw Finn creeping along behind them.

He caught Vola's glance and squeaked before ducking out of sight behind a stall.

Vola fought the urge to go after him. She was not his keeper. She wasn't responsible for him. She had her own people to worry about, and she couldn't watch their backs if a street urchin with more mouth than sense distracted her.

With a half-hearted sigh, she forced herself to face Lillie and made encouraging noises every time the wizard turned to solicit her opinion.

"Red, do you think?"

"Black," Vola said. "If Sorrel's getting black, I want black, too." Although she couldn't help eying the red satin Lillie held up. Orcs didn't get dressed up much, and when they did, it was usually with the bones of their slaughtered enemies. Vola'd never really had the chance to wear anything like what Lillie was sorting through.

Vola scanned the crowd, watching for anyone who seemed too interested in their group. Virvalim was still hunting Lillie, and the longer they could keep him from realizing she was back in the city, the better.

However, the group of workmen hanging around the next stall over were clearly focused on Vola, not Lillie. One ogled her armor and then spat.

"Look at that orc masquerading as a paladin. Who do you think she's fooling?"

Vola raised her eyes to the sky and turned her shoulder so she wouldn't be tempted to bare her teeth at the man.

"She could be serving one of the Obstacles," another said, sounding bored.

"That just proves my point, don't it? They're all evil—Ouch!"

Vola couldn't help glancing back at the workmen. Finn stood beside them, hands clenched at his sides. "Leave her alone."

"What the hell does it matter to you—"

Finn wound up his right leg and kicked the man in the shin. Again, from the sound of it. "She never did anything to you."

The workman growled and grabbed Finn's arm, hoisting him up on his toes. "Look, kid—"

Finn twisted and planted his elbow in the man's gut, just like Vola had shown him.

Vola sucked in a breath, almost as if Finn had knocked the air out of *her* lungs. *He was listening. If he paid attention to what I said about that, what else did he hear me say?* For a second, she didn't see Finn hanging from the man's hand. She saw a girl with green skin and tusks, fighting to protect someone else because she didn't know how to protect herself.

A breath of warm air and the pressure of a body beside her made her jump. The smell of fresh grass and a sunshine drenched riverbank washed over her.

She looked up to find a woman with gold skin and masses of dark curling hair cascading down her back. She wore a black robe with a fish knife tucked into her belt.

"Not your responsibility, huh?" Her voice was full of the rush of wind and the *shing* of a blade being drawn.

"Lady," Vola started.

The corner of the woman's mouth quirked up, and she extended a hand. In it was a short sword with a worn leather scabbard.

The same short sword Finn had stolen and Vola had left as an offering on the temple altar.

"Vola," Sorrel said. "Check out the—Oh, hey, Cleavah."

"Sorrel," Cleavah said. Her eyes held Vola's. "The sword."

"Yes, lady," she said.

The woman walked away, pulling up a dark hood which she hadn't been wearing moments before. She stepped behind a column at the edge of the market and didn't come out the other side.

"I wish Maxim would talk to me personally," Sorrel said with a sigh. "Maybe he could tell me what to do with his Warhammer." She tilted her head. "What's it like to have a goddess come talk to you every time you get something wrong or you have a question?"

"Uncomfortable," Vola said.

"So what was this one about?"

Vola handed Sorrel the lead rope of the swamp monster and clutched the scabbard before stepping toward Finn and the workman.

"Him," she said and grabbed the workman's forearm where he still held the boy. She squeezed until the man yelped and dropped him.

"Excuse me," she said. "This one's mine."

The man opened his mouth, but she squeezed just a little harder and he gasped. She released him and he stumbled back, cradling his arm.

"S-sorry," he stammered. "He's all yours."

He jerked his chin at his cronies and they scampered off.

Sorrel stepped out of their way and cocked her head as Finn picked himself up off the ground and glared up at her. "What did you do that for? I was trying to protect you. Now I owe you for the rescue."

"Don't try to keep score, kid," she said. "By the time I'm through, you'll never be able to catch up."

His brow scrunched. "Huh?"

She ignored the noise and held out the short sword balanced on both her palms. Finn's eyes latched onto it.

"When a knight trains a paladin, he gives the boy or girl two gifts. A sword to signify that the trainee is ready to use his strength in service to his master. And a shield when the training is done to signify that they're ready to protect the world."

She touched the hilt over her shoulder briefly before returning her hand to the scabbard. "My trainer, Henri, gave me this one, and I still remember him when I carry it."

Vola held the sword out to Finn. "If you want to protect people, then I'd better teach you how to do it the right way."

His mouth fell open, but he didn't reach for the sword.

She shook it a little. "This means I will teach you. It means I will feed you, clothe you, and equip you. I will protect you until you can protect yourself and the ones you choose to serve. It means you'll obey me, follow me, and learn what I'm willing to teach you."

"But, why? You didn't like any of the things I gave you."

"This isn't something you've earned, Finn. It's my gift to you. We'll work on the rest later."

She took one more step until the sword hit him in the chest. His hands rose to curl around the scabbard.

"One more thing," she said before he could take it. "No more stealing. I'm responsible for your actions. Anything you do, I have to answer for. Both the good and the bad. Understand?"

He gulped. "You'd do that for me?"

Had Henri felt this same lump in his throat when he'd handed her a sword? "Yeah," she said around it. "I will."

She let go, and he kept hold of the sword, clutching it to his chest. He nodded, his bright hair flopping into his eyes. "I promise," he said, even though she hadn't asked him to say it.

She took him by the shoulder and steered him back toward Sorrel. He walked woodenly, his hands cradling the sword.

As the boy came into range, the swamp beast's eyes narrowed and its head lashed forward. Sorrel was too slow to yank it back.

But instead of taking a chunk out of Finn, the swamp monster butted its head into his shoulder and...cuddled?...him.

He chuckled and reached up to stroke the thing's scaly cheek.

"There's a plus side already," Sorrel said.

"Who would have thought the thing had a heart."

"Well, it did love Henri, remember?"

"Yeah, but everyone loves Henri." Vola took the dangling lead rope from Sorrel's hands and handed it to Finn. "First lesson is responsibility," she told him. "You get to keep this…thing. Make sure it's fed and watered and stabled correctly. And above all, make sure it doesn't eat anything still alive. Including people."

"What's going on?" Lillie said as she came toward them, Talon in tow. Her hands were full of packages.

"We're parents," Sorrel said, throwing her hands in the air. "Vola just adopted him. Isn't he cute?"

"Oh?" Lillie said, peering at Finn. She glanced between Vola and the boy. Vola inhaled, ready to defend her decision, but Lillie just smiled. "I suppose we shouldn't be surprised."

"What?" Vola said. "Why?"

Talon snorted. "You have to protect everyone and everything. You're a paladin. It's what you do. You adopted all of us, didn't you?"

Vola sighed and rubbed the back of her neck. "Only by accident."

ELEVEN

THAT NIGHT VOLA made sure Finn was tucked up tight with the swamp monster in the inn's stable, before the party headed for the ball. She hoped that the two might keep each other out of trouble. There were already teeth marks in the wood walls of the stall where the swamp monster had tried to eat its way out, and the stable boys were terrified to venture down to that end of the stable. But Finn sat placidly between the beast's front legs as it snuffled his hair.

Vola just shook her head and left them to their own devices for the night. Tomorrow morning she'd figure out what she was going to do with the boy. He wasn't any older than she was when Henri started teaching her. Maybe that was her best bet. She couldn't go wrong if she followed the path laid down by her own teacher. No one was better at taking awkward, gangly youths and turning them into honorable knights than Henri.

She left them murmuring to each other and met the rest of the party just outside the inn. They all seemed a little overdressed to walk through the streets, but in a city with so many stairs, carriages weren't really a thing.

After less cajoling than Vola had anticipated, Lillie had convinced her to try the red dress. It felt two sizes too small, squeezing her in all the wrong places, but Lillie insisted it was just right. The skirt would have been far too narrow if it weren't for the knee-high slit that allowed her legs to move. She would never admit it out loud, but she'd checked herself in the mirror five times before they'd left just to make sure it was really her who looked this good. At least she was armed. That made her feel more like herself.

"I still think the sword strapped to your thigh ruins the line of the dress," Lillie said, glancing down.

Vola touched the bulge of the hilt and scowled. "Well, there's nowhere else to put it," she said. "And I'm not walking into a party with one of our suspects without a weapon. Besides, this isn't even close to a sword. It's a dagger."

"A very long dagger."

"If this goes according to plan, we won't even need weapons to flush out Lord Tildon."

"That's easy for you to say," Vola said, turning to lead them up the hill toward the upper tiers. "You *are* a weapon."

Lillie flushed and lifted her skirt to go up the next flight of steps.

Her gown was a deep blue the color of the sky just before full dark. It fit her form through shoulders and hips before falling in a full skirt below her knees. The blonde beauty normally down-played her looks under a plain blouse and bodice, but tonight she'd pulled out all the stops, drawing her hair back to accentuate her face and lightly pointed ears.

Talon shifted from foot to foot, fussing with the long flaps of her gauzy jacket. She and Lillie had landed somewhere in the middle on design and color with fitted pink trousers beneath a long blue coat whose tails nearly trailed the ground behind her. Talon had been letting her hair grow out from a shaggy cut, and she'd pulled the sandy locks back from her face with a couple jeweled pins.

Her eyes flitted from shadow to shadow, and she buried her fingers in Gruff's neck, a sure sign she felt the need to hide. But her feet remained planted on the cobbles, and she didn't bolt.

Talon frowned down at herself. "Not having weapons makes dressing as a girl way less comfortable," she said. "I'd feel better if I knew I could stab someone."

Vola glanced at her sidelong. She'd bet her shield that Talon had at least two knives hidden on her person at the moment. But she wasn't going to point them out.

"You look really good," she said instead. "Do you like the outfit?"

"I like the color," she said, still frowning. "But I don't look like the rest of you. Everyone's just going to look at me and know I'm not really a girl."

"But you are a girl," Sorrel said, skipping ahead to hop on a railing and walk along the edge. "No matter what you look like."

She wore a sleeveless black top and flowing pants that fastened at the ankle. She'd convinced Maxim's Warhammer to disguise itself as a particularly ornate fan which swung from her wrist. No one would know it was a god's weapon unless they looked closely at the little paintings, which depicted angels in battle against a dark tide of roiling mist.

Talon shook her head. "It's more than just the clothes. It's the way you move and talk and fight."

"I think it's more about how you feel about yourself," Lillie said. "If walking and talking like a girl is going to make you feel more like yourself, then by all means, let's practice."

She took Talon's hand and lifted the edge of her own skirt to demonstrate. "Smaller steps. We don't go tromping about like we're wearing boots when we're wearing slippers. It hurts your feet."

Vola glanced down surreptitiously and tried to take smaller steps.

"Lift your skirt on stairs so you don't tear your hem. And we don't scratch in public. At least not so everyone can see."

Sorrel caught herself itching her nose and dropped her hand to her side.

Talon tripped over her feet and growled.

Lillie smiled sympathetically. "And we don't growl during polite conversation."

Talon opened her mouth to protest, but Lillie cut her off.

"Even if they say something stupid. We laugh and tell them they're so funny but in a way that makes it clear they aren't funny at all."

"Wouldn't stabbing them tell them they weren't funny?"

Lillie opened her mouth, then hesitated like she couldn't quite bring herself to say no. "Well, yes. But we're trying to avoid bloodshed."

"Why?"

Lillie sighed. "Let's stick to the movement thing and polite conversation."

They reached the upper tier where streams of elven nobles converged from other houses and tiers to make their way to a tall wrought-iron gate which guarded an elegant facade. Wizard's fire lit the scene and magical lights twinkled in the evening.

Human guards in red livery stood on either side of the open gate and nobles streamed inside, chatting and laughing.

According to Lillie, Lord Tildon attended the Elven Exile ball every year. They should be able to find him and flush him out. How exactly, Vola wasn't sure yet. Lillie's plan revolved around poking at the noble until he exploded and they could arrest him for some indiscretion. But Vola was with Talon on this one. Poking him would go so much better with blades than with words. Still, Lillie's plans usually worked much better than the rest of theirs.

A woman in a dress covered in feathers glanced at their party, her eyes traveling between the four of them. Vola felt it like a bucket of ice-water when her gaze landed and stayed on Vola. The woman's chin raised, and she sniffed before leaning to whisper in her companion's ear. They tittered together.

Normally, it didn't bother her. At least not too much anymore. But tonight…

"I should have worn my breastplate," Vola muttered as Sorrel led Talon toward the gate.

Lillie turned her face up to Vola's. "What?"

"I could have come as your bodyguard or something. This way I'm…exposed."

Lillie beamed at her. "No. You're perfect." She took Vola's hand and tucked it under her arm, then marched them forward and into the fray.

Past the gate, pillars of glowing mage lights lit a large garden, each one colored differently so patterns wound up and down the pillars. Marble paths meandered through the perfectly manicured lawn. Several manors opened onto the shared space, their doors flung wide. It was all very impressive, but the thing that caught Vola's eye and held it was the structure directly across from them. A series of interlocking arches rose ahead, forming a beautiful barrier between the garden and the space beyond.

"The Diaphadon," Lillie said. "A sacred space for elves everywhere. They built it just after the Exile as a reminder of home. Until a couple of years ago it was actually illegal for anyone other than an elf to enter. They weren't technically allowed to kill non-elves who trespassed, but they often did it, anyway."

Vola glanced around. "I see a lot of elves here tonight." There was a smattering of other races, but the party hardly reflected the diversity of the city below them.

Lillie's smile went quiet and calculating. "Yes. Most other races still avoid this space." She didn't elaborate. She gestured Sorrel and Talon over. Sorrel bounced on her toes while Talon frowned at the ground where the skirt of her jacket dragged.

"You two, okay?" Vola said.

Sorrel shrugged. "There's food everywhere, but I haven't seen a decent beer yet."

"Well, we're not here to drink. Lillie has a plan." Vola cocked her head at the wizard who'd come up with the whole scheme.

"Sorrel and Talon stick to the edges of the party," Lillie said. "You're less conspicuous right now. So keep an eye out for our suspect. Lord Tildon is an old elf. Ancient, really. His house colors are blue and silver. Once you have him in sight, I just want you to listen. Remember everything he says. Every joke he makes, every person he talks to and about what."

"And where will we be?" Vola asked.

"Walking right down the middle," Lillie said with a grin as the other two dispersed.

"What?" Vola said, but Lillie stepped out, and with their arms entwined, Vola had no choice but to follow.

Lillie sailed through the party, nodding regally to the other guests, wiggling her fingers at another group across the way, and laughing as if Vola was the funniest thing in the world.

"What's your game?" Vola whispered, trying to keep an eye on Sorrel and Talon and watch her feet at the same time.

"Why, what do you mean, my dear? Oh, look. There's Rilla. We really must say hello to the princess." Lillie towed her to a long table covered in a pristine tablecloth and piles of food. Literally piles. A tower of strawberries rose beside a fountain of sparkling white wine, while a replica of the city made entirely of stacked pastries loomed on the other side.

Rilla stood beside the table, a bright pink drink in her hand. She cradled the delicate glass as if it was the only reason she'd come. She wore a sleek green dress with gold around the plunging neckline. A wide gold headband with green jewels held back her hair. A figure in plate armor and a slitted helm stood behind her, still as stone.

"Princess," Lillie murmured as they stepped up to the table. "So nice to see you."

Rilla's gaze sharpened on them and her eyebrow went up. "Wasn't expecting you four here. Anything I should know about?"

"We didn't get a chance to brief you," Vola said. "We have a lead on one of Virvalim's toadies. Lord Tildon is supposed to be here tonight and we're going to flush him out."

Rilla's face brightened. "And I thought this was going to be one of those boring parties." She waved a hand. "Have at," she said. "And let me know if you need help with anything. Aside from the drinks, these things are always incredibly dull."

She tossed back the rest of her pink drink and set the empty glass on the table.

"You say that like we're going to cause a scene," Lillie said. "We can be discreet."

"Like a house on fire," Rilla agreed. "You're aware that Sorrel is over there chatting up the dean of the Wizard's University and Talon is using the table as a back scratcher."

Vola spun and sure enough Talon was discreetly inching along the edge of a table across the way, rooching up and down so the edge would scratch her back, while Gruff growled at anyone that came close. Apparently, she'd taken Lillie's admonishment about scratching in public to heart and found an alternative. Though Vola doubted that had anything to do with gender and everything to do with growing up with a pack of wolves.

Sorrel's voice carried across the lawn as she sidled up beside an old white man with a long gray beard. "You're supposed to be smart, right? Do you have any experience with the weapons of a god? Studied their properties or know how to use them properly?"

Vola rubbed her forehead. "All right, so we're not perfect."

"Hmm, I don't think they've found Lord Tildon, yet." Lillie tapped her lip. "Time for phase two. I was going to show Vola the Diaphadon. I think she'll really appreciate the architecture."

Rilla's eyes narrowed, and she glanced between Lillie and the stretching archways beyond the garden. "You were?"

Lillie smiled brightly. "I am."

"Are you sure you know what you're doing?"

"I do. You should come along, too. You did say you didn't want to be bored."

Rilla tilted her head as if conceding the point. "I did. I think I'll give you a head start, though."

"Very thoughtful of you," Lillie said and started forward.

Rilla gestured the golem in armor forward and whispered in its ear.

"What are we doing?" Vola said. "Isn't this the place that elves don't like non-elves going?"

Lillie gave her a sidelong look. "You were paying attention. Don't worry, they abolished that law years ago. Rilla was part of it, I believe, citing that there should be no limitations in the city based on race or class. Still, you might want to signal Sorrel and Talon to stay close."

Vola obliged, keeping the hand gesture down near her waist but making sure to meet both Talon and Sorrel's eyes to be sure they saw.

"This is politics again, isn't it?" Vola said as they approached the lowest archway, wide enough to admit five people at a time. "I hate politics."

"Vola, politics is just tactics without the swords. And you love tactics." Lillie slowed her steps as if she wanted to be sure everyone saw them and where they were going.

Vola sighed and followed as Lillie finally stepped inside the Diaphadon. Then she had to catch her breath.

Marble arches rose around them, interlocking repeatedly until they formed an intricate pattern surrounding a large empty space paved with gleaming stone. But that wasn't its only beauty. A ball of burning wizard's fire trapped behind a globe of perfect glass hung suspended in midair directly in the center of the space. It sent out rays of light to glitter along the intricate archways, sparks of color zipping along each pathway, creating a pattern of endless light and color.

Vola stepped forward, jaw dropping. "Holy Cleavah."

"Mmhmm," Lillie said as they moved further, directly under the ball of wizard's fire. "You can almost see why the elves wanted it all for themselves."

That brought Vola back from the moment, and she snapped her chin down to glance around the space inside the arches. Several people milled, but every single one of them was tall and willowy with sharply pointed ears. They murmured to each other, speaking behind their hands while their eyes shot accusations at the two of them.

"Ah, there he is. Right on time," Lillie said as a tall elf with flowing silver hair and a blue tunic strode into the Diaphadon after them.

"Lord Tildon?" Vola whispered.

"As predicted. Let's see what happens."

"What do you think you're doing?" The ancient elf spoke forcefully, face florid with outrage.

"What do you mean?" Lillie blinked innocently and twined her arm through Vola's. Vola caught sight of Sorrel and Talon slipping into the Diaphadon behind him, sticking discreetly to the walls.

"You profane this sacred space by bringing anyone outside of the blood here. An orc no less."

Lillie let her mouth fall open as Vola drew herself up. "I just wanted her to see the beauty of this place. It's not against the law, now, is it? Lord Tildon?"

Oh my goddess, Vola thought. She did this on purpose. That's why she dragged me in here. To draw out the racist bastard and get him to say something stupid. Vola glanced at Lillie, who was doing a wonderful job of acting half as clever as she really was.

Lord Tildon jerked back and ground his teeth together, his jaw working with the effort. "No," he grated out. "No thanks to those frauds who sit on the Thrones of Southglen."

Lillie's fingers tightened on Vola's arm, but her expression remained pleasant. "Oh, you don't agree that the city should be free for all its citizens?"

"Freedom is beside the point," he spat, silver eyes flashing. "Standards must be maintained. There are those of us who are just better at knowing what's best for all. A bunch of young women who haven't the breeding or experience to know better should not overturn our sacred traditions."

Over his shoulder, Vola saw Rilla slip into the Diaphadon. She leaned against the archway, listening intently.

"But shouldn't we allow others to experience those traditions, so they may grow and appreciate them as well?" Lillie said, her voice gaining weight. "If we continue to grind the rabble under our boot, how will they ever become more than what we've made them?"

Lord Tildon drew back his lip and sneered. "Dress a pig up as a noble steed and it's still just a pig underneath." He gestured to Vola.

Vola felt the growl start in the back of her throat, but she strangled it when the wizard laid a hand on her shoulder.

"Please don't insult my friend so, my lord."

Lord Tildon's eyes bugged out. "Friend? Surely you mean pet."

Vola bit her tongue, reminding herself that this would all backfire if she was the one to lose her temper.

Lillie stepped back as if affronted and placed her hand on her throat. "What we call each other in private is none of your business, sir."

Vola choked and tried to turn it into a cough.

The lord's nose wrinkled in disgust. "You would sully yourself with this filth?" He gestured to Lillie's ears. "You corrupt your own noble heritage."

Vola's gaze flicked back to Rilla. Lillie's plan was solid, but if Vola could get Lord Tildon to really lose it, they'd have everything they needed to arrest him. Then Rilla could take it from there.

"Well, the princesses say I'm all right," Vola said. "They say I'm equal to the likes of you even." She jerked her chin up at the glowing arches above them and leaned in toward Lillie. "It's pretty enough, *pet*. But I can show you much better." She drew a finger down Lillie's arm, suggestively.

Lord Tildon snarled and drew a line of white light in the air. A blade coalesced in front of him, and he grasped its hilt. "I will spill your heathen blood for that. Then maybe the bitches on the Thrones will see what they've done to this city."

Lillie grinned in triumph at his blade and dropped Vola's arm to free up her hands. "Oh, yes, I'm sure they will."

"Tell me more, Lord Tildon," Rilla said from the doorway as her golem came through with a clank. "I'm absolutely riveted."

Lord Tildon spun, his hair flaring behind him, to stare at the princess of the Dagger Throne. He glanced at his sword and gulped.

"I might be a dumb orc, but I believe it's treason in any country to draw steel in the presence of royalty," Vola said.

Rilla examined her fingernails.

Lord Tildon's eyes widened, and he sneered. But panic

underlay his confidence, and his frantic gaze took in each of them, Lillie and Vola standing in the center, Rilla and her golem blocking the door, Sorrel and Talon flanking them, and a scattering of shocked nobles standing around the space. And Lord Tildon realized he was screwed.

"Give up, Lord Tildon," Vola said, conversationally. "Come quietly and we'll find you a nice sumptuous cell."

His brows drew down, and his pale cheeks filled with a flush of rage. "Never."

He threw his free hand into the air and drew down, like he was calling another sword, but this time several points of light grew in an arc around him until three glowing chimeras stepped out of thin air, onto the shining marble of the Diaphadon. The massive beasts crowded the space, stretching their mismatched necks as if waking from a nap.

An elven woman screamed and fainted into her companion's arms.

The nearest chimera whipped all three heads around to stare at them, lion, goat, and dragon eyes fixed on Vola.

"Well, shit." Vola said, and a little strike of lightning hit the chimera on its dragon muzzle. "That escalated quickly."

She yanked up the slit in her skirt and drew the dagger she'd smuggled in strapped to her leg. Talon flipped back the tails of her jacket and pulled out two.

Sorrel leaped on the nearest chimera, Maxim's Warhammer already morphing into a staff. The next one over stalked toward Vola and Lillie. Without her shield, Vola felt particularly unprepared to defend anyone, but she thrust herself between Lillie and the monster, anyway so Lillie had a chance to fall back, her lips moving with a spell.

The chimera took a swipe, and Vola ducked, rolled, and came up slashing. Her short blade cut into the beast's lion claw and it howled. It lunged for her, and Vola stepped back. She trod on the edge of her skirt and tripped. There was a violent tearing of silk and suddenly she could move her legs. Too late, though. The chimera used the moment of hesitation and pounced.

Its claws dug into her shoulders as she fell backwards, but just as her back struck the stones, the monstrous weight disappeared with a crackling pop. Vola glanced up to see Lillie lower her hands.

"Wow," Vola said, pulling herself to her feet. She gestured to the other two chimeras. "Do that again."

"Are you kidding? I can't believe that worked the first time. I'll never get up enough steam for another," Lillie cried. She yanked the back of her skirt up between her legs and tied it around her waist to leave her legs free for running. "It's mostly fire from now on."

Lord Tildon booked it across the space toward the front of the Diaphadon.

"You cover the others," Vola called. "I'll make sure this bastard doesn't get away."

"Forward," Rilla's voice called from the other side of the chimeras. "I said forward, you hunk of metal."

"Authorization not recognized."

Vola gripped her blade and sprinted for Lord Tildon, who had reached the doorway of the Diaphadon. A crowd had gathered outside, peering in at the commotion, but he could push through to escape easily.

Behind Vola, flames erupted, sending a wave of heat across the marble. Lord Tildon glanced back just as Vola tackled him with a flying leap. They hurtled through the doorway, limbs tangled. Party guests scattered before them, screaming.

Lord Tildon shoved at her and brought his sword up between them. Vola rolled away to avoid the slash and struck the legs of the nearest table. It collapsed in a cascade of pastries and fruit, and the fountain of sparkling wine crashed to the marble in a wave of alcohol.

Vola pushed free of the wreckage and shook a large strawberry off the end of her dagger.

Lord Tildon lunged for her, his fist lashing out, and Vola had a split second to realize his hand was covered in cracked stone. She raised her free arm to protect her face, but he went for her other hand instead, bringing his weighted fist down across her wrist.

Vola cried out, her blade skittering away across the marble. She sucked in a breath, bent over her smashed wrist, and glanced at her blade, which was too far away to retrieve.

He drew back his sword arm and aimed for a strike.

"Vola!" Lillie called from too close. The wizard limped through the wreckage of the table as she gathered a spell in her hands. But instead of throwing it at the lord, she thrust her fist down into the ground.

Thunder sounded, spearing Vola's ears, and a shockwave rippled out, smashing the marble at their feet.

Lillie tugged at the edge of one of the broken pieces. "Here."

Lord Tildon growled and charged her.

Lillie scrambled back, slipping in some sort of pudding. Vola ignored the pain in her wrist and grasped the edge of a large flat piece of marble and lifted it as a shield.

She threw herself in his way, and Lord Tildon's blade shattered against the stone.

A glow formed at his feet and chains made of white light snaked out, tangling his legs and reaching up to manacle his wrists.

Lord Tildon froze, caught in the light as Rilla and Sorrel and Talon trotted up beside them. The scattered nobles around them cowered back from the princess's golem, which lumbered along behind.

"There," Rilla said. "I'd like to see you get out of those. That power comes directly from my Throne."

"The chimeras?" Vola gasped out. She couldn't get her feet under her, and it seemed much better to kneel there on the broken marble.

"We got them," Sorrel said. "Are you all right?"

Vola shook her wrist and nearly passed out. Black crept across the edges of her vision.

"You should take care of that," Lillie said. "You probably shouldn't have lifted that last stone with it, but I didn't want you sliced in half without a shield."

Vola put her other hand to her head, trying to think straight. "Is anyone else hurt?"

"No," Talon said. She'd made it through the fight unscathed. The bottom edge of her jacket was a little frayed, but she hadn't tripped over it at least. And Sorrel looked fresh enough to take on another chimera.

Lillie took her chin in her hand and gave her a rare but firm look. "We're all fine, but I think we'd feel better if our paladin was in top shape."

Vola placed her hand over her wrist and winced. "Lady bless," she gasped. White light seared between her palm and her wrist, and the pain instantly receded.

As Vola's head cleared, she noticed a lady at the door of the Diaphadon screaming and holding her head.

"The hostess," Lillie said, catching the direction of her glance. "She's not exactly pleased."

Rilla stood, staring at Lord Tildon, mouth set in a crooked line. "Well, that's not how I expected my night to go." She speared Vola and Lillie with a glance. "You know this doesn't actually prove he's part of the plot, right?"

"No," Lillie said. "But he's arrested for treason now, and you have an excuse to seize and search his property and everything else that might be relevant. If you can't pull the truth out of that…" She held out her hand, palm up.

"Then I don't deserve the Dagger Throne," Rilla finished for her.

"You used me," Vola said, though her voice didn't hold much heat.

Lillie flushed. "No. I showed you something beautiful. It was his racism I used."

"Clever," Rilla said. "Not how I would have done it, but I can't deny it got the job done."

TWELVE

"Do you suppose it will be enough?" Sorrel said as Lillie laid an armful of white flowers on the altar of a local temple.

"The hostess said to make a donation to Helena, goddess of apologies, and she would think about forgiving us for ruining her party," Vola said. "That's all we can do."

"How much more do we have left?"

"There's another two baskets worth of flowers and fruit on the swamp beast," Talon said, laying down her armful.

"'Cause I wanted to talk to the priest," Sorrel said, glancing over her shoulder at the temple acolyte, who watched them with a furrowed brow. This wasn't a terribly big temple, only dedicated to four of the minor Virtues, so he probably didn't get many visitors.

"Go ahead," Lillie said. "This was my fault, anyway. I've got the rest."

Sorrel skipped over to the man, pulling Maxim's Warhammer from her back. Vola stepped to the front door to check on Finn, who stood at the swamp monster's head, holding it steady as they unloaded it. Little planters stood on either side of the steps, holding dead bushes. Clearly the upkeep of this place suffered from its lack of popularity.

"Next time you crash a nob's party, can I go with you?" Finn said, his wide grin lighting up his face.

"It's not like it was fun," Vola said with a sigh. "It was work, and we got attacked. We had to fight for our lives. In dresses."

"Even better," Finn said, letting go of the swamp monster to swing his arm around like he carried an invisible sword. She'd made him leave the short sword behind. She didn't want him carrying it until he knew the basics. "You showed the bad guy not to mess with you."

She narrowed her eyes. "Being strong isn't about being able to beat the crap out of the other guy."

"No, it's about making sure no one will mess with you again."

She frowned. "Look, if you were holding a sword, it would be all wrong. Here." She stooped to pull a long dry stem from the shrubbery beside the door. "Hold your hilt like this. Fingers here. Feet apart, weight on your toes. Otherwise, I can do this."

She shoved the tip of her finger into his shoulder, and when he wobbled, she stepped into his space so he fell on his butt.

He gaped up at her, and she extended a hand. "Your job isn't to look strong, it's to be strong. To be steady so those around you can depend on you."

He didn't meet her eyes as he climbed to his feet. "Nobody depends on me. I'm just Finn the failure."

She stared at him until he flushed.

"Who calls you that?" she said.

"No one. Just me."

"Plant your feet like I showed you. Grip your hilt. The right way. Better. Keep your weight on —"

"My toes, yeah. You said."

She tilted her head. Then she stepped forward and tried to tip him again. He swayed with the poke, but his feet held firm.

She raised her eyebrows. "See. Not a failure. Just unpracticed. Prove you're someone who can be relied on, and people will begin to depend on you."

He opened his mouth again, hair falling in his eyes, but she cut him off.

"Just practice. That's where the strength comes from. It comes from discipline. It comes from determination. Those are all in here." She tapped him on the chest. "Not up here." She poked his forehead. "I'll show you some more practice drills when we get back to the inn. You run them over and over again, and you'll be able to do them in your sleep."

"That doesn't mean anyone will ever look at me different." He spoke to the ground.

She slipped her finger under his chin and tilted it up. "You heard what they said about me in the market, right? That's why you attacked them."

He shrugged.

"Lots of people think that way about orcs. But look." She pointed to Lillie, who took the steps carefully, her arms laden with the last two baskets. "They don't. They rely on me. They trust me. Whose opinion do you think I care about more?"

He didn't answer, and she didn't make him, but when she turned away to check on the others, he was raising his stick, grip firm as he rearranged his feet.

She stepped back into the temple.

Talon and Lillie had finished unloading the baskets of offerings and were arranging them on the altar. Lillie kept adjusting them, as if looking for the perfect balance of color and symmetry. Talon tried to emulate her, but Vola couldn't see any difference.

Sorrel trudged over, hands in her pockets, her staff across her back.

"What did he say?" Vola asked.

"He said its power is divine." Sorrel scowled.

"Well, yeah. We knew that."

"Well, the closest thing to divine power in this world is magic. I think that means I've been going about this all wrong. I really am just bashing people on the head with a divine stick. If I want to use Maxim's Warhammer to its full potential, I should be using it like a wizard's staff."

Vola frowned and opened her mouth to say something about how the staff changed based on who was holding it, and it wasn't a wizard's staff when Sorrel held it.

Before she could speak, a sharp squeal came from outside and Finn's voice raised in ire.

Vola rushed for the doorway, Sorrel right behind her.

Finn lay on the ground as if thrown there, the swamp beast huffing and snorting over him. Vola's jaw clenched as she drew her gaze up, taking in the square-jawed, black-haired man standing beside the steps. He wore brown, trimmed with yellow, but the cut of his tunic and the quality of the fabric made the effect much more impressive. Several guards behind him wore the same colors over their armor, their scabbards and shields well-used.

The man raised his chin when he saw Vola and Sorrel. "Is the bitch inside hiding?"

Vola's eyebrows shot up. "Excuse me?"

His lips pulled back, and he clenched perfectly manicured hands at his sides. "You heard me. It's just like a bitch to cower in a temple seeking forgiveness for her sins."

"Not sure who you're talking about, buddy," Sorrel said. "But you might want to find a new insult. It loses its effectiveness the more you use it."

Vola stalked down the stairs to help Finn to his feet. "Did he hit you?" she asked quietly.

He rubbed his nose with his sleeve. "I remembered what you told me about my feet. But it doesn't work if they have steel."

"No, it doesn't. We'll get to that as soon as I deal with this."

"You tell her to come out," the man said. "Or I'm desecrating this temple with her blood. The gods will forgive me, I'm sure."

There was a rustle at the door, and Lillie appeared with Talon at her side. Her breath caught when she saw the man, but she did not retreat, she did not back down.

"Virvalim," she said, voice flat.

"Lilliara Ephyra." His lips curled in an unpleasant smile, and Vola felt the rage rising in her, tinging the edges of her vision red. "Lord Tildon told me you'd returned to the city."

Vola's fingernails dug into her palms. She'd hoped that bundling Lord Tildon off to prison last night would prevent that sort of information from getting back to Virvalim.

"After all the time I've chased you through swamps and back-waters, this is where I find you." He spat on the step.

"Boy, you really don't care about blasphemy, do you?" Sorrel said, glancing at the glob of spittle.

"You murdered my son," Virvalim cried, pointing at Lillie. "You murdered my boy and left him bleeding in a privy."

"Your son was a vicious rapist who deserved to be put down like the rabid pig he was," Lillie said, without a trace of hesitation or uncertainty in her voice.

Virvalim screamed, and he lunged up the steps.

Vola launched forward, placing herself squarely in his path.

He bounced off her chest and down the steps. The guards reached for their weapons.

Vola held up a hand. "Aren't there rules about this sort of thing?" She glanced back at Lillie, who was white as milk but hadn't flinched. The guards exchanged glances but didn't charge. Vola let her hand drop. "Execution among nobles isn't illegal," Vola said. "Right?"

"She has to be able to defend her actions. Physically." Virvalim scrambled to his feet, looking a little less poised this time. "She can't hide anymore. She has to meet me or be declared a fugitive from the law."

"Yeah, but you can't just brawl in the street." Vola waved her hand vaguely, trying to think like Lillie. "There's tradition and honor to uphold."

He sneered up at Lillie. "Fine. I challenge your execution. Meet me in the Justice Hall tomorrow to defend yourself or you'll be declared a murderer, and I'll hunt you down and slaughter you the same way you slaughtered my son, you bitch."

He spun on his heel and snapped for his guards to follow.

Vola blew out her breath and turned to face the others. Sorrel and Talon both glanced back at Lillie, who held her head stiff and proud.

"Well, that could have gone worse," Sorrel said. "He could have actually come up with something more original to call you."

Rilla paced from one edge of the Throne room to the other, hands clenched behind her back.

This space in the very heart of the palace was lined in tall windows and drenched in light. Blue stone inlaid the white marble floor in a starburst pattern radiating out, each point ending in a throne. Fifteen seats of power arrayed around the circle.

Vola squinted, but she couldn't see anything outwardly that indicated these fancy chairs chose the rulers of Southglen. They all looked like cold lifeless marble, short in the back and uncomfortable looking. Each one had a symbol carved into the back rest. Nothing particularly magical about them at all.

Also, there were fifteen Thrones. But there were not currently fifteen princesses in the room. Only eight.

A severe looking older woman with long white hair tied intricately behind her head occupied the Shield Throne. Justice and Law were present, both middle-aged, one with a sharp nose and the other with thin lips. War and Magic. Education. And one frumpled princess darted in late and sat in the Sewage Management Throne.

The rest were working or traveling. According to Rilla, they didn't live here all of the time. The only time they were all present was during a quorum or a coronation.

"Lord Virvalim has issued a public proclamation calling Lilliara Ephyra, daughter of the accused Lord Ephyra, to defend herself in challenge to her execution of his son, Otis Virvalim," the princess of the Law Throne said, voice ringing around the chamber. She had pulled her graying brown hair back into a no-nonsense knot, and she wore a sensible shirt and loose trousers, all in a pale green.

Her blue eyes settled on Lillie, who stood in the center of the circle, Vola, Sorrel, and Talon arrayed behind her. "Did you in fact execute Otis Virvalim?"

Lillie raised her chin. "I did."

"A barbaric custom we would do well to eradicate this instant," the princess of the Justice Throne said. "So other nobles don't take it into their heads to murder each other for sport." She glared at Lillie.

Vola cleared her throat.

"You disagree?" the princess of the Justice Throne said. She wore her silver blonde short accentuating her slightly pointed ears.

Vola's mouth went dry under her gaze. Talking to Rilla was one thing. She was like the terse friend you'd just met in the bar. This scrutiny made Vola feel like an ant at a picnic. "Lillie would never murder someone for sport," Vola said. "You could just ask her what happened."

The Justice princess glared while the Law princess hid a smile behind her hand.

"I wouldn't have had to murder anyone if the law was doing its job," Lillie said and suddenly the princess of the Law Throne wasn't smiling anymore.

"Oh?" she said, dangerously calm. She tapped the arm of her Throne.

"Otis Virvalim was trying to rape a serving girl. I drew his attention away from her, toward myself."

"So you could kill him," the Justice princess said.

Lillie's jaw twitched. "The law protected me. It did not protect her. So yes. I used it to execute him."

The two princesses exchanged a look. Clearly Law and Justice worked together a lot, and Vola wondered if they were so in tune with each other that they could communicate with a couple of finely arched eyebrows.

"I can't say I'd rather have a man like Otis still in this world," the princess of the Law Throne said. Then she unbent enough to murmur to the Justice princess. "Seriously, who names their kid Otis?" She straightened again to jerk her chin at Rilla, who still paced between her Throne and the empty Treasury Throne.

"Did you know about this when you hired them?" she said.

"Of course, I did," Rilla snapped. "I'm not incompetent."

"Kind of a conflict of interest there, Dagger," the Justice princess said.

"We didn't know Virvalim was involved in this treason plot beforehand." Rilla spun to point at Vola and the others. "And you guys were supposed to lie low."

"Sorry we caught one of your bad guys for you," Sorrel said, rolling her eyes. Vola kicked her ankle. "Ow."

"This isn't the end of the world," Vola said. "Virvalim doesn't know there's any connection between us and the Thrones. You just happened to be there when we took down Lord Tildon. It isn't our fault the moron drew steel in the presence of the Dagger Princess."

Rilla's chin jerked up.

"So you're prepared to meet his challenge?" the Justice princess asked.

"I don't see that I have a choice. Do you?" Lillie said.

"You could run again," the Law princess said, her eyes narrowing.

"I will not do that," Lillie said quietly, squaring her shoulders.

"Do you think you can actually beat him?" the Law princess said.

Lillie opened her mouth and then hesitated. Vola saw the stiffness in her shoulders, and this wasn't the resolve of confidence. Despite the number of people Lillie had set on fire for them, she'd just been struck with a moment of doubt.

"She's not alone," Vola said, stepping forward. Sorrel and Talon mirrored her.

"You're claiming a champion, then," the Justice princess said, as if unsurprised.

Vola's brow drew down, ready to argue that Lillie was perfectly capable of defending herself, but Lillie ducked her head. "Yes."

"It is your right," the princess said. She speared Vola with her glance. "But make sure this is the end of it. We want the matter resolved and we want it resolved yesterday. No loose ends. Not even a shred of proof she might be guilty according to the law."

Vola placed her fist on her breast and bowed. "Yes, Your Highness."

THIRTEEN

THE DAY of Lillie's challenge dawned bright and clear. Not even a wisp of fog marred the view across the plain.

Vola adjusted her breastplate as they walked, feeling much more at home now that she carried her weapon and her shield. Talon and Sorrel were fitted for battle as well, carrying their usual range of weaponry. Lillie walked beside them, quiet and pensive.

Finn trailed along behind them. He wore his short sword at his side, but Vola had tied the hilt to its scabbard to keep him from drawing it.

"I don't want you swinging it around until I teach you how to use it," she'd told him that morning.

"But then what's the point of carrying it?"

"It's a statement," she'd said. "I think we'll need all the strength we can muster today. If things go iffy, you can use this." And she'd handed him an unassuming sling and a pouch of rocks.

His lip lifted in disgust. "That's for kids."

"It's this or nothing."

He'd chosen the sling.

At the top of the hill, people streamed into the central court of the Justice Hall. But this wasn't the common rabble they'd seen a couple of days before. These men and women were dressed well, with silks and brocades and jewels that glinted in the sun. They laughed among each other as they picked their way through the court.

"What's the occasion?" Sorrel said, glancing around.

Vola noticed the looks they were getting from the crowd. Especially Lillie. "I think we are."

"A challenge duel is always a bit of a show." Lillie stared straight ahead as if ignoring all the looks. "It's entertainment and justice all wrapped up in one. People will want to see who is in the right but also place side bets."

The courtyard where Rilla waited for them was recessed with tiers of seats leading down into a sandy bowl where the combatants would fight. Cracked arches surrounded the top tier indicating the antiquity of the place, and while someone had replaced the sand below, dark stains still stood out around the pit. Rilla tapped her foot at the edge, arms crossed and eyes wary.

"How are you feeling?" she said under her breath as they drew even with her.

Vola shrugged, answering for all of them. "Good. It's nice to finally face the threat head on rather than skirt around it."

"Keep that confidence. There's no room for mistakes with this one." She hesitated a moment before jerking up her chin and saying. "Good luck."

"Thanks, Rilla. Or should we call you Dagger?" She looked at the princess out of the corner of her eye.

Rilla snorted. "Only if you want to sound like a pompous ass." She gestured up toward the palace. "We use our Throne names between ourselves as a formality, to remind ourselves of our respected jurisdictions. And the rest of the world uses them because they can't be bothered to remember our real names. But if a princess gives you her real name, it's because she wants you to use it."

"Then maybe we should call you Allellarilla," Sorrel said, cocking her head.

"Try it and see what happens," Rilla said, fingers sliding down the hilt of one of her many knives.

Sorrel's grin pulled into a grimace. "Okay, maybe not."

Rilla stepped back a pace. "I shouldn't be seen playing favorites," she said. "Head down to the fighting floor. You'll sit on this side."

A railing surrounded the floor below where sand had been strewn to absorb any splattered blood. It reminded Vola of the training ring at the paladin academy. Her teeth clenched in reaction. A lot of paladin trainees had stood behind that railing and mocked the half-orc who'd dared to be a knight. Of course, she'd also made a lot of them eat sand in that same training ring, so the memory wasn't all bad.

The princess for the Justice Throne stood in the center of the ring, waiting motionless. She wore a long sleeveless dress in pristine white linen, which hung in uninterrupted folds from her shoulders.

Across the way, Virvalim settled into his area behind the railing along with his guard contingent. Two heavily armored knights stood with him beside the bench.

Vola raised an eyebrow at the plate armor and glanced at Lillie.

Lillie followed her look. "Otis's cousins. I believe he was an only child, so they are his closest relatives besides Virvalim. They'll have a stake in this as well."

There was a lot of shuffling as the spectators settled themselves in the tiers above, but as soon as the Justice princess raised her arms, silence fell across the space.

"The challengee has chosen to be represented by a champion. Lord Virvalim, your response."

Virvalim smirked across the way, then bent his head to converse with the two knights.

Sorrel pulled Vola back a step while Lillie stood stiff beside the railing. "What's going on?" she whispered. "Why doesn't she want to beat the crap out of this guy for herself? Doesn't she know she can do it?"

Vola glanced across at Virvalim's smirk and remembered the way Lillie's brothers had ruffled her hair and talked down to her. The only ones who'd been surprised when Lillie had chosen to be represented by a champion had been her party.

"Maybe it's not that," Vola whispered back. "Maybe it has something to do with being back here where everyone underestimates her. Maybe she's underestimating herself."

"Or she's just being clever about it," Talon put in.

"What do you mean?" Vola asked.

"A noble is only as good as the people they command, right?" Talon said, meeting her eyes. "Maybe this is a way to prove her strength by proving ours."

"Lord Virvalim, your answer," the Justice princess prompted.

Virvalim finally looked up. "I will use a champion as well. Since the bitch is too frightened to face me herself."

"Language, my lord," the Justice princess said, sending a mild glare at Virvalim. Rilla climbed down the tiers to join her in the middle of the ring. "Very well. Principals, choose your champions."

One of Virvalim's nephews climbed over the railing without even waiting for acknowledgment.

"Antony," Lillie murmured before turning to her party. "He's a brute, but he does know what he's doing. Watch for feints; he loves to trick his opponents. It makes him feel smart."

"Your champion, Lilliara Ephyra?" The Justice princess said.

Lillie looked at Vola. Rilla looked at Vola. They all looked at Vola.

But Vola thought about what Talon had said about proving their strength.

"Sorrel," she said quietly. "You're up."

Lillie blinked, opened her mouth to protest, and then stopped, looking thoughtful. "All right," she said. "This should be interesting."

"Oo, fun," Sorrel said and then ducked under the railing. She stepped forward into the ring, her small figure dwarfed by the empty space and the monstrous knight towering across from her. A murmur spread through the crowd.

Rilla frowned and stepped closer to them. She caught Vola's gaze. "Are you sure?" Her eyes flicked to Sorrel. "No offense."

Sorrel's smile went flat. "Why do people always say 'no offense' and then insult you, anyway?"

Vola bared her teeth. "I'm sure."

"This is a challenge match," Lillie told Sorrel. "Not an execution. You just have to put him down so he doesn't get back up again."

Sorrel's shoulders drooped. "Oh."

"We don't need another death to fuel Virvalim's temper," Vola said. "He'll abide by the results. Right?" She glanced at Lillie.

Lillie's mouth pulled in a grimace. "Theoretically."

Talon drew her daggers and leaned on the railing. She huffed when Vola looked at her. "Just in case."

"Any other rules I should know about?" Sorrel said.

"You can use whatever you need to take him out. Magic, skill, strength. The idea is that if the gods favor you, you'll be able to win regardless of what the other guy brings with him."

"All right, then." Sorrel turned back to her opponent and squinted, looking him up and down.

Very deliberately, she pulled her staff from her back and tossed it back to Vola. "Hold this."

Vola caught it, raising her eyebrows. But she wasn't about to second guess Sorrel.

The Justice princess rolled her eyes before raising her hand. "Then let it begin. And let this be the end of the matter between you two."

She and Rilla stepped to opposite sides of the ring, one on either side of the two combatants.

The brute across the way, Antony, glanced at Sorrel standing unarmed and unarmored in the center of the ring. He lifted his visor so Vola could see his eyes moving uncertainly, and he turned to check with Virvalim.

Virvalim waved him on. "Why are you standing there? Attack. Should your cousin go unavenged?"

Antony shrugged, then shut his visor with a clank and settled his grip around his longsword.

Sorrel waited, fists at her side, stance steady. Vola knew her well enough to see her attention was focused but not panicked.

Suddenly, Antony roared and charged, sword raised. Sorrel side-stepped, ducked, and stuck out her foot.

The armored knight went sprawling, spraying sand into the air as he skidded to a stop.

Instead of pressing the advantage, Sorrel straightened and dusted off her hands. She tilted her head at her opponent. "Would you like to try again, now that you're ready?"

Antony growled and clambered to his feet with much clanking. Then he lunged for Sorrel again. This time she spun out of the way, but he was ready for it and followed her quicker than Vola would have thought possible encased as he was in all that metal.

Vola straightened, eyes steady on the two of them.

He swept his blade around, and Sorrel leaped over the tip. As he staggered through the swing, Sorrel brought her fist down on his arm. Antony grunted and yanked back.

The gathered nobles gasped and murmured as he switched his blade to his other hand and shook out the one that Sorrel had struck. Vola could imagine his grimace.

He settled himself once again, but before he could press forward Sorrel rolled, came up behind Antony, and delivered a blow to the back of his knee that sent the knight into the sand again. She leaped for him, but he kept hold of his sword and lashed out, making her dodge back out of the way.

Sorrel spun with a kick, keeping Antony on the defensive and on his knees. He had to shuffle around to keep track of her frenetic movement.

She darted behind him and her foot lashed out, landing a blow to the back of his head that would have had Vola seeing stars.

He shook his head, lumbered to his feet, and wove unsteadily, trying to line up a blow with his sword.

Sorrel stopped moving and planted her feet in the sand, almost like she wanted him to hit her. But Vola saw her close her eyes. One foot slid to the side and then back, and Sorrel brought her hands together in front of her.

Vola raised her chin in expectation.

Sorrel flickered and her figure wavered and flashed behind the hulking brute. They'd seen the move before. Sorrel had learned it from a former monk in Brisbene.

She reappeared, almost as if out of thin air, except there was no portal. Then her hand shot out, palm open, and there was a crack of thunder as the knight flew across the ring. He struck the railing opposite them and slid to the ground, the wood splintered above him. He lay in the sand, unmoving.

Silence rang around the arena as Sorrel straightened and shook out her fist.

"Sorry," she said. "I meant to make that last longer."

Vola couldn't help the grin that spread across her face, but there was a collective rumble from the gathered nobles above them. And it didn't sound triumphant. If what Lillie had said was true, they'd been looking for more of a show.

Virvalim jumped over the railing and raced to his fallen nephew, but even Vola could see that the knight still breathed. He was just out cold.

"Trickery," Virvalim hissed, his fingers checking for a pulse. He raised his gaze to glare at Sorrel and then at Lillie. "Deceit. There is no way a halfling could beat a full Glenhaven knight."

Sorrel planted her hands on her hips. "Excuse you. You mean a full monk of Maxim. And it's not my fault he couldn't last. You should have taught him to pace himself."

A susurus of displeasure moved through the crowd as neighbors leaned to whisper and point.

Vola swung her leg over the railing to join Sorrel. Just in case.

"That's it, Lord Virvalim," the Justice princess said, stepping into the ring. "The matter is over."

Virvalim's face turned a dark purple. "It's not over," he spat. "Not when your deceit is clear for all of us, finally." He spun, facing Rilla, who had just vaulted the railing. "You used the Dagger Throne's magic to win."

Rilla stopped short. "Careful, you fool. Words are weapons I am vastly familiar with."

"Your Throne's power is wrapped in trickery and subterfuge," he said with a sneer, pitching his voice to carry to those who had gathered for the show. "How are we not to draw conclusions when a pint-sized outsider uses trickery to beat one of the best knights in the city?"

"Hey," Sorrel said. "No one helped me. Every skill I have, I earned. If you were in the right, the gods would have let you win despite being incompetent."

"Virvalim, you're making a fool out of yourself," the Justice princess said, stepping forward. Her lips pulled in a hard firm line. "I represent the Justice Throne and as barbaric as this tradition is, the halfling is right. We honor the decision of the gods."

"False magic can muddle even the gods. The Obstacles themselves are corruptions of the Virtues. You used the power of the Dagger Throne to cheat them of their justice." He spun to point a finger at Rilla.

She crossed her arms with narrowed eyes. "Why?" she said. "Why would I cheat?"

Virvalim's mouth tipped in a smirk. "Because those people are working for you."

Vola's chin jerked up, and she glanced at Rilla.

Rilla's face went very still.

"They're working for you," Virvalim said, turning so his voice carried across the tiers. "They caused the scene at the Elven Exile celebration so you could arrest Lord Tildon without a fair investigation. They stay in the same inn that you frequent down in the city. They work for you, and now your honor is wrapped up in theirs." He swung his finger around to point at Lillie, who drew herself up with a scowl. "You had to make them win. Otherwise, you would have gone down with them."

He spread his hands to the crowd. "This is just proof that the magic of our Thrones is corrupted. Their power isn't reliable anymore if it's used to choose princesses who would cheat and steal from the honest citizens of Southglen."

"Treason," the Justice princess hissed.

"No," Virvalim cried. "Truth. At last. The Thrones are corrupt. The princesses are unreliable. And all we have to defend ourselves is our righteousness."

He raised his hand and his guards swarmed over the railing,

along with his other nephew. Rilla spun, daggers drawn, but Virvalim himself went for the Justice princess. He lunged and grabbed her around the neck as two of his guards went for Rilla.

Screams erupted from the stands as Vola pulled her sword and shield to defend the princesses.

Figures clambered over the railing, shedding coats and cloaks to reveal more of Virvalim's livery. He must have had guards scattered amongst the crowd.

Vola caught one against her shield and thrust him back to fall on the sand. She cast a quick glance behind her to check her party. Talon stood on the first tier behind the railing, bow drawn and trained on the enemy below while Gruff held her targets in place for her. Sorrel held out her hand and Maxim's Warhammer screeched across the space to slap into her palm.

A ball of fire struck the ground at Vola's feet, warping around her to blast Virvalim's guards back against the sand. Lillie had entered the fray.

A skinny figure at the edge of the fight swung a measly sling, and a rock whizzed by Vola's ear. She sighed and sprinted over to Finn.

With one move, she slashed the bindings on his sword.

His eyes went wide. "You mean it?"

"Keep the blade up, defend yourself. Goddess, I wish I'd had time to show you more." She gripped his shoulder and nearly yelped when light sprang from her hand, outlining him in a brief white light.

"I'll keep an eye on him," Cleavah said in her ear.

"Thank you, lady," Vola said fervently.

Guards staggered past, clothes on fire as Vola sprinted for Virvalim. Rilla spun, blades flashing, and from past evidence, Vola trusted she could protect herself for the moment.

Virvalim staggered back, his arm choking Justice as he dragged her with him. His guards coughed and beat at their flaming livery, but several still had the presence of mind to cover their lord as he retreated. They fell in between Vola and Virvalim.

Vola lowered her shield and threw one aside. The next came at her with his left side wide open. She parried and kicked his left knee so he staggered to the sand. She ran him through and pivoted to find an opening to Virvalim.

The lord had fetched up against the railing, but he didn't look like the cornered rat he was. He held her gaze with his teeth bared as he raised his hand, a glowing stone in his palm.

"A spell," Lillie called through the smoke. "He's going to teleport—"

Vola threw herself at him, her sword whistling in an arc.

A flash of light threatened to blind her and wind sucked into the space where Virvalim had just been. Vola's blade lodged in the railing as Virvalim's guards and his two nephews disappeared, leaving empty air. The gust of displaced wind knocked the rest of them to their knees, gasping.

The only ones left on the fighting floor were Rilla, Vola, and the rest of her team. Even the tiers had cleared of any innocent bystanders.

"Shit," Rilla said, pushing herself to her feet.

Vola hissed and put her boot up to lever her sword out of the railing. Lillie and Sorrel sat up out of the sand while Talon reappeared behind the first tier of seats. Finn crouched beside the far railing, blade still in his hand, shaking his head as if his ears rang.

Rilla hunched, hands on her knees, cursing.

Virvalim and his men were gone. Along with the Justice princess.

"Sooo, that just happened," Sorrel said.

Talon hopped down onto the sands and clapped her on the back, making her stagger. "Congratulations. You fought so well, you started a coup."

FOURTEEN

RILLA PACED from one side of the throne room to the other. Five more women stood beside their Thrones, faces pale and drawn. One wrung her hands. Another picked her nails, making them bleed.

"He's taken four," Rilla said. "Four of us. Justice he grabbed right there in the arena where any of us could have stopped him. The rest he managed to nab with a combination of surprise and strength. His cronies broke into the residences of the princesses and stole them right out from under us."

Vola held out her hands to calm the occupant of the Dagger Throne. "You can't blame yourself. Like you said, he surprised us."

"But this is what I'm supposed to do. This is what I'm for," Rilla cried. "I'm supposed to protect Glenhaven and the Thrones from this sort of treachery."

"Then use this as a learning opportunity and move on," one of the other princesses said. She had coppery colored skin and straight black hair that fell in waves down her back, and she stood in front of the Education Throne. "We will fix this. Who does he have?"

"Justice, Law, War, and Shield."

"And Magic," a breathless voice added. A golem came into the room, supporting a young woman around the waist. Soot smeared her round cheeks, and she limped heavily, favoring her right side. "We were discussing new regulations for our healers when they broke in and tried to take us. I barely escaped."

The golem deposited the young woman on the Health Throne and Education rushed to her side.

Rilla's lips thinned, and she halted her frenetic pacing. "He went for the ones he deemed the most important. The ones who could stop him or rally the city to fight back. Damn, I wish he hadn't gotten War or Shield."

"He did not get you," Lillie said quietly, but her voice carried enough that everyone in the room looked sharply at Rilla.

The Dagger princess took a deep bracing breath and then blew it out. Some of the tension left her shoulders with it. "Right." She stood straight. "I'm recalling everyone from their work. Most of the others are still in the city somewhere, but I know Faith and Treasury are traveling. All the Thrones need to be gathered here for safety, but also for our offensive. Virvalim might have taken those he deemed the strongest, but he's underestimated the rest of us."

Rilla seemed determined, at least, but a couple of the other princesses glanced at their Thrones with a wince. The princess of Administration wrung her hands.

"You four—" She glanced at the party, and her eyes slid to Finn, who stood awkwardly beside them. "Er, five. I need to know where Virvalim is holed up. I will stay here to recall the other Thrones. You find out where he's keeping the ones he kidnapped."

"How do we even know if they're still alive?" the princess of the Public Works Throne said. "If this is a bid for power, he could have executed them already."

Rilla shook her head. "He'll keep them around. I'm sure of it. He doesn't have all of us, which means his basis for seizing the Thrones isn't secure. He'll use them as leverage for our cooperation." She speared Vola and the others with a glance. "Which means we can't leave them in his hands."

"We'll find them," Vola said, holding her eyes.

"Do so. And with your cover blown, I don't care if you have to tear down the city to do it."

The princess of Public Works squeaked. "Oh, no. Don't do that."

Rilla rubbed her forehead. "Okay, okay. Leave the city standing. But do whatever else you have to do. Go."

Out in the city, the wind seemed to have shifted. Merchants nailed boards to their windows as housewives hurried past with the last of their shopping slung over their arms. Workmen scurried home in the middle of the day, casting worried glances at the upper tiers of the city.

"They'll hunker down until things settle," Lillie said as they headed down the stairs. "They know something is amiss and staying home is safer."

"What can we expect from everyone else?" Vola asked.

"The nobles will be picking sides," Lillie said. "No one with a title will be safe by just staying out of it. This is the moment when all those alliances, all those friendships come into play, and you have to decide who you will stand with. Because after this is all over, there will be one winner. Either the princesses or the traitors. There will be no middle ground for those too scared to fight."

"If you're not with us, you're against us, eh?" Vola said.

"Exactly. You can bet Rilla is going to be collecting heads when this is done."

"Then we'd better make sure she gets the right heads."

A couple of the royal guards accompanied them to Virvalim's manor just to make sure nothing obviously nasty waited for them, but they high-tailed it back to the palace almost immediately. All the guards and golems were being recalled to defend the palace and the princesses.

But of course, Virvalim hadn't made it easy. He wasn't holed up in his manor with the kidnapped princesses. And it wasn't like he'd left any helpful notes about where to find him like Lillie's brother had. In fact, it looked like someone had been through just before them to clear the place out and destroy anything incriminating.

Vola poked through the ashes of the fireplace in Virvalim's study, looking for anything still intact. "Nothing," she said. "Damn, we should have moved faster."

A tiny lightning bolt struck the carpet at her feet, but it seemed half-hearted at best.

"Well, we could search the whole city," Sorrel said, surveying the desolate room. "See if anyone spotted him and his hostages. But Rilla's probably got people for that."

"She's expecting us to do something only we can do," Talon said.

"Yeah, no pressure," Sorrel said.

"No, wait." Vola pushed up from the hearth. "We do have resources Rilla doesn't."

"We do?" Sorrel said. "You remember she's a princess, don't you?"

Vola frowned at her. "Who told us about Lord Tildon?"

Lillie straightened. "My brothers."

Vola nodded. "And I'll bet they're not hiding away or picking sides. They're stuck down there with all that information they've been gathering. They said they had more they could give us after they'd followed up on it. Virvalim has more friends than just Lord Tildon, he has to. He couldn't pull this off alone. If everyone's picking sides, we just have to find out who Virvalim has on his side. I'll bet that's where he's keeping the princesses. And Lillie's brothers might know who they are."

Of course, that meant they had to take another swim in the river. At least Glenhaven lived in perpetual spring and summer and didn't seem to get much rain.

Vola didn't feel right leaving Finn on the wharf this time, but the swamp beast loved the boy and had no problem towing him under the waterfall.

They climbed onto the shelf in the cavern and stood dripping on the rock ledge. Lillie wrung out her hair and called for her brothers.

This time Kellan came out of the passage first, but he didn't run to greet them. He nodded to Lillie. "Sister."

Her brow furrowed at the strange greeting. "Are you all right?"

He shook himself and gave her a little uncertain smile. "Yes. Yes, of course. What's going on? Did you need something?"

"Virvalim's made his move. He's kidnapped several of the princesses. We need to find him and where he's keeping them." She stepped forward to take Kellan's hands, and he jumped. "Do you know who he's working with? Which of his allies are likely to shelter him against the rest of the Thrones?"

"Virvalim's started his coup?" Xavier said, stepping out of the passageway beside them. He hadn't bothered with the plate armor this time, dressed only in a pair of trousers which had once been neat and clean but now bore greenish stains from the dank cave.

Xavier ran a hand through his hair. "Damn the man." He glanced sharply at Vola. "You were supposed to kill him if he actually challenged my sister. That would have gotten him out of the picture."

"Don't blame us," Vola said, crossing her arms. "It's your rules that got in the way." Besides, wouldn't he know that the trial by combat wasn't to the death?

"Well, what's done is done. Next time you encounter him, you'll have no excuse. He's a traitor now. The Thrones will have no objections if you take him out. Before he kidnaps anyone else."

"Will do," Vola said dryly.

"You want to put some clothes on there, Xav," Sorrel said, cocking her head.

"Why? I don't mind you looking at me."

"Xavier," Lillie cried.

Sorrel didn't even flush. She just rolled her eyes, clearly unimpressed. Xavier wiggled his eyebrows at Vola, who gave him a once over and then sniffed.

"Xavier, do you know who Virvalim might be working with? Where he might have hidden the princesses?" Lillie said, voice sharp.

Xavier sighed and moved away from Talon, who sagged. "Yes, of course. But you have time. It's not like Virvalim will kill them. He needs them if he wants to wring any control out of Allellarilla and the others."

"Give us the names," Vola growled. "And we'll decide our timeline, thanks."

Xavier held up his hands and wandered back into the passageway. "Yes, fine. Innis, can you jot down the list of Virvalim's conspirators?" he called.

Lillie's last brother was still in the back, in the cavern they'd made into their living area. He wore a shirt at least, though it was clear the brothers were suffering from a lack of civilization.

He brought Lillie the list he'd made. "These are his known allies," Innis said. "The ones he's been currying favor with over the last few months. But if this coup started just this morning, things will have shifted considerably. I'd look at Lord Brecken. He's been fortifying his manor recently. We thought it was odd, but if he was expecting Virvalim to be bringing prisoners—"

"Then maybe that's where they're holed up," Lillie said, taking the paper from him.

"What about the one who was sending messages?" Finn piped up.

They all turned to look at him, and he flushed bright red under his freckles.

"Who?" Xavier said.

"The one who was sending messages. From outside. The person who's working with the traitors. He sent the message that said he was ready when they were ready." He glanced desperately at Vola.

"Finn's right," she said. "That's how we learned of the plot in the first place."

Xavier's eyes narrowed. "And Finn is?"

"My protege," Vola said. "I'm training him."

His eyebrows went up. "Then he should know that a true knight doesn't interrupt their betters."

Vola's teeth clenched. "Unless he has good reason. Virvalim is working with someone outside the kingdom. And he said he was ready to move on the Thrones when the traitors did. Which means we'll be dealing with him now, too. And whatever it is he's set to do."

Xavier shook his head. "The stolen research on the Thrones? That was just a red herring to get the Ephyra family arrested. Virvalim will stop at nothing to see us disgraced. Focus your efforts here, where it will actually do us some good."

Vola opened her mouth, ready to protest that the messages Finn was carrying weren't a red herring. They had been real enough, but they had no more information on that lead. Unless

Rilla's people could track down where the message had come from.

Xavier glanced at Finn again and sniffed before taking Lillie aside to whisper in her ear.

Vola stepped back to put her hand on Finn's shoulder. "It was a good thought."

He shrugged, dislodging her touch. "Maybe."

"What's wrong?"

"Nothing. It's just…" He cast a glance at Lillie's brothers. "You almost had me believing I could do this. Be something different. But all they see is someone worthless."

Vola hid the rush of red that crowded her vision and crossed her arms over her chest. "You're going to give up because one self-important noble looked down at you? Who would you rather believe, him or me?"

"It's not just him, Vola. It's everyone. You're the only one who ever told me I could be something different."

"I must not be telling you loud enough then."

His lip twitched like he wanted to smile. "Loud enough to drown out the world?"

Vola rubbed her forehead. "Henri never seemed to have a problem being loud enough," she muttered.

He raised his head. "Who's Henri?"

"My trainer. He took an angry half-orc and turned her into a half-decent paladin. And he always seemed to know exactly what to say to do it."

"He taught you?"

"All the same things I've been trying to teach you." Vola hooked her thumbs in her belt. "First time a paladin candidate called me an agent of the Obstacles, I tried to kill him. I outweighed most of them by that point, too, but Henri just picked me up by the back of the shirt and held me there, hanging, until I promised I wouldn't run the guy through."

Finn listened, his eyes wide.

"Later, he told me good is a choice. Everything is a choice. How you react, how you behave. And you always have that choice."

"Yeah, but some people are just better at it than others."

"Who?" she said with a snort.

"You. And Sorrel and Lillie. I'm not sure about Talon yet, but…"

"No one's sure about Talon. She's really good at keeping her thoughts behind her teeth. But she hasn't admitted to murdering anyone like Lillie."

His eyes went round. "What?"

Vola nodded to the wizard who was biting her lip and making notes on the list. "Lillie executed someone without a trial. That's what that whole mess this morning started with. She looks all calm and peaceful, but when you break her code of honor, she's got a vicious streak a mile long."

His mouth hung open before he snapped it shut. Then he glanced at Sorrel.

Vola followed his look. "Sorrel is possibly the blood thirstiest person I've ever met. And she's supposed to be a monk."

"What about you?" Finn grumbled.

"I've just had a lot of practice." Vola chewed her lip, staring off into the distance. "Every new person I meet, every new town I walk into, I have to watch what I say, what I do, and make sure I don't do anything stupid that proves them right and me wrong."

She leveled her gaze on him. "Good is a choice. One you have to make every day sometimes. If you don't want to be good, that's your decision. But you can't sit there and say you'll never be good because you were born this way. I chose. So can you."

FIFTEEN

LORD BRECKEN LIVED in a fortified manor much further down in
the city than most of his noble friends. Vola and the others slunk
through alleys the entire length of the tier in order to avoid
walking right up to the front gate. Lord Brecken's wall stretched
half again as high as the others around him made of smooth
plaster over stone. Several guards patrolled the wide walkway on
top, wearing enough armor to stand a siege.

Vola signaled the others to stop at the corner of a nearby
bakery and squinted up at the walls.

"We need to make sure the princesses are actually in there
before we do anything," she said. "As soon as we get their position
we can field the problem of getting them out over to Rilla. I doubt
she'd want us just breaking down the door on our own."

"There's a spot just there where the two patrols meet." Talon
said. "I can get in there without anyone noticing as long as I time
it just right, when they've both turned." She glanced down at the
black wolf beside her. "Gruff would have to stay here, though."

Vola frowned. "You're the best bet to do some scouting," she
said reluctantly. "But I really don't like the idea of sending you in

there alone. If anything happens, we can't get in there with you. You'll be completely cut off."

"Pfft," Sorrel said. "She wouldn't be going alone. We can be in and out with the information we need in five minutes. Ten tops."

Vola wasn't quite as confident, but she certainly wasn't going to get away with scaling walls and sneaking through a manor full of guards.

She glanced at Lillie. "Anything you can cast to help them out."

Lillie bit her lip. "Not much, really. I could cast a magical darkness but…" She looked up at the sky, which burned fierce in the mid-afternoon sun.

"Probably a little too noticeable right now," Vola said.

Sorrel brightened. "Hey, maybe Maxim's weapon can help out." She reached behind her to pull the staff from her back.

"Is that a good idea?" Vola said.

Sorrel frowned. "I want to learn how to use it right. And that means wielding its magic."

"Yes, but is right now the time to figure it out?" Vola gestured up at the walls towering over them. "It's working just fine as a glorified stick. But if you get in there and try something new and it goes wrong, you'll alert Virvalim and Lord Brecken."

"And if they know we're aware of their alliance, they'll either move the princesses or kill them outright," Lillie said, voice serious.

"All right, fine," Sorrel said with a glare. "I won't use it, except in the extreme case of needing to knock a guard out."

Vola winced as Talon and Sorrel crept along the back wall. "Don't let it come to that, either, please," she whispered. But she couldn't be sure they heard, and she didn't want to rush after them. She clanked too much while they moved silent as shadows along the bottom edge of the wall.

At the spot between two guards, Talon stooped and Sorrel

scrambled up her back, taking a running jump at the wall. The halfling scampered up the sheer face nearly six times her height, using her feet to propel herself higher and finding minuscule grips in the cracks between cut stone.

Vola held her breath until the monk perched on the top of the wall, then hunkered down and held her staff straight down the wall. Talon jumped and used the staff to pull herself up. The two disappeared without raising an alarm.

Lillie barely waited till they were over the wall before pulling out a book. Vola hadn't even seen her carrying it. The wizard literally could read anywhere. She'd read while trekking through a swamp once. It hadn't gone well, but then Lillie didn't seem to mind falling into puddles so much anymore.

Gruff paced from one side of the alley to the other, eyes trained on the spot where Talon had disappeared. He let out a small whine before flopping down on the cobblestones.

"I know how you feel, buddy," Vola said quietly. She reached out a tentative hand to scratch his head. He huffed as if heaving a resigned sigh and let her pet him.

"Aren't you supposed to protect them?" Finn said, glancing between Vola and the wall. "Isn't that what paladins do?"

Vola sighed. "Yes. And part of that is letting their strengths carry us when we need it to. If I constantly try to smother them and keep them out of danger, then I'm just weakening the whole party. I need to protect them so they can do their jobs well. In this case, I'd be no good in there. But I will sit here and make sure to cover their exit if they have to leave in a hurry."

Finn's mouth twisted as he stared at the wall. "Does that make it any easier to wait?"

Vola blew out her breath. "Not even a little." She eyed him where he stood, lanky arms hanging awkwardly at his side. "Do you want to help?"

He rolled his eyes. "Yes, please. Don't make me just stand here."

"Come here, then." She placed him behind them, facing back up the alley toward the main thoroughfare where housewives hurried by with baskets on their arms and nursery maids towed gaggles of children. "You're watching our rear which is normally my job. And while you're watching, you can do those strengthening exercises I showed you. They don't make much noise."

He straightened his shoulders and nodded. Then Vola hunkered down beside Gruff to wait, facing the manor.

She kept her eyes on the wall. She'd set him Finn behind them for a reason, but she expected trouble to come from inside the manor. They should be able to hear any alarms Talon and Sorrel raised from out here, but how would they be able to join the other two if they managed to get into trouble.

Vola scanned the route the ranger and the monk had taken. There was no way she and Lillie and Finn would get over the same way. There was a postern gate down the next alley over with guards situated over top. Could they get in there without a lot of fuss?

The hair along the back of Vola's neck raised just as Finn let out a yelp.

She spun, catching the flash of a uniform back down the alley, and four of Lord Brecken's guards came into view.

Shit, the danger had been behind them, not in front.

The guards shouted and charged forward. Finn stumbled but managed a credible block when the lead guard raised his sword against him.

Lillie dropped her book, hands flying to summon a spell.

"No fire," Vola whispered and sprang forward. They had to stop this before the rest of the guards around Lord Brecken's manor heard the commotion.

Vola caught Finn as he staggered and thrust him behind her.

"Watch our backs. Make sure no one comes at us from the manor."

Vola trapped a guard's blade against hers and thought furiously. She didn't generally deal in non-lethal attacks, but they couldn't leave a bunch of dead bodies on Lord Brecken's doorstep if they wanted to remain undetected.

She ducked under the guard's blow, twisted his wrist to disarm him, and struck his helmet with the hilt of her sword.

The metal rang around the alley, and Vola winced.

Lillie whispered fiercely and threw out her hands. Two of the guards crumpled where they stood, snoring softly.

The last one charged for Finn.

Vola tossed down her sword and shield, grabbed his arm as he passed, and swung him face first into the wall.

He folded against the cobbles.

Vola froze, the clangs of their short battle still ringing in her ears, and she listened for any cries of alarm from the manor.

Silence.

She blew out her breath and leaned against the wall.

"Wow, are you going to teach me that one, too?" Finn asked, jerking his chin at the guard lying at her feet.

Vola rubbed her forehead. "Really only works in close quarters. But I did see Henri use it to fell a full ogre once. He used its momentum to cave its head in."

Finn whistled through his teeth as Vola bent to check the guard's pulse. He'd have a very colorful face in the morning, but he'd live.

"Are you all right?" Lillie asked.

A boot scuffed the cobbles, and they sprang upright, ready for another round.

Sorrel and Talon stood at the mouth of the alley. Sorrel planted her hands on her hips and raised an eyebrow. "Looks like you guys had some fun."

Gruff rushed to greet the ranger.

"What did you find?" Vola said.

"Exactly what we were looking for." Sorrel raised her hand, and Talon gave her a high five without looking.

"Virvalim isn't in there, as far as we could tell," Talon said. "But Lord Brecken is. And he has five unhappy guests."

"Definitely recognized Law and Justice and I think War," Sorrel said. "And I'm gonna bet the other two were Shield and Magic. He's got them trapped in some kind of magic circle."

"So, we have our target," Lillie said.

"Which will be useless if we don't get this cleaned up." Vola gestured at the slumped guards. "If Lord Brecken learns we were here, he'll batten the hatches and any hope we had will be gone."

"Or he'll move them again, and we'll have to start all over," Talon said. "So whose brilliant idea was it to kill a bunch of guards on his doorstep?"

"A necessary adjustment to the plan," Vola said. "And they're not dead."

"If you would all just hush a moment, I could fix this," Lillie said. She knelt beside one of the slumbering guards with a wince.

Vola loomed over her shoulder. "What can you do?"

Lillie glared her into silence and held a hand over the nearest one's forehead. "You should take your buddies here for a stroll down by the scarlet district. You can spend a wonderful day and night down there without Lord Brecken getting in your way. Don't come back until tomorrow."

The man's eyes fluttered open. "That does sound nice," he said, words slurring a bit like he'd already enjoyed a pint or two.

"Doesn't it?" Lillie said. "Relaxing."

"Yeah." He shook his companion awake and helped him to his feet. "Come on. We're going to go see some ladies. Lord Brecken won't miss us for the night."

"I like ladies," the other guard said.

They each hauled one of the unconscious guards upright. The one Lillie had originally spelled frowned at the bloody face of the one Vola had run into a wall. "What happened to him?"

"He, er, got into a fight with one of the ladies," Lillie said, glancing at Vola. "She objected to the way he addressed her, but they've come to an understanding and he'll feel a lot better in the morning. I promise."

The conscious guard nodded as if that made perfect sense and staggered down the alley with his burden. They disappeared around the corner, looking like they'd already finished a night on the town.

"They won't report back to Lord Brecken until tomorrow at the earliest," Lillie said. "Hopefully by then it will be too late."

"I didn't know you could just make people do whatever you wanted," Vola said, rubbing her arms where goosebumps had formed.

Lillie winced. "It doesn't work exactly like that. It has to be something they actually want to do but wouldn't have decided for themselves. I wasn't even sure it would work. I've never been that strong with illusions."

"Let's not waste it, then. We'll get back to the inn and send a message to Rilla. We have what she needed. She can tell us if she wants to mount a rescue yet or not."

They were careful on their way back to the inn. They moved through the mostly empty streets, checking to be sure they weren't followed. But Lillie's spell seemed to be sticking because none of Lord Brecken's guards came after them.

Back at the inn, they trotted up the stairs, but at the top a shadow separated from the wall, and Vola jumped. She drew her sword and shield, placing herself in front of Finn.

"Nice reflexes," Rilla said, coalescing from the shadow. "Glad you're on alert." She gestured with one hand and two other figures stepped out of the wall behind her. Vola recognized the mousy princess with the big spectacles from the Throne Room. The other was the Health princess, who now had a fresh scar across her temple.

Vola blew out her breath and sheathed her weapon. "I didn't know you could walk through walls."

Rilla grimaced. "I can't. But I can remain unseen when I want to."

"What's going on up the hill?"

Rilla rubbed her forehead. "I've got the palace on lockdown. We've made a lot of noise about fortifying our position up there, and I left Faith and Treasury in charge of keeping it that way. I'm hoping it will look like we're all still there and concentrating our efforts on defense."

"So, they won't be expecting you to be coming up behind them," Vola said with a nod. She pushed into their room and gestured the princesses inside. Lillie darted around her and snatched the cushions up off the floor, tossing them back on the sofas before offering the princesses a seat.

"Sorrel and Talon scouted Lord Brecken's manor and found War, Magic, and the others," Vola said.

"He has them in some sort of magic circle," Sorrel said. "Not sure what it does."

"It has to dampen their magic somehow, otherwise the War princess would have burned that place to the ground already," Rilla said, planting her hip on the back of the sofa.

"Could you draw it for me?" Lillie asked, pulling out her notebook and a pencil.

Sorrel bent to draw on the paper while Talon took up the narrative. "He's got guards all along the walls with way more inside. The gate is the heaviest concentration of firepower. I noticed at least two wizards keeping watch at the front."

Vola frowned. "I doubt we could all sneak in the same way you two did. We're bound to be noticed, and as soon as he's on the defensive, any surprise we might have had would be shot." She glanced at Rilla. "You've still got the royal guard and all those golems at your beck and call, right? Could they smash through the gates and punch through the defenses enough to get us inside? No element of surprise, but if we have enough force and we're quick enough, it might work."

Rilla grimaced. "It goes against my grain," she said. "And we need to play to our strengths, not theirs. We don't have War with us. Or even Shield. But we do have subterfuge on our side. And some other unexpected cards we can stack the deck with." She glanced at her fellow princesses, who'd sat silent until now.

"Costa, can you get us in?" Health asked the mousy princess.

She snorted and pushed her glasses up. "Does Brecken shit?"

Vola blinked. "Uh, what?"

Rilla rubbed her lips as if to hide a smile. "She's being literal," she told Vola. "Everyone shits, right? Even Lord Brecken."

"I assume so," Vola said, eyebrows lowered.

"Can't say we've ever witnessed it," Sorrel said.

The mousy princess—Costa—nodded. "And isn't it handy that my Throne and I have made sure the entire city has all the conveniences of modern plumbing?" She cocked her head and smiled serenely at Vola. "It was mandatory, even for some of those nobles who think their poop doesn't smell."

"I take it you're the princess of Sewage Management."

"Yeah," the princess said with a grin. "But call me Costa. You can't believe how depressing it is to be named 'Sewage.'"

Vola nodded in sympathy.

The princess of Sewage Management smirked at Rilla. "I can get the fighters in," she said. "I'll just need a strong swimmer."

Vola's mouth twisted in a satisfied smile. "I have one of those you can borrow. Just avoid its teeth."

"Teeth?" Her eyes widened.

"Don't ask."

"You want to go over the wall, then, Dagger?" the Health princess asked, her round cheeks flushed with decision. "You can take me with you. We'll meet in the middle and rescue the others. I believe that's called flanking."

"We won't have Magic to break the circle," Rilla said. "Lillie, can you undo whatever it is Lord Brecken's done to keep them cut off from their Thrones?"

Lillie tilted the paper, squinting. "I think so. If it's a standard diagram in conjunction with somatic and verbal elements then all I have to do is disrupt the diagram portion and the whole paradigm should collapse."

Vola turned to Rilla. "That means yes."

SIXTEEN

IT TURNED out there was an entrance to the sewer through the basement of the inn. They didn't even have to leave the building. Although the innkeeper did look at them funny when Vola led a princess, a monk, a wizard, a ranger, a teenager, a wolf, and a swamp monster through his kitchen. But then he glanced back at Rilla, who waited by the door to see them off, and he just rolled his eyes toward the ceiling.

Vola wondered what other strangenesses Rilla had housed in this inn.

Even the swamp beast fit through the big grate at the back of the kitchen, which meant Vola didn't have to squeeze too much.

The plop on the other side was pretty gross, though.

A cramped tunnel stretched away under the inn with slick tile walls arching low enough Vola had to duck, and they could only walk in a single file line.

"Which way?" Sorrel asked from near the front.

"Up," Costa said. "We only have to go one or two tiers, but the city is built into a cliff. Vertically. All the shit flows down."

"I think you just like saying shit," Sorrel said as the princess moved out, walking down the pipe with one hand on the wall to keep steady.

"It's literally in my job description," Costa said with a grin over her shoulder. "Also, it's kind of fun to see people jump when a princess swears."

Lillie squinted at the surrounding walls. "I expected more, er, shit. This is pretty clear."

"Yeah, that's my doing. I'm keeping it at bay, otherwise we'd be up to our ears. These tunnels weren't built for manual maintenance."

Lillie started. "You're keeping the tunnel clear? Is that the power your Throne gives you?"

"Like Rilla can create traps and hide in shadows and stuff?" Sorrel said.

"Exactly. My Throne allows me to control fluids."

Vola grimaced at the dirty sludge trickling away past her boots. "You mean more than water?"

The princess cast a pointed look back over her shoulder. "Fluids. Do you really want me to break it down for you?"

"No."

The tunnel ended abruptly at a wall, but when Vola glanced up, there was a hole leading to the next level of "fluid management." The next tier.

Sorrel scampered up with a coil of rope over her shoulder. The slick surface didn't even slow her down.

She lowered the end, and Talon used it to help herself up the sheer face.

"Someone give Gruff a boost."

Vola glanced at Gruff, who raised his lip in a snarl.

"Gruff," Talon barked, and the wolf subsided.

"Any volunteers?" Vola said, raising her eyebrows.

Lillie and the princess avoided her eyes. Finn whistled and stuck his hands in his pockets. The swamp monster spit.

"Fine," Vola said and bent to shove her shoulders under Gruff. The wolf grunted and scrabbled at the edge of the opening when she got him high enough. Talon grabbed his ruff and pulled, and the wolf's back legs disappeared into the upper tunnel.

Talon and Sorrel reached down to grasp both of the princess's hands and hauled her up, then did the same with Lillie. Vola gave Finn a leg up and tossed him to the next level.

An ominous dripping echoed through the tunnel as Vola and the swamp beast stared at each other.

"You're sure we need it?" Vola called up to the princess.

Costa's head appeared over the edge of the opening. "For the idea I have…yes."

Vola sighed. "Give me the rope."

She tied the end around the barrel chest of the swamp monster, then put her shoulders under it as the others strained from above.

As Vola lifted, sharp teeth bit into her scalp.

"Ow!" She heaved and practically threw the thing up into the upper level. Then she rubbed her head and glared up at the swamp monster, which bared its teeth in what could only be a grin.

She pulled her hand away to find blood tinged with slime. "Ew, it drooled on me, too." The faint acid burn of the thing's saliva superseded the sting from the wound.

"Look at it this way," Sorrel called, sending the rope down again. "Whatever that thing's got in its mouth is probably going to be more aggressive than any of this sludge. So unless it turns you into another swamp monster, you're probably not going to die of disease. Like dousing your wounds in alcohol."

"And if it does turn you into another swamp monster," Lillie said, panting as Vola put her weight on the rope end. "We promise to love you just as much."

Vola clanked as she clambered through the hole. "Gee, thanks."

Costa was already moving down the next tunnel, hands feeling the walls on either side. She didn't seem to mind the layer of slick coating the tiles. Every time there was a branching, she veered without hesitation, leading them further and further from the inn.

"How do you know which way to go?" Talon asked.

"I built these tunnels," she said. "Also, the…fluid talks to me."

"Oh my gosh, she talks to poop," Sorrel whispered back. The susurus bounced off the walls.

"Here." The princess passed through a narrow gate. A valve hung on the wall beyond. "This is the first piece of my plan." She stepped just a few feet more to a spot where the tunnel veered up again. "And this is the second piece."

Sorrel sidled up beside her and squinted. "What's up there?"

"Lord Brecken's manor. These pipes lead directly to his plumbing."

"There's something blocking them," Sorrel said.

"Exactly. The system is designed to allow movement down. But not movement up. Usually a good thing. Imagine sitting down on a nice toilet and having this—" She dug a toe in the sludge at their feet, "shoot up your butt."

"I'd rather not, thank you," Lillie said, pursing her lips.

The princess cocked her head in a "fair enough" gesture.

"How do we get around it?" Talon asked.

"By overloading the system," Costa said with a pleased little smile. "We blast it with enough sewage, and that will overwhelm the magic and the back-flow valves. But that's why we need that." She pointed back down the way to the gate where the swamp monster still stood. "Those gates are designed to keep such a thing from happening. But if someone can keep the valve open while the shitstorm happens, I can direct the tidal wave right at Lord Brecken's manor, and ta-da, we're in."

Vola glanced between the valve and the swamp beast. "Oh," she said, shoulders slumping. That's why they needed a strong swimmer. And someone with thumbs. The swamp beast would be able to hold her in place while she kept the valve open.

But it meant she was going to have to trust it.

She glared at the creature. "Don't screw this up."

It gave a wet huff, spitting a wad of mucus at Vola's breast-plate. It hissed where it struck.

"All right, everyone get to a safe distance, probably back down one of those side passages we passed," Vola said, wrapping the monster's lead rope around her wrist.

Lillie's eyes went wide. "Why does it have to be you? Any of us could volunteer."

Vola snorted. "And if the swamp monster fails and you have to hold against the tidal wave of shit?" She glanced up to see if a lightning bolt would accompany the word, but apparently if it was literal poop, it didn't count because Cleavah stayed quiet for once. "I'm the best bet and you know it."

Lillie pursed her lips, but before she could protest further, the princess shrugged and led the rest of them back down the passage. "It doesn't matter to me who does it. As long as that valve stays open."

"Yes, ma'am," Vola said and saluted as she went past.

The others disappeared around a bend in the passage, taking Finn and Gruff with them.

Vola yanked the wheel valve over to the open position and gripped the swamp beast's crest just above its shoulders. They glared at each other right before Vola yelled, "Ready when you are."

Too many moments went by with nothing more than the trickle at Vola's feet gurgling monotonously.

Then there was a dull murmur that grew to a low hum, one

Vola could feel as a tingle in her feet. Then a rumble. And finally, a roar.

Vola risked a peek around the solid gate, and her eyes widened as a wall of sludge raced down the passageway.

She slapped the swamp beast, startling it so it leaped forward just as the wave of sewage reached them. Vola held the valve open with one hand and clung to the swamp monster's crest with the other.

It squealed right as Vola took a deep breath and the sludge closed over top of them. She felt the swamp beast kick out and swim desperately against the current, bobbing and jerking as the sludge tried to sweep them away.

Her hand slipped on the valve once and it started to turn, closing the gate to prevent exactly what they were trying to do.

Vola pulled against the swamp beast to position herself again and grabbed hold of the valve once more, forcing it to stay open.

The force of the flow didn't slow or ease, and Vola's eyes remained squeezed shut. Thick sludgy liquid filled with chunks of who knew what flowed past.

Beside her, the swamp beast flailed. Then Vola felt a set of teeth chomp down on her wrist. She screamed wordlessly through her clenched lips and shook her arm. The teeth let go, and she felt the lead rope of the swamp monster ripped away in the current. She spun, losing her grip on the valve. She kicked out, trying to right herself, and as her head broke the surface of the sewage, the force went out of the current. Like a dam that had broken and now the torrent eased.

Vola was pushed another ten feet before the flow of sludge subsided entirely, depositing her on the slick tiles of the pipe.

"Vola!" Sorrel called as she and Lillie and Talon pounded down the tunnel toward her. "Are you all right? Phew."

Sorrel jerked to a stop and held her nose.

Vola coughed and spat as she rolled to her hands and knees

and surveyed herself for damage. Her eyes stung and watered, but other than her nose and clothes, there appeared to be no casualties.

"What happened to the swamp monster?" Talon asked.

Vola glanced down the tunnel as the princess stepped to the pipes at the end and squinted up, checking to see if their way was open.

"I don't know," Vola said. "I think it got swept away."

"Millford?" Lillie said with a slight pout.

"Good riddance," Sorrel said.

Lillie shot a glare at her. "That's not very charitable."

"It tried to take a chunk out of me as it went." Vola lifted her arm to show the teeth marks along her wrist. "And at least there's water for it down here."

"Yeah," Talon said. "Think of it like releasing it back into its natural habitat."

"Good news," Costa said. "It worked. We broke right through. Good work, Vola."

"Great," Vola said flatly. She pushed herself to standing and frowned down at her dripping clothes.

"I can help with that," Costa said. She held her hand out, three inches from Vola's chest, and the damp cloth under her breastplate heated against her skin. She started to steam.

Lillie gagged and held her hand over her mouth.

When Costa was done, Vola raised her arm to examine her sleeve. It was stained and wrinkled and a little stiff with some-thing she'd rather not think about, but at least it was dry.

"I can't do much about the smell," Costa said. "Sorry. But that at least should help." She jerked her head at the pipes. "We should hurry. The blast could have been quite spectacular from above and we'll have to move quick if we want the element of surprise. Who wants to be the first one up?"

"Oh, me," Sorrel said and scrambled up to the pipes. Costa

gave her a boost, and the halfling braced both feet on either side of the pipe and shimmied her way up.

Vola knelt to give Talon a hand just as Sorrel disappeared past the broken backflow valve above.

"That is truly disgusting," Sorrel's voice floated down to them. "But on the bright side, we're all clear up here. Figuratively, of course."

Talon clambered up through the pipe, and Vola lifted the princess to follow. This was a little easier than the last time since the pipe was a little smaller. There was more for them to grab hold of. Gruff even squeezed through,with a little help.

Unfortunately, though, it meant Vola's shoulders got stuck halfway up and the others had to yank and pull until she popped out into the room above like a cork from a very icky bottle.

Here was more evidence of their entrance. The noble bathroom, complete with marble tile and a claw-foot tub, was painted floor to ceiling with a new shade of yuck. The fancy wooden seat complete with padding had been blown clean off the pipe where they'd climbed up and lay broken and pitiful in the corner.

"At least I'm starting to get used to the smell," Talon said. "It doesn't burn my nose anymore."

"There is something to be said for numbness," Lillie said. "I'm just glad no one was in here when it erupted."

Sorrel tapped her on the shoulder and pointed to the opposite wall—where there was a very clear outline in the sludge. A figure with its hands raised in horror.

"Oh," Lillie said, shoulders drooping.

Vola moved to the door and peered around the edge. "We need to get to the princesses. Rilla will provide a distraction at any moment. Talon, Sorrel. You know where we're going. You lead. I'll bring up the rear."

Talon took point, slinking down the passage outside the bathroom, both daggers drawn and ready. Sorrel followed her on silent feet. The two of them scouted the way, before turning to wave the others forward. Lillie and Costa and Finn scampered after them, while Vola protected their rear, her sword and shield drawn.

Lord Brecken lived more opulently than the Ephyras, with wide hallways and thin porcelain vases on stands. But the corridors were mostly devoid of people, and Vola wondered if the other inhabitants of the manor knew what kind of treason was going on here. Once or twice, they had to wait and hide while a harried servant rushed by, eyes large and frightened.

On the ground floor, just outside a pair of big double doors that had to lead to a great hall or a dining room of some kind, Talon and Sorrel stopped.

"This is it," Talon whispered while the party waited.

Vola crept up to glance around the corner. Four armored guards stood watch outside the room, and pairs of them walked the hallways outside on a strict rotation.

"Are the other doors guarded like this?" Vola whispered.

"All of them," Talon replied. "We'll have to wait for the distraction."

Vola scooted back to the others. "Costa, let Rilla know we're in place."

The princess took a water skin from her belt and poured a handful into one palm. Then she cupped her hands together and whispered.

The reflection in the water's surface shimmered and a pair of light brown eyes blinked back at them. "Costa?" a tinny voice said.

"Rilla," Costa said. "We're in place. Commence distraction plan number one."

"That's still a stupid code phrase," Rilla said. "But we're on our way."

Costa let the water dribble to the carpet, being absorbed without a trace. Then she shook her hands dry.

"Can you teach me that?" Lillie said.

Vola rolled her eyes and returned to Talon. "Be ready," she whispered along the line.

They didn't have to wait long. There was a crash and a boom from somewhere outside, and an alarm bell rang just seconds later.

The guards outside the room exchanged a look before one of them directed the closest pair to go investigate.

As soon as they were out of sight, Vola turned to her party. "Now. Quietly."

Sorrel flashed across the space, disappearing between one step and the next, and reappearing directly beside the closest guard. He didn't even have time to scream before she'd knocked him flat.

They swarmed the four remaining guards. Talon took out the next two, blades silent as a striking snake, and the fourth fell to the floor, eyes closed, snoring deeply, before Vola could even reach him.

They dragged the prone guards out of the way, careful not to wake the one Lillie had put to sleep. While Vola made sure the bodies were stacked somewhere out of the way, Talon cracked the door open and peeked inside. She raised a hand, five fingers up.

Vola nodded, then stepped up to the door as Talon slipped inside.

When she heard the first scream, she threw the doors open and the rest of them raced inside. A rushed survey showed Talon standing over one guard toward the back of a large dining room. Four more were placed around the bare open space in the middle where a chalked diagram dominated the floor.

A pillar of crystal obscured five shadowy figures frozen behind the hard surface.

That was all Vola had time to take in before a guard in chain mail loomed in front of her, his mouth slack with shock.

She charged him, kicked his legs out from under him and bashed him on the head with her shield. He went limp.

The others made short work of the remaining guards. Sorrel took one, Lillie lobbed a fireball at another, and the princess held her hands together and yanked as if pulling something up out of the ground. A piece of the floor gave way and fountain of sewage erupted, swallowing the remaining guard and dragging him down into the floor.

Distantly, Vola thought she heard a delighted squeal.

A door on the far wall flew open and the four guards on the other side rushed in, weapons ready.

"Finn, princess, block the other doors. Lillie, start freeing the princesses. Sorrel and Talon, with me."

Finn and Costa raced to shut the door they'd come through and the one on the far end of the hall, while Sorrel and Talon and Vola rushed to meet the new enemy. Sorrel met them first, but instead of sweeping her staff around to knock one off his feet, like Vola was expecting, she skidded to a halt and braced herself, holding the staff out at arm's length.

"What are you—"

Flame spouted from the end of the staff, harmlessly arcing away over the enemy's heads. The guards all glanced at the flames, then down at the halfling.

"Damn," Sorrel said. "That always works for Lillie."

"You're not Lillie," Vola called and tossed herself into the fray, taking advantage of their confusion.

"No, but I am the bearer of a god's weapon." Sorrel danced out of the way of one of the guards and raised the weapon again. "And I can master it."

She poked the end of the staff into the guard's gut, making

him stagger back, and frowned at the length of carved wood in her hands. "Come on, come on."

Talon leaped on one of the guards, slicing across his neck while Gruff pulled another off his feet and went for his throat.

The last guard charged for Sorrel. Sorrel squeezed her eyes shut as lightning shot out of the end of the staff and engulfed the guard. He stiffened and buzzed as arcs of electricity raced across his figure. Then he slumped to the ground, smoking.

Sorrel cracked an eyelid open. "I guess that works," she said. But she sounded disappointed that it hadn't come naturally.

"You know you're not a wizard, right?" Vola asked as she and Talon closed the doors with a bang. She put her back against the door to hold it closed.

Sorrel scowled. "No need to rub it in."

"That's not what I—" There was a thump against the door that nearly threw Vola aside. She braced her feet. "Never mind. Lillie, how's it coming?"

Lillie knelt at the edge of the diagram, crawling awkwardly on hands and knees around the chalked markings. "It's gonna take a second."

"We don't have a second," Costa yelled from the other door. She'd dragged a table in front of it, but it screeched across the floor as the guards on the other side shoved the doors open.

Vola checked Finn, who was braced against the last door, feet wide and planted.

Lillie moved slow, yes, but also deliberately, clearly not dawdling as she worked her way around the diagram. Vola's eyes followed the lines to the center of the room where a long table would normally stand. Instead, there was a towering pillar of crystal. Pale purple, but still translucent enough to reveal five women standing in varying poses of outrage and horror. Vola recognized the princess of the Shield Throne, the older woman with the long silver hair and the serene expression. Another, tall and fierce with shining gold curls piled on her head and a hawk nose could only be the princess of War.

They all stood frozen as living statues, artwork caught in a moment of surprise.

The door thumped again, making Vola jerk. Talon threw herself against the door next to her.

"We can't hold them forever," she said.

Sorrel had scampered over to help Finn.

"I know," Vola growled. "But we have to hold them for long enough for Lillie to finish."

The banging ceased and Vola frowned. "What are they up to now?"

Talon laid her ear against the crack in the door and listened, a frown pulling her brows down.

"Duck," she said, suddenly.

She yanked Vola away from the door, and they went tumbling just as it exploded in a shower of splinters. Vola raised her shield to protect them, then scrambled to her feet.

But instead of an army, one man strode through the door, flanked by his guards.

"Lord Brecken, I presume," Vola said.

The man smiled. He wore a thick maroon surcoat over shining mail and he carried his helm under one arm, the plume waving in the dusty air.

"You will regret invading my home," he said in measured tones, as if they discussed cold tea or a particularly annoying house guest.

"Just as you will regret kidnapping your monarchs, I'm sure." Vola settled her shield on her arm and raised her blade.

"You do know it is not illegal for a noble to murder, don't you?" He narrowed his eyes.

"Gonna be hard for you to do that when you're dead."

He sneered. "Stop them," he told his guards, and as they

stepped forward the other doors burst inward, letting in waves of maroon clad guards.

Lord Brecken settled his helm on his head and drew his longsword. Then he launched himself at Vola.

Vola ducked and dodged around him, moving faster than most people expected a heavily armored orc to move. She got in a slash across his back before he turned and danced out of the way. They circled each other warily.

Talon spun past, her blades a blur, Gruff snarling at her heels. Across the room there were shrieks as a tidal wave of sludge washed guards off their feet. Sorrel wasn't bothering to stand her ground anymore. She raced around the room, staying one step away from the enemy while she shot fire over her shoulder. Half of her shots missed.

Finn had found a table and broken off the leg. He swung the makeshift club, intercepting one of the guards chasing Sorrel, then bashing another on the head as they floated past on a wave of sewage, and catching one just as he was about to spear Lillie.

Vola kept circling Brecken until she positioned him directly across from the crystal holding the princesses. Then she stepped back instead of forward, throwing him off for a crucial second. She brought her sword around in a feint and when he went for it, she bashed him with her shield, sending the noble stumbling back over the edge of the diagram into the crystal encasement.

Sparks shot out and Lord Brecken screamed. Then he jerked himself away, holding his shoulder.

He growled and sprang for Vola. She stepped sideways, but her boot caught the edge of a carpet and made her fumble just long enough for Lord Brecken to slash at her unarmored leg. Vola cried out and fell to one knee.

A dark shape hurtled between them, flinging Lord Brecken back. The shape hit one of the guards beside them, and the man went down with a gurgle. When it stood still for a moment, Vola recognized Rilla.

She saluted with her sword. "Nice of you to join us."

Rilla grinned.

As Lord Brecken staggered to a standing position, another figure swept through the door. The older princess of Health.

The woman looked at Lord Brecken and without warning Lord Brecken screamed in agony. He fell again as his limbs jerked and bent.

Vola winced. She was pretty sure knees weren't supposed to look like that.

"Funny how fragile human joints are, isn't it?" the princess asked with a small, sharp smile.

"You and I have different definitions of funny."

Rilla stepped up beside her.

Vola left them to it with a shudder and limped to Lillie, who still crawled around on the ground even amidst the slaughter.

She caught one guard on her shield as he tried to charge the wizard and flung him back. Her leg buckled, and she went down, just as Lillie sat up with a triumphant smile. She raised both hands and the crystal in the center of the room cracked from top to bottom. Then, with a ringing noise that echoed through the hall, it shattered.

A shock wave swept across the room, knocking the rest of them off their feet.

The princesses blinked, then breathed deep, and finally shook themselves as if waking from a long sleep. Shield was the first to recover, squinting at the destruction around her.

"Looks like they've had all the fun," she said, turning to War.

The princess of War with her lovely hair piled on her head, making her neck look long and graceful, smiled. It had edges sharp enough to cut. "Not quite all the fun," she said. She raised her hands. "This place is still standing and it shouldn't be. Don't you agree?"

SEVENTEEN

THE FLAMES from Lord Brecken's manor lit the rest of the city like an awful torch. The princess of the War Throne stood outside Rilla's inn with her arms crossed, the light from the fire reflecting across her face as she stared up at the manor on the tier above them.

Vola had made the mistake of suggesting they call the fire brigade as they'd fled the manor, and she'd been glared into silence. But even as they'd traveled down to the next tier, she'd glanced back. Neither of the manors on either side of Lord Brecken's had caught fire, and the flying sparks seemed to hit a wall before falling toward any other buildings.

Someone was protecting them. Vola suspected the princess of Public Works.

"I'm keeping the others up at the palace to make sure attention is focused up there," Rilla said as she herded them inside. She was the only one brave enough to tear War away from the sight. "But the rest of us are staying here. It's time to plan a more concerted attack. This rebellion ends now."

War bared her teeth. "Lord Brecken will serve as an example to the rest."

Vola, Sorrel, Talon, and Lillie retreated to their room while the princesses invaded Rilla's. Finn followed the party and plopped in front of the fireplace as if too tired to move again.

"Take a rest," Vola said. "Who knows when Rilla will need us." She sniffed, then glanced down at her stiff, stained clothes. "After a bath."

The others let her use the tub in the washroom first. She'd never had a bath in a tub big enough for an orc. Not even at the paladin academy. It seemed like a lot to ask half a dozen servants to cart hot water up from the kitchens, but after trekking through the sewers and getting hit by a tidal wave of shit, she deserved to splurge.

It was kind of nice not having to make all the decisions, she thought as she lay back in the tub. Rilla could handle this one for once.

By the time she returned to the room, Lillie snored delicately on her bed, Sorrel curled against a pillow with her eyes closed, resting if not asleep, and Finn paced in front of the fire. Vola didn't see Talon at all. A smaller tub had been dragged in front of the fire and wet towels lay in a pile near the door. It looked like the rest had taken turns cleaning the worst of the muck off.

"What's wrong?" Vola asked Finn, combing her fingers through her long wet hair.

Finn started. "Nothing." His shoulders slumped. "Couldn't sleep. I feel like I should. We just fought a noble and about a hundred guards. I should be tired. Right?"

"Or you're wound so tight your body doesn't remember what tired is." She braided her hair quickly then picked up her sword and the short sword she'd given to Finn. "Come on."

She led him out the door that opened onto the central courtyard. A narrow set of stairs led down to the flagstones below.

Here she finally saw Talon, nestled beside Gruff against the benches on one side of the courtyard, face turned away.

Vola let her be, striding to the practice dummies opposite. She dumped the swords, then positioned Finn before one of the dummies.

"Stand," she said.

He positioned his feet the way she'd taught him, letting his hands fall loose and ready at his side.

"Good." She snatched up the short sword and held it out to him, hilt first.

He took it without hesitating.

"Point up, step, thrust."

The boy followed her steady instructions.

"Form two," she said, and he flowed into the second stance.

"Step, slash, dodge."

He did so, then looked up at her expectantly.

"Good," she said. "Really, really good."

He beamed, then his shoulders sagged a little. "I thought maybe I was learning really slow."

Vola shook her head. "It always feels slow at first. Henri dumped me on my butt at least ten times a day in the beginning."

His mouth fell open. "He dumped *you*?"

"I was a little smaller then. More your size. But yeah, Henri can still dump me nine times out of ten."

"Is he a really great knight?"

Vola snorted. "No, actually. He always resented being called a knight. He said he was just a trainer. But I finally realized in the end that Henri wasn't limited to being a great knight, because he was more than that. He was a great man. Now keep going."

Finn turned back to the dummy with renewed vigor. "Do you...do you have any more stories about him, like the ogre one?"

"Sure. I could tell you about the time we went in to clear out a goblin horde and Henri talked them all into attacking their leader."

"How did he do that?"

"I'll tell you when you've done thirty more repetitions," she said with a smirk.

He groaned but smiled at the same time.

Vola retreated a few steps so she wasn't in his peripheral view as he went back to practicing his forms.

Talon had raised her head, though her hood remained up, and Vola moved across to sit on the bench beside her.

"Hey," she said, keeping her eyes on Finn's figure. He flagged once or twice but always corrected himself to keep going.

There was no answer from Talon.

Vola glanced down at her.

The ranger twined her fingers over and over through Gruff's ruff while the wolf lay patiently with his head on his paws.

Vola's brow drew down. "What's wrong?" she said quietly.

Talon raised her startled gaze to meet Vola's eyes for a moment before she dropped it again to concentrate on Gruff's fur. "Nothing."

"Try again," Vola said, leaning back on her arms.

Talon sighed. "It's not that big of a deal," she said. "It's just… Things were supposed to change. After Brisbene. But I don't feel like I'm doing that good of a job being…being a girl."

Vola sat back up.

"At least, not all the ways we've tried."

"It wasn't really supposed to be about being good at it," Vola said. "We were going to try different things to find something you liked. Something that made you feel more like yourself. Have you found anything you liked?"

Talon's hood turned away. "I don't know. I guess I like wearing the clothes as long as no one's looking at me. But I felt like I was just doing everything all wrong. I don't look or walk like Lillie at all."

"Neither do I," Vola said.

Talon hesitated, then shrugged as if conceding the point. "True," she said. "It's just the only time I've felt like myself this whole time has been with daggers in hand."

"So?" Vola said.

"So, that's what I've always done. Nothing's changed."

Vola pushed herself to her feet and swiped the dust off her butt. Then she held out her hand to Talon. "Come on."

"What?" Talon said.

"Spar with me."

The light struck through her hood enough to highlight her eyebrows drawing down in confusion. "You want to fight? But we were talking. I thought girls preferred talking."

Vola snorted. "Some do. Some are completely weirded out by it and need to whack something to feel normal."

Finally, Talon grabbed her hand and allowed herself to be pulled to her feet. Vola stooped to pick up her own sword and took a two-handed stance in the wide-open area of the yard.

Talon stood uncertainly opposite her, hands on the hilts of her daggers.

"You gonna just stand there?" Vola said.

"I'm not sure exactly what we're doing."

Vola shrugged, then advanced, sword swinging. Talon ducked and rolled, then drew her daggers. She caught Vola's next swing on her crossed blades and thrust the sword away.

"I don't understand," Talon said, then leaped back to avoid another slash. Her hood fell down.

"This is the kind of girl I am," Vola said. "I'm the bash them in the face if they threaten my friends kind of girl. The maybe I like to dress up once in a while and read romance books kind of girl.

The *I don't like to talk about my feelings, but I will if I have to* kind of girl."

Talon's mouth fell open in an o.

Vola pulled back and stood, sword down and loose in her right hand. "You don't have to lose any part of yourself to become a girl unless you want to. If you want to be tough and slice up bad guys, then you're the type of girl who is tough and likes to slice up bad guys. If you want to dress up occasionally, wear jewelry and heels, and feel pretty, that doesn't make you any less strong."

She leveled her gaze at Talon. "You are a girl, right? So, you choose what that means to you. None of us can teach you how to be something you already are."

Talon bit her lip.

"So what does being a girl mean to you?" Vola asked. "What made you want to live like one in the first place?"

"I wanted to be myself," Talon said quietly.

"Then be yourself." Vola tilted her head. "You can be the strong, silent type of girl. The type who shaves and wears night-gowns and kicks butt. Be yourself, Talon, and that's the type of girl you are."

A couple hours later, Sorrel joined them, yawning. She stretched out on a bench to watch as Talon and Vola each sparred with Finn, introducing him to different fighting styles.

Lillie appeared on the steps to their room, wrapped in a fluffy bathrobe, her hair a mass of wet strands over her shoulder. She leaned on the railing, combing her fingers through her wet hair.

Something made the back of Vola's neck prickle and she rubbed it self-consciously, glancing around. But the courtyard was clear.

Funny. It had felt a little like the nudge Cleavah had given her to go after Finn. But there wasn't anything here.

A tinkle, like a shingle falling from the roof, made her gaze snap up. Five figures masked and wearing leather armor crept along the roof line.

"Well, that can't be good," Sorrel said, sitting up.

"You don't know that," Lillie said. "Maybe they lost their keys."

"No one wears a mask and creeps along roof lines because they've lost a key."

The nearest one realized they'd lost the element of surprise and dropped on Vola in eerie silence.

Vola yelled. She didn't have either her shield or her breastplate, but the man who jumped her wasn't anywhere near her size. She caught him and threw him aside with a roar. But a zing of pain along her shoulder told her she hadn't gotten away unscathed.

Despite her talk of lost keys, Lillie didn't hesitate. She drew her hands together and shot a fireball at the remaining figures on the roof. They dove out of the way, two of them jumping to the courtyard and two scrambling through the window that led to Rilla's room.

"Assassins," Vola bellowed. "Rilla, to arms!"

The first one she'd thrown aside rolled to his feet as if unscathed and spun the knives in his hands. His eyes crinkled at the corners like he smiled under the mask. Like he thought this was going to be easy.

Talon struck him from the side, and he went down with a smack on the flagstones. She stooped for the kill, but the assassin disappeared in a puff of black smoke that made the ranger cough and stumble back.

Vola growled and spun, searching for him. But there were

only two other assassins in the courtyard now, circling Sorrel and Finn.

Sorrel spun and kicked, her bare foot landing squarely in the assassin's chest. He flew back, but before he could hit the ground he flipped and righted himself.

Slippery little bastards.

Sorrel threw out her hand and above them, glass shattered. Maxim's Warhammer flew through the air and snapped to Sorrel's waiting palm. The next assassin tried to go for Finn, but Sorrel aimed the staff at him and lightning flew from its tip. The force of it threw Sorrel back as the lightning arced over the assassin, making him duck.

Finn took advantage of his distraction and used the step-thrust pattern he'd been practicing to get in a solid hit.

No way she was letting her protege take on an assassin alone. Vola charged him, red flickering at the edges of her vision.

The man ducked out of the way, and she stumbled headlong past him. She slashed as she passed, but he leaped and flipped backward.

She pivoted, changing directions and tactics faster than he was prepared for, and swept him off his feet before he could dodge, but when she brought her blade down on his head, he vanished in a puff.

He reappeared behind Talon. She spun too slow to catch his blow, but Gruff was there with a snarl and a flash of teeth, and the assassin barely cried out before he went down with a gurgle.

Sorrel aimed her staff at the other assassin again, but this time, as the lightning crackled forth, the man disappeared, too.

And reappeared behind Lillie.

Lillie screamed as he struck and a gout of flame sprang up between them. Lillie crumpled to the stairs as the assassin's clothes caught fire. He sizzled as he died.

Heart in her throat, Vola lunged for the stairs, but the air moved behind her. She spun, fast enough to see the first assassin reappear, but not fast enough to dodge his blow.

But Finn had already been moving, and he speared the assassin just as the man tried to do the same to Vola.

She stepped out of the way as the dead man slumped to the flagstones.

Finn stared at the corpse, chest heaving. "That trick only works if you don't have anyone watching your back."

"Good," Vola said, breath coming too fast. "Very good. Are you hurt?" But even before he shook his head, she could see he was unscathed while Lillie lay groaning on the stairs above them.

She signaled the others. "Talon, Sorrel, get to Rilla and the princesses. Finn with me." She sprinted up the stairs to the wizard. "Careful, now," she said as Lillie sat up with a wince.

"I'm all right," she said. "I think."

Vola hid her scowl as she checked Lillie for injury. She'd heard those words before, and believing them without a second look had landed Lillie with a permanent limp.

But this time, a thorough search revealed nothing more than a fist sized bruise high on the wizard's neck.

"It was…it was strange," she said as Vola took the bruise into herself, healing Lillie completely. "He reversed the blow at the last second. Like he was trying to knock me out instead of kill me." She rubbed her shoulder.

"Why would assassins attack but then not try to kill us?" Vola said as Lillie hauled herself to her feet. They hurried along the balcony toward Rilla's window and door where Talon and Sorrel had disappeared.

Vola pushed through the door before Lillie could come up with an answer and caught Rilla with her hands in the air. Ropes of green light snaked up around an assassin's legs, pinning him to the wall. One strand wrapped around his throat, holding him just high enough he had to stand on his toes to avoid strangling.

A bloody smear in the corner beside the princess of the Shield Throne was the only remaining evidence of the last assassin.

The princesses had turned the large room into a war room, with the center table covered with a map which now lay askew. Colored chess pieces lay scattered on the floor where they'd been knocked.

The princess of the Dagger Throne advanced on her captive, her face drawn and eyes set. "Why were you sent here?"

"To kill you," he said, then spat. "You couldn't figure that out?"

Rilla drew her knife and plunged it into the wood beside the assassin's ear. "Who sent you?"

"I'm not telling you anything."

The rest of the princesses gathered behind her, looking on.

"You think they'll be able to protect you?" Rilla said, lowering her chin. "You just tried to kill your monarchs. Nothing is going to save you from a traitor's death. But if you tell us who hired you, we can make it the quick death at the end of a long rope, instead of a long death at the end of a lot of pain."

"I'm not talking."

"Did you really think you'd get away with it?"

"Shouldn't have been anyone left to tattle on us. Except that one."

He jerked his chin at Lillie.

Rilla narrowed her eyes. "What's that mean?"

His mouth went hard and thin, and he refused to speak.

"The one outside went to a great deal of trouble to not kill me along with the others," Lillie said quietly.

Rilla grasped the hilt of the knife she'd left in the wall. "You had orders not to harm her?" she said. "Why?"

The assassin just smirked.

"They probably needed a scapegoat," War said, glancing at

Lillie whose face had gone white. "And the Ephyras are already under suspicion."

Vola frowned. That didn't quite add up.

Sorrel tilted her head and prodded the assassin with her toe. "Why are your clothes wet?"

Vola leaned closer. Sorrel was right. He didn't exactly drip on the floor. But he was leaving a damp mark on the wall behind him.

"I went swimming," he snapped. "What's it matter to you?"

Vola's breath blew out in a whoosh, and on a sudden suspicion she stepped forward and took the assassin's sleeve between her fingers. Trapped between the fibers was a scattering of glowing dust, almost invisible in the afternoon sun. A familiar dust they'd seen before.

Orders to spare Lillie. Dust from glowing mushrooms. Swimming.

Fuck.

Vola turned to Lillie, eyes wide.

Lillie stood, hands clenching in an uneven rhythm before she whirled and raced for their room, the ties of her robe streaming behind her. Vola and the others followed, leaving the princesses to take care of the last assassin themselves.

EIGHTEEN

With the swamp beast lost somewhere in the sewers under the city, they had to make their way under the waterfall alone. That didn't end up being such a hardship with Lillie's anger to drive them. The wizard swam faster and stronger than ever, and Vola was able to concentrate on getting Talon and Finn to the cavern.

They made it through the current and popped up among the glow from the fungus.

Vola rubbed the water out of her eyes as Lillie hauled herself up onto the rock shelf.

Before Vola finished helping the others out of the water, Lillie strode off toward the back passage, leaving a wide trail of water.

Vola exchanged a glance with Talon and Sorrel before hurrying after her.

She caught up just in time to hear Lillie snap, "Xavier!" as she huffed into the back cavern where the Ephyra brothers had set up their living quarters.

Xavier had his foot up on a stool, fastening the shin guards of his greaves. He froze as Lillie's voice rang from the bare rocky ceiling.

Innis lounged half-armored on a ripped sofa, polishing his breastplate. "She knows," he said without looking up.

"What makes you say that?" Xavier drawled as he finished with his strap and put his foot back down on the ground. He straightened and adjusted his loose linen shirt on his shoulders.

Lillie's face went red, and she strode across the room to plant herself with her hands on her hips directly in front of her eldest brother.

"You sent the assassins," she said without preamble. "You tried to kill the princesses."

"Tried?" Xavier raised an elegantly curved eyebrow and tossed his honey-colored hair over his shoulder. "They didn't succeed, then."

Lillie sucked in a noisy breath. "You don't even deny it?"

"Why should I? You've already worked it out for yourself."

"How could you do this?" Lillie cried.

Kellan slipped into the cavern beside Vola, making her narrow her eyes and shift her weight. But the younger boy just stood there, gazing straight ahead. Sorrel and Talon crowded behind them, peering around Vola's broad shoulders.

"Father taught us duty and honor and above all, loyalty to a higher ideal. An ideal represented by the Thrones," Lillie said. "How could you betray that?"

"No, those are the things he taught you. Pretty words for a pretty head to parrot. Ideals without weight or practicality. We —" Xavier gestured to himself and his brothers. "Learned that to make those ideals a reality, good men have to force the issue. Southglen can't thrive under a cadre of princesses chosen by cold, emotionless Thrones who don't share those ideals."

Lillie drew back with a grimace and flashed a glance at Kellan. "You don't believe that," she said. "I know you don't."

"I believe in duty and honor and loyalty," Kellan said, voice flat.

Vola's teeth creaked as they clenched. This didn't sound like the same young man who'd been so worried about Lillie the first time they'd visited.

"You have to take those things if you want to make them yours," Kellan finished.

Xavier stepped forward to pat Lillie on the head. "I don't know why you're so upset. We told the assassins not to hurt you. And now that you're here, you can help. After all, we're family. We're not doing this just for us."

He brushed past her, and Innis rose to help him don his breastplate, tying the straps he couldn't reach. Xavier returned the favor for Innis.

"Does Father know what you've done?"

Xavier rolled his eyes. "Of course not. His stubbornness runs even deeper than yours. He would have stopped us, unlike you."

Lillie's lips pulled back. "I'm not going to help you sit your own asses on the Thrones."

Xavier smirked at Vola. "Did you teach her to swear? I wouldn't have thought it possible." He turned back to Lillie. "We're not going to sit on the Thrones. We're destroying them completely. The system is broken. The Thrones are choosing people to rule who are bad for Southglen. It's time to institute a new system. You can be part of it."

"Never," Lillie spat.

Xavier huffed a laugh. "You say that. But you've already been helping us. Lord Tildon was such a pain. He wouldn't let us move any faster. And Lord Brecken was too reckless, never listening to our advice. It's too bad you couldn't take down Virvalim as well. He's going to be a problem in the end. He thinks he should be king."

Ice trickled down Vola's spine as she traced their actions back and found the brothers lurking behind each and every one. They'd been the ones feeding them names and ideas. Turning them away from inconvenient suspicions and guiding them to strike at their enemies.

"Oh my goddess, we've been working for you this whole time," Vola said as the blood drained from her face.

The slaver. Finn had even reminded them that the slaver was a lead. He'd sent the message to Virvalim that they'd intercepted. But Xavier had brushed him off, and Vola had let him.

Xavier smirked and stepped as if to push past Vola.

Vola gave the signal, and Talon leaped for the eldest brother.

Xavier seemed to expect the blow and backhanded her across the room. Sorrel leveled her staff at Innis, but Kellan threw out his hand and a sheet of white spread in front of his brother, and the lightning crackled across its surface. It reflected back at Sorrel, sending her reeling into the wall.

"Stop, stop!" Lillie cried, and Vola wasn't sure who she was speaking to, them or her brothers.

The wizard rushed to place herself between Xavier and the door. "Don't do this. Don't force me to stop you."

Xavier tilted his charming smile at Lillie. "Now Lilliara, we both know that's not going to happen."

Lillie thrust her hands out and flames sprouted from her fingertips, crackling with her anger.

Xavier's smile crooked sideways, and he stepped closer, daring Lillie to strike. He stepped so close his boots hit her toes.

Vola waited, breath held, eyes flicking between Xavier and Lillie. A part of her wanted to will Lillie forward, to strike. But how could she urge her to kill her own brother? Even one as obnoxious as Xavier.

Lillie raised her chin, eyes meeting Xavier's.

Then her shoulders slumped, and the flames in her hands died.

Xavier stroked her shoulder. "Don't worry, Lilliara. We'll take care of things. Just like we always do."

Vola's fingers clenched, but if Lillie didn't make the decision to strike at her family…Vola wasn't going to make it for her.

Xavier signaled Innis and Kellan, and they disappeared through the portal at the end of the hall with a flash.

Vola raced to Talon's side and checked her for injury. "You all right?"

"Just hit my head," Talon said, voice muzzy.

Vola held her hand over the back of Talon's head where she was rubbing and whispered, "Lady bless." White light flashed between their flesh, and Talon sat up, eyes clear again while Vola took the ache into her skull.

"Sorrel?" Vola called.

"To hell with this Warhammer. I'm going to kill that regicidal maniac with my bare hands."

Finn was helping the halfling to her feet, but from the strength of her anger she was fine.

"Lillie," Vola said, standing. Lillie still stood in the doorway, head down. Hands clenched. "Lillie. I'm not asking you to come with us, but we can't let them—"

"You're not asking, but I'm coming anyway," Lillie said. Then paused. "No. I'm not just coming. I'm leading."

Vola wanted to ask what made her think she'd be able to strike out at her brothers if she hadn't been able to two minutes ago, but she knew well enough not to underestimate Lillie's anger when someone had betrayed that damned moral code of hers.

She had just enough time to stand as Lillie rushed for the portal where the Ephyra brothers had disappeared.

"Wait—"

But the wizard disappeared with a flash, and Vola urged the others through before plowing into the light herself.

She hit the ground on the other side running and instantly struck a wall. She bounced off and clanked against the dusty ground.

Vola blinked up at her surroundings.

Bare rock walls surrounded her, open to the late afternoon sky above. A barred gate was the only break in the stone. And staring down at her was Lillie's father, blinking myopically. Lillie herself stood with a hand raised to her lips, eyes wide with horror.

"Well, hello," Ephyra said. "Nice of you to drop in? Though I do wonder what the occasion is."

"Oh, no." Vola lurched to her feet. There was no one else in the cell. Just the three of them. "Oh, no."

She staggered to the gate and rattled the bars. Locked. And a golem stood just outside.

She stepped back and angled her head up. "Sorrel?" she called. "Talon?"

"Here," came a voice from somewhere over the wall. "We uh, we seem to be in the prison. How about you?"

"Same."

"We have Finn and Gruff with us. Do you have Lillie?"

"And her father."

Ephyra watched all this with patient curiosity.

"Well. That sucks," Sorrel said.

"Kellan was right. She did follow."

Vola whipped around to see Xavier outside the bars, arms crossed. The golem had shifted aside to make room for him.

Vola threw herself at the bars, trying to catch the gloating noble against them, but he danced back with a laugh. "I'll admit. I thought it was a long shot, but Kellan convinced me we should prepare the portal just in case you decided to come through. A good idea." He smiled down the corridor at his youngest brother, who was just visible.

Kellan didn't respond. Just stared straight ahead.

"Xavier," Ephyra said. "What the hell is going on?"

"It's time for the final play. It's too bad the assassins didn't do their jobs, but you really can't trust hired help, can you?"

The blood left Ephyra's face, leaving him pale and sweaty. "What?"

"But here's the thing. We won't need to worry about killing the princesses if we drain the Thrones of their power. They'll be powerless. Helpless. And without the Thrones, Southglen will be looking for new leadership."

Vola's mouth went dry. "Draining the Thrones…you can't do that. Can you?" She glanced at Lillie, who bit her lip hard enough to turn it white.

"Thanks to a friend outside the country, we can. We wanted the government. He wanted the power from the Thrones. And since we needed the Thrones gone anyway…" Xavier shrugged. "It was an easy trade. It wouldn't have worked if Father hadn't done all that research, telling him exactly how to achieve the impossible."

Ephyra gasped. "You stole the research," he said. "You sent it under my seal."

"Well, yes. Your arrest was an unpleasant side effect but—"

"Unpleasant side effect? You've betrayed me. You've betrayed your house and your honor!" Ephyra stepped forward, face drawn, mouth grim.

"I'm taking my honor for myself," Xavier spat. "You only ever talked about loyalty and honor as if they were things you had to keep and protect. Not things you could use and seize from others. You were never willing to go further than what was given to you. Our family is even older than the Thrones. The Ephyra line is ancient and powerful, but our power is chained by a few silly girls who don't even have a drop of nobility in their blood. The princesses have warped this country. They've warped our noble purposes and calling, and they've made you think that it's right. No more."

He snapped, and Kellan stepped down the hall to stand beside him. "It starts now," Xavier told Kellan.

Xavier disappeared while Kellan raised his hands and spoke. "Passcode alpha," he said. "Follow."

The golem lurched with a clank and then spun on its heel to follow Xavier.

Shit, they had access to the golems. Rilla was going to be so pissed.

"Kellan," Lillie said before her last brother could leave. "Kellan, don't do this. You know it's not right. What's wrong with you?"

Kellan froze, one foot in the air. He shook his head as if to shake off the sound of Lillie's voice. But then he glanced back at Lillie.

"Can you see magic, sister? If you could, you'd know that sometimes magic gives us no choice."

Lillie's hand shot to the circlet she wore across her forehead. A gift from Rilla after they'd finished their first job for her. And it did allow her to see magic.

Lillie gasped and threw herself at the grating between them, flinging a spell at her brother. "Kellan!"

Kellan was already moving down the hall and the spell missed, bouncing off the walls and zipping back into the cell.

Vola threw herself across Lillie and Ephyra, dragging them down out of the way.

By the time she shot back to her feet, the brothers were gone.

Lillie knelt on the dirt floor gasping, but Vola was enough of a healer to know it wasn't pain keeping her pinned to the ground. At least not physical pain.

Her own family. Her own brothers had used her, betrayed her, and tricked her into this prison cell. And now they were off to commit the worst treason. There was no one to warn Rilla and the other princesses that the Ephyras were going to drain the power from the Thrones and take over Southglen.

Vola rubbed her forehead. What could she do? What could any of them do, locked in here like this? She was only good at one thing. Protecting people. And how could she do that from in here?

She blew out her breath. "Talon?" she called. "You guys still all right?"

"Yes. Though Sorrel is climbing the walls."

"You heard Xavier."

A pause. "Yes."

Lillie lashed out, striking the wall with her fist. She winced, and cradled her hand against her chest.

"Feel better?" Vola said.

"Not really, no," Lillie said, head bowed. "I can't…I can't help thinking this is all my fault."

Vola snorted. "How do you figure?"

Lillie looked up, eyes wide but not really seeing. "I left," she said. "I ran away. Maybe if I'd been here…"

"Your brothers would have chosen differently?"

She grimaced away from the idea. "Maybe not. If they chose this…then it was already too late when I left. My family…" She covered her face with her hands. "How can I fight this, Vola? How can I hate my own brothers so much? Xavier was right. I can't strike at them. Everything I've done in my life, I did to protect them. Because family is everything."

Vola glanced at Ephyra, knowing exactly where Lillie had gotten that sentiment.

Ephyra stared down at Lillie, his brows drawn together, his mouth creased and unhappy.

He knelt, taking Lillie's wrists in his hands and pulling her hands from her face. "Yes. Family is everything," he said, quietly. "I was so worried for you. When you left. I worried about you out there in the world without any of us to protect you. You'd lived in the shelter of the Ephyra house your whole life. How could you survive on your own? But here's the thing I never even thought of. Not until you threw yourself between me and my executioners. And then stayed your hand on the word of someone who was a stranger to me." He glanced up at Vola. "You found a new family. You made one for yourself. They protected you. They strengthened you. And they helped you to grow. You are not the daughter that left here after murdering a rapist."

Lillie gasped and stared, water standing in her blue eyes.

"You're not the daughter that ran away. Because of them. You chose your family. And I'm so proud of you and who they've helped you become."

She swallowed a couple times. Then ducked her gaze and sucked in air.

"Family isn't just who you grew up with," Ephyra said. "It's who you choose to protect."

Vola waited, heart in her throat.

Lillie stood and raised her chin. "You're right," she said. "I'm done protecting people who have chosen over and over to hurt me and the people I care about."

Vola carefully crossed her arms, masking the way her hands shook. "So we're going after them," she said. "How? How do we keep them from draining the Thrones?"

Lillie stretched her hand out toward her father in question.

He shook his head, eyes narrowed. "I'm not sure. They were built with divine power. Each of the Greater Virtues poured their power into a Throne, imbuing it with their personal code. But there are plenty of ways worldly power can corrupt the divine. Only divine power can protect them."

"And your brothers will be there to keep us out," Vola told Lillie. "How will we get past them?" Finding a way to counter the divine could wait till they knew if they could even reach the Thrones.

Lillie's lips thinned. "Kellan," she said.

"What about him?"

"What he said there at the end about magic making it so you don't have a choice. It wasn't an excuse. It was an explanation. A hint." She touched the circlet on her forehead. "To use this and see the magic holding him. He has some sort of spell binding him. That's why he was acting so strange and wooden. He's being controlled. And he was trying to tell me. If we can break the control on him, we'll have him on our side. And we'll know everything they know."

"I'm glad to know all of my sons haven't gone bad," Ephyra said dryly. "But that only works if we make it out of here. Have you ever broken out of prison before?" He raised his eyebrows at Vola.

Before she could respond, someone cleared their throat above them.

They all looked up to find Sorrel sitting on the top of the wall swinging her feet. Talon, Finn and even Gruff knelt beside her, silhouetted against the afternoon sun.

Sorrel waved cheerily. "I knew that would come in handy."

Vola rubbed her lips. "So literally climbing the walls."

Talon quirked a grin. "You seemed to be focused on your conversation. We didn't want to interrupt."

Sorrel wiggled her sandaled feet. "These are excellent. Rilla really knows her footwear."

NINETEEN

SORREL AND TALON gave the rest a hand up and out of the prison cell. From the top of the wall, Lillie could see the trap spells laid out along the plain here above the city, and all they had to do was tiptoe around them to make their way to the edge of the cliff.

They dropped over the side beside the palace. Vola headed for the stairs but froze when she heard a bashing sound traveling over the Justice Hall courts and the manicured greens.

"Sounds like someone's trying to break down the palace door," Talon said. "Should we investigate or leave it to the golems?"

"The golems are under Kellan's control," Vola said. "And Kellan is under Xavier and Innis's control. Maybe."

"To the palace, then," Ephyra said, setting off as if to storm the gates himself.

No one crowded the courts of the Justice Hall today, and the city below them lay quiet and still like it was holding its breath. Everyone must have been lying low to avoid all the head chopping and property burning that usually went alongside a coup.

"What are we going to do when we get there?" Finn asked. "What's the plan?" He didn't ask like he was worried or charging into trouble. He asked like he was thinking through all the possibilities and the things he could contribute.

"Xavier and Innis are going to drain the Thrones of their magic with the help of the slaver we've been chasing. That's who sent the message to Virvalim that started all this." Vola nodded to Finn.

He bit his lip. "That sounds…pretty bad."

"But not hopeless. Ephyra says divine power is the only thing that's going to be able to save the Thrones. They were made by the gods, and it's the only thing that will be able to prevent the traitors from tampering with them. Luckily, we have some of that with us."

Vola glanced pointedly at Sorrel, and Sorrel craned her neck to look over her shoulder. Her eyes crossed as she focused on the staff slung across her back. "Oh. Oh, no."

"Not oh no," Vola said. "This is good news."

"Yeah, but I still haven't figured out how to use it. I just keep blasting myself out of the fight or shooting lightning off into the distance."

"That's because you're doing it wrong."

Sorrel threw her hands in the air. "That's exactly my point!"

"I didn't mean —" Vola paused in the middle of the wide paved path that turned the corner and led to the palace in just a few hundred feet. The others went on without noticing. "Look. Can I see it for a second?"

Sorrel shrugged dejectedly and tossed the staff to Vola. As it hit the paladin's hand, the weapon morphed and shifted, becoming a perfectly balanced longsword, its hilt fitting her hand as though it was made for her.

Vola narrowed her eyes at it, settled it in her grip, and swung it a few times.

"Maybe you should just use it," Sorrel muttered.

Vola tilted her head. "Does it still want to be a quarterstaff when you hold it?"

"Yeah. I have to concentrate if I want it to stay a wizard's staff."

"And does that feel…I don't know, natural?"

Sorrel shrugged. "It's certainly distracting, especially in the middle of a fight."

"Sorrel," Vola started slowly. "The weapon changes based on who's holding it. I think that must mean that the power adapts to you. That means you don't have to change anything about the way you fight. You're not good at making it work like a wizard's staff because you're not a wizard. Lillie would be great at it."

Sorrel opened her mouth. "But that priest said—"

"Maxim didn't give his Warhammer to that priest," Vola said. "Or to Lillie or me or anyone else. He gave it to you. So he must want you to use it the way you would."

She handed the sword back to Sorrel, and in the halfling's hands, it shimmered and stretched to become a long staff carved with knots and wrapped with leather around the grip. Sorrel stared at it.

"It's divine no matter what you do, so use it. The way you were meant to. The way you were trained to." Vola flicked Sorrel's forehead. "Stop trying to make this harder than it is."

Sorrel rolled her eyes. "Like that's ever worked for us before."

Another crash sounded from ahead, and Vola winced. "Make it work, cause we're out of time to experiment."

They turned the last corner separating the Justice Hall from the palace proper in time to spot War and Shield lobbing some sort of magical battering ram at the large palace doors. Rilla and seven of the other princesses stood behind them in varying states of distress and frustration.

Had the traitors already seized the palace from the other princesses? Kellan's portals could have gotten them into the palace proper without a fuss.

Behind the princesses, a line of golems waited, standing at attention. No one watched them because no one needed to. They were trusted servants.

Vola sucked in a breath and exchanged a look with the others. She opened her mouth.

"Yeah, we know," Sorrel interrupted. "Don't explain, just run."

They sprinted across the lawn even as the golems shook themselves and slowly stretched their limbs, reaching for their weapons. The big armored figures closed in on the princesses.

"Rilla, behind you!" Vola called as she ran. She pulled her sword from behind her back.

Rilla turned, eyes wide, in time to catch the first golem's fist across her jaw, rather than the back of her head.

The princess of the Shield Throne flung out her hand, and Rilla landed with a soft thump.

"Authorization code: War Eternal," War shouted. "Stop where you are. Immediately. Cease. Desist."

The golems kept coming. "Authorization not recognized."

"Oh, hell." War raised her hands and a wall of fire sprang up around the princesses. The nearest golem caught on fire, flames licking up its plate armor. It ground to a halt, standing half in and half out of the flames.

The rest seemed to hesitate as well. Maybe whatever they were made of under the plate wasn't resistant to heat.

Vola leveled her shield and charged into the nearest Golem, knocking it back a step.

Sorrel zipped past and leaped for another. She struck the

golem in the back with both feet, and the thing stumbled and fell flat to the ground. The halfling sprang out of the way as Vola lunged for the prone golem and brought the pommel of her sword down on its head. The helmet caved in and the figure seemed to collapse in on itself.

Sorrel scrambled up the next golem's back and perched on its shoulder to smack it over the head so hard its helmet rang.

Lightning zipped between the golems, making their armor sizzle, and Vola cast a grin back at Lillie. But it wasn't their wizard who stood with her arms raised, it was Ephyra.

Vola turned to take on another golem, but the one she targeted fell with an arrow through its visor, and Gruff followed it down with a snarl.

Finn pounded up beside Vola, sword drawn, his grip firm and ready. She caught his gaze. "I'll take them down. You finish them."

He nodded, no trace of hesitance in his expression as she rushed for the next golem. The thing moved with uncanny speed, but she ducked and slid under its strike and swept its legs out from under it. Finn followed her with a strike to its helmeted head and it went limp.

Talon paused on the edge of the battle and raised her bow. Her arrow took off another golem's head, and it lumbered in a bewildered circle before collapsing to its knees.

Vola breathed a sigh of relief. This wasn't so bad. They were winning. Golems were big, yes, but they were also dumb.

A clanking sound rang around the cliff walls, making her spin and raise her sword.

More golems poured out from the wings of the palace and closed in on them, trotting in time together. And the ones scattered on the ground around them twitched as if rallying themselves. One sat up and reached for its own severed arm. It held it like a club and lurched to its feet.

"Don't these things have an off switch?" Sorrel called, raising her staff once more.

Vola cast a glance at Rilla. The princess of the Health Throne was tending her, a glowing white light making the fingers of her hand indistinct where she held them over Rilla's head.

The princess of the Dagger Throne sat up, holding her temple, and glared at the incoming golems. "Stupid, fucking technology. On my authorization, halt your fucking movement. Self-destruct sequence initialization."

One of the golems shuddered in mid-step, then kept moving as if nothing had happened.

"I'm going to kill the wizard that sold me these things," Rilla growled.

The wall of plated figures closed in, and Vola backed up, shoving Finn and Talon behind her. "Talon cover us," she said. "Finn, protect the princesses. Sorrel, keep doing what you've been doing. Lillie, you got anything that will slow them down?"

Lillie stepped around Vola and raised her hands. She whispered a couple words and threw out her arms. Her hair stood straight out from her head as lightning zipped and crackled over the golems, arcing from one to another, making them all pause in their relentless march.

"That's more like it," Sorrel said, sprinting for the nearest one. "Now let's find the off switch."

"Try passcode alpha," Ephyra called after her. "That's what Kellan used."

Sorrel climbed the front of the golem and flipped back its visor. She drew back her fist and said, "Passcode alpha, you worthless piece of tin. Self-destruct sequence initialization, and don't let me catch you slacking."

Her fist whistled through the air, and she planted it in the golem's face with a resounding crack that echoed off the cliffs.

The golem shuddered, and Sorrel flipped free as it fell in a heap of loose armor, pauldrons rolling away across the flagstones.

The entire phalanx of golems all shuddered in their tracks and fell in heaps of metal and leather fastenings.

Sorrel dusted off her hands and spun with a grin. "One dead army at your service, Your Highnesses."

Vola's shoulders relaxed as the princesses all climbed to their feet behind them and War dispelled her fire barrier.

"What the hell just happened?" Rilla snapped. "Who usurped my command of them? Was it Virvalim? I'm going to execute that man with my bare hands," Rilla said, cracking her knuckles.

"Er," Lillie said. "Actually…"

Ephyra wrung his hands behind her.

Rilla's eyes fastened on their guilty faces. "Actually what?"

"We found the real traitors, Your Highness," Vola said. "I mean more of them, at least. Virvalim is definitely plotting against you. It's just…these guys might be worse."

Her eyes narrowed. "Who?" she barked.

Lillie flinched. "Xavier and Innis Ephyra," she said. "And I believe they hold Kellan Ephyra captive with them." She didn't cower, just raised her chin in acknowledgment of her family's duplicity.

Rilla blew out her breath. "Wonderful. Between them and Virvalim, no wonder we can't get in." She turned back to the doors—and the other princesses.

"All right. One more time. This time without the interruption," War said.

Rilla rolled her eyes. "This is stupid. I can get us in through a side entrance if you'll just give me two seconds. If you knock down the door, they'll know we're coming."

"They locked us out of our own palace and took the others captive inside. They know we're coming for them. I'm not going for subtlety here."

War stepped to the front and raised her hands. The other princesses reached out to place their hands on her shoulders. It got a little crowded with ten of them, but they didn't seem to care, their faces set with determination.

Vola's grip tightened on her hilt. She didn't like all of them clustered here in one place. One wizard could take them all out at once.

She glanced at War's face. Or maybe not. With all their power mustered together, surely, they could protect themselves.

War's hands began to glow with an ominous red light, and she raised her chin to glare at the door.

Between one moment and the next, the light sputtered.

War's eyes widened as it flickered and went out entirely. "What—"

Behind her, Shield clutched her head and fell. Health doubled up with a groan and collapsed.

Vola sucked in a gasp as one by one the princesses all toppled to the ground.

TWENTY

Vola dove to catch Rilla.

Rilla blinked up at the sky, eyes full of shock. "The Throne," she gasped out. "The Dagger Throne. I can't feel it."

Her hands fluttered at her sides, and Lillie knelt to hold them.

"I can't feel my Throne," Rilla said, voice weak. "Gods, what's happened to it? Why can't I reach it?"

Lillie glanced up at Vola, terror reflected in her wide blue-green eyes. "They've started draining the Thrones of their power."

Vola's lips set in a thin line. "Rilla. Rilla, we need some other way into the palace. We need to get in to stop them, otherwise the Thrones will be gone forever."

The princess seemed to rally and pushed herself up from Vola's arms. She rolled to her hands and knees and took a deep breath.

"Yes," she whispered. "Yes. There's a side passage. Through the Justice Hall. It's probably locked. But I can have someone open it for you."

"How?" Sorrel asked. "If you don't have your magic—"

"I have the magic I learned before the Throne bound me," Rilla snapped. "Enough to call for help."

Ephyra knelt beside them. "I can get them to safety. We can hole up in the Ephyra manor while you stop whatever it is Xavier and Innis are doing."

"We'll head to the Throne room, then," Vola said.

Rilla's hand gripped her arm, and she lifted her head to stare up at Vola. "End this," she hissed.

Vola saluted with a grim smile. "Yes, ma'am."

Vola and the others crept through the Justice Hall again to find the side entrance Rilla had talked about.

The door stood open a crack, manned by a girl in a neat black gown and crisp apron who waved them in quickly.

"Miss Dagger said you were coming," she whispered, shutting the door behind them. "The traitors went through the main halls of the palace straight to the Throne room. But if we go up through the servant's quarters, I think I can get you in unseen. Would that be all right?"

"Of course," Vola said. "You know your way around better than we do. And we trust Rilla's people."

The girl flashed a smile at her. "Yes, we do, too. You'll fix this, won't you?"

"It's ending now, one way or another," Lillie said.

Finn puffed up his chest. "But don't worry. We're here to protect you," he said. "It's what we do."

Sorrel hid a snort behind her hand while the girl tilted her head and gave him a quick once over before she ducked her gaze again.

"I feel safer already, sir," she said, batting long eyelashes.

Vola would have laughed, too, except she'd never seen pride

in Finn's face before, and she wasn't about to do anything to erase it.

The girl led them through deserted halls, scouting the way when she had to before darting back to tell them it was clear. Rilla trained her people well.

The girl paused at a corner where the servant's quarters became the hallway into the main palace. She checked that the way was clear before she gestured them forward and scurried across the open space.

Vola followed with the others.

A figure stepped around the corner the girl was aiming for, and she squeaked in surprise.

Before Vola could rush forward, the man raised his hands and a cloud of green noxious gas swept over them, dropping the girl to the polished floor.

Vola's lungs burned, and she fell to her knees, coughing as her eyes stung and watered. She hacked and gasped, trying to draw a clear breath, but it felt like her lungs were trying to crawl their way up her throat.

Tears blurred her vision, but she could still make out a tall familiar figure at the end of the hall.

Virvalim.

She couldn't find clear air, and black started clawing at her from the edges of her consciousness. She dropped her chin and a dim glow caught her eye. Her emblem had swung free from her breastplate. Cleavah's fish knife glinted in the light.

Vola grabbed it and held on. With no air in her lungs, she prayed in her head. *Lady, protect me.* Warmth tingled across her palm and suddenly she could draw a full breath. She sucked in the clean air and cleared her throat.

Finally, she managed to raise her head.

Sorrel lay next to her, staring at the ceiling, gasping. Talon's figure lay not far away, as did Finn's.

But Lillie stood in a pocket of clear air, the slight breeze that kept the gas at bay ruffling the ends of her hair.

Virvalim stood at the edge of the noxious fumes. "There," he said with a sharp smile. "Now you have no one to hide behind."

Lillie's eyes slid to Vola and their gazes met.

Vola wanted to struggle to her feet. She wanted to fling herself in front of Lillie and bring Virvalim down before he could attack the wizard. But Sorrel, Talon, and Finn lay, fighting for breath. She could crawl to them, but it would mean leaving Lillie alone and undefended.

Lillie held her gaze, then jerked her chin at the others.

Vola's eyes narrowed as if to say, "are you sure?"

Lillie's lips went thin, and Vola recognized the look. She shrugged. "Fair enough," she muttered.

"What do you want, Virvalim?" Lillie snapped, turning to her adversary. "You were defeated. Your challenge was met, and I won. You have no more legal right to this conflict. Now get out of our way."

Vola did a quick assessment and crawled for Finn. The boy had the least amount of experience with this sort of thing and as long as she worked quickly, she could get to all of them in turn.

Virvalim's eyes narrowed, and he lowered his chin. "It wasn't a fair fight," he said. "If you fought instead of hiding, you would have been dead on the ground."

Lillie crossed her arms. "I didn't make up the rules. I didn't make up the fact that I could have a champion fight."

Virvalim smirked. "Well, now it's even. Now I can kill you without your friends interfering."

Vola snorted as she reached for Finn. "He says that like it's going to be easy," she muttered.

Lillie's eyes flicked to her briefly, but Virvalim chose that moment to strike, sending a spike of ice straight toward her chest.

But Lillie pulled her hands apart and sent a wave of fire forward to melt the ice into a harmless puddle.

The flames leaped for Virvalim, and he chanted a spell to wrap himself in a cloak of water.

Vola wrapped Finn's hand around her emblem, and the boy's eyes flew open as he gasped for clean air. She gave Finn a few moments to recover, then gestured him to the outer edges of the room to get out of the gas. Finn heaved a deep breath of clean air and then started crawling for safety while Vola made for Sorrel.

Finn paused in his retreat to grab the girl and drag her free of the gas as well.

Vola ducked behind Lillie to get to Sorrel, but the two wizards were locked in combat and didn't even notice.

She'd never actually seen a wizard's duel before. The lights and flashes were pretty, but how did anybody win if every spell and attack had a counter?

From Sorrel's side, Vola could reach out and drag Talon closer. She wrapped their hands around her emblem all at once.

Lillie threw a spell at Virvalim, and he grunted, doubling over in pain. He gazed at his hands, which shook and turned a strange sort of gray. His fingers curled and froze in place. The stone crept up the flesh of his wrists, threatening to engulf him completely.

Virvalim growled at Lillie, but instead of retaliating with magic, he surged forward, hands outstretched as if to wring her neck.

Lillie drew her fist back and punched the ground between them. A clap of thunder rang around the hall, and Virvalim flew back. He crashed into the wall and slid to the floor.

The green cloud dissipated just as Talon and Sorrel gasped for clean air and blinked away the tears in their eyes.

Vola checked the others over, but Talon and Sorrel recovered quickly. Finn was helping the serving girl to her feet.

Vola surged upright and took a couple steps to stand behind

Lillie's shoulder where she stood over Virvalim. Sorrel and Talon joined them, weapons drawn.

The lord scowled and used the wall to lever himself to his feet, cradling his stony hands.

"Congratulations," he said. "Now you have someone to hide behind again."

Vola snorted and sheathed her sword, relaxing into a parody of parade rest. Sorrel and Talon followed suit. Finn glanced at them and then lowered his sword reluctantly.

Vola crossed her arms and made sure Virvalim had noticed their relaxed state. His eyes widened and flicked to Lillie, whose face had gone still and grim.

She opened her hands, palm out. "Try me."

Virvalim's mouth twisted in a sneer, and he pushed himself off the wall to step forward.

Right into the large puddle his ice had left.

Lillie knelt to touch the floor, and the water froze around Virvalim's boots and climbed up his legs, locking them in place. Then she straightened and flung out her hands. Flames spouted, catching Virvalim right in the face since he couldn't run.

He screamed and fell.

Immediately, Lillie pulled back on the fire, and Vola stepped up to his smoking figure. He grimaced, his face lined with soot.

"You know why we protect Lillie?" she asked the prone lord. "Because she's our cannon. When she hits a thing, it stays down."

"What do we do with him?" Talon said.

"He is a traitor," Finn said hesitantly.

"Aw, but I really hate killing people who are lying down," Sorrel said.

Vola leveled her gaze on the lord. "Beg for mercy," she said. "Tell us about the man who's draining the Thrones, and we will argue for exile instead of execution."

Virvalim's face twisted, and he spit at Vola. "Get out of my way, greenskin." He shoved Vola as he surged to his feet and stomped away. Not even pretending to flee. Just walking away in a huff.

"Wrong move," Lillie said quietly. "She's the merciful one."

She pushed both hands out from her chest, and a wall of air rushed out and through the hall, striking Virvalim and slamming him against the corner. His hands shattered into little shards of rock and the rest of him crumpled to the floor and didn't get up again.

"Damn, Lillie," Sorrel said.

Vola stepped to Lillie's side and put her hand on her shoulder. She squeezed.

"Let's go," Vola said, quietly. "This part is over."

Lillie hesitated only a moment before nodding and following Vola toward the Throne room.

TWENTY-ONE

Now they were out of the servant's quarters of the palace, thick maroon carpets covered the marble floors and gilded furniture graced the empty spaces along the walls. Dour paintings of ancient princesses dressed in ruffles and starched collars glared down at them from the paneling.

The serving girl led them to the end of the hall where a pair of wide double doors stood. Kellan stood guard outside.

"He's alone," Lillie said. "We just have to figure out how to break the compulsion on him."

The whisper of her voice rose up the ornate walls and bounced off the ceiling, making Kellan look up. He stepped away from the door and moved toward them, his arms held stiffly at his sides. The blank sheen in his eyes sent a shiver down Vola's spine. Whoever or whatever was driving Kellan's body peered out at them, but she couldn't see any trace of Lillie's brother in there.

Lillie's breath hissed through her teeth, in anger or fear, Vola couldn't tell.

Vola drew her sword, not to kill him, but to be ready, just in case. Lillie's lips thinned, and she raised her hands.

A few feet from the door, Kellan staggered. He put his hand to his temple and then collapsed onto the carpet with a moan.

"Well, that was fast," Sorrel told Lillie.

"That wasn't me," Lillie cried and rushed for him. She fell to her knees beside her brother.

"Wait, it could be a trick," Vola said, reaching for Lillie.

Beside Vola, Finn jerked.

Vola froze, caught between the wizard and her protege.

"Finn?" she said. "Are you—"

The boy stepped forward, sword naked in his hand, and slid the blade into the serving girl's back.

The others swarmed forward, yelling as Vola stood, hands shaking in shock. She shook her head, forcing herself to move.

"Finn!"

Finn spun, blade raised against her. His face had gone slack, so devoid of emotion and personality that she barely recognized him. Behind them, the serving girl slid to the floor, silent.

Vola brought her arm down to knock the sword from Finn's hand, but he twisted, dodging the blow faster than she knew he could move, and he countered with an aggressive strike of his own. Vola lunged back, narrowly missing the swipe he made for her stomach.

"Finn, stop this," she called. "Fight this, whatever it is."

He advanced, unrelenting, but she refused to actually hurt him. She waited for his next blow and side stepped, catching his blade on hers and twisting until his sword fell against the carpet with a thump.

Finn reached for her face, fingers curled into claws.

Kellan lifted his head from the floor and groaned. Lillie leaned over him as he grated out, "Shield. Raise a shield."

Lillie's eyes went wide, and she snapped out three quick words, forming the spell with her fingers. A translucent bubble sprang up around them, sealing them off from the outside world.

Finn's eyes rolled back in his head, and he fell, legs going completely limp. Vola dropped her sword to catch him against her chest.

Her breath came in quick, shallow bursts as her fingers clenched the fabric of his shirt. His face was just as slack now as it had been two seconds ago, but this was the quiet of unconsciousness, not unawareness.

The serving girl lay just feet away, eyes staring glassy at the ceiling. An innocent, slaughtered in cold blood. Maybe if Vola had gotten to her sooner…if she hadn't been fighting her own protege. If Finn hadn't stabbed her in the first place.

"Finn, Finn, what have you done?" Vola whispered.

"Not him," Kellan croaked. He pushed himself up to his elbows, head hanging limp while he breathed. He cleared his throat and tried again. "It wasn't your boy. He…he has a mind control spell."

"Xavier?" Lillie asked.

Kellan shook his head and sat up completely. "No. No, the man funding all this. The one who's draining the Thrones for Xavier and Innis. He can control people. But he can only handle one person at a time. He had to drop the spell on me in order to cast the one on him." He gestured to Finn, who still lay in Vola's arms. "And the shield disrupts his magic."

"Then he's nearby," Talon said, voice flat. She glared at the walls full of ancient paintings as if one might come alive.

"No." Kellan sagged. "I don't know where he is. But he can work from afar, obviously. He cast the spell at your boy through me."

"Why?" Vola said around the lump in her throat. "Why would he take over Finn?"

Kellan shook his head again. "I don't know. It's…it's all very fuzzy when he's driving you. Maybe he wanted to get to you and couldn't. I don't know how it works. Maybe he was trying to get him to stab you in the back. But Finn was strong enough to divert him."

Vola's brow drew down, and she stroked the hair away from Finn's brow. "Good boy," she whispered, though her chest was tight and painful.

"So as soon as this shield comes down, we're vulnerable again?" Talon said. "What do we do when that happens? We can't stay in here forever."

Kellan sat up and held his head like it hurt. "I don't think he'll try again. Not so overtly. I got the impression he's not very good at it. At least not yet. He needs a weakness in order to worm his way in. Obliviousness or arrogance usually. If you're alert to it, he won't be able to break in. I think."

It wasn't a huge advantage, but Vola would take it. She'd be extra aware of any thoughts that didn't seem to be her own. Extra vigilant to any actions that were out of character for the rest of them.

But that didn't help Finn or the girl he'd just murdered. "Why is he still unconscious? Will he be all right?"

Kellan licked his lips. "When he takes over, it's pretty traumatizing. It...it feels like a curtain lowers between you and the world. You can't control yourself, and you don't even know what's going on. I didn't remember the first episode. Not until much later. By then it was too late."

Lillie laid her hand over his. "What happened?"

Kellan shook his head like he didn't want to remember. But he spoke anyway. "I disagreed with them," he said. "I disagreed with what they were doing and how they were doing it. They kept their plans from me until after you got home. But when I realized they were using you to take out their rivals in the nobility, I told them to go to hell. The next morning, I woke up and I couldn't remember anything. By the time I realized what was going on, they never let me go."

"Xavier and Innis did this?" Lillie asked, voice low and dangerous. "They didn't like you disagreeing, so they had this man control you for them?"

Kellan nodded. "He's been monitoring them from afar. Making sure they were on track. I thought, maybe they were being influenced as well, but no. They actually want this. They want to take the power out of the Thrones. They want to gut the princesses' authority. They want Southglen for themselves."

"And they were willing to get rid of the rest of us to do it," Lillie said.

Kellan hung his head and nodded.

Vola's teeth clenched, and she rolled Finn gently onto the carpet, against the wall as if tucking him into bed. "Lillie, can you make this shield hold? To protect Finn."

"Yes. For a bit."

Vola cast a sharp glance at her. "How much more fight do you have in you? You've been throwing around a lot of spells."

Her eyes narrowed. "I have enough," she said. "Kellan?"

The young man stood, his knees shaking a bit, and he stretched his fingers. "Plenty."

"Then I suggest we go pay your brothers a little visit. Rilla told us to end this. Let's make sure it ends today."

TWENTY-TWO

VOLA DIDN'T BOTHER TRYING the door first. She strode up to them and planted her foot at the level of the latch, expecting them to slam open.

They didn't budge, and she hopped backward on one foot, hissing.

Talon rubbed the back of her neck, and Sorrel whistled toward the ceiling while Kellan stepped up to the doors to check them.

"They've sealed them from inside," he said, running his hands along the carved panels. "I think they've used the stolen power of the Thrones to do it, too. We won't be getting past them through any normal means."

"What about your portal spell?" Lillie said.

"What about it? I don't have a portal here."

"No, but I think I can tweak it to be a teleportation spell. I'll have to hold the diagram in my head in order to complete the paradigm, but it should work. And I think we can take one or two people with us at a time, too."

"Lillie, do you know how dangerous—"

"I'm not letting a pair of doors keep me from this, Kellan. Either help me or get out of the way so I can get us inside."

Vola carefully didn't interrupt as Lillie glared at her brother.

Finally, Kellan rolled his eyes. "Fine, but if you get me killed, I'm haunting you."

Lillie took hold of Vola's arm while Kellan grabbed Sorrel.

"You're sure this is safe?" Sorrel said.

"Well, it's not like we've had time to practice so—" was all Kellan had time to say before the whoosh of air drowned him out and Vola found herself staggering on the other side of the doors. Lillie was gone and back again with Talon in tow by the time Vola managed to straighten up and get her bearings. Sorrel clutched Kellan's arm nearby, looking a little green.

"Okay, chalk one up to experimental spells," Vola said, then advanced into the room.

Within the cavernous space, Xavier knelt beside the War Throne, checking a diagram chalked on the floor around the stone chair. Innis mirrored his pose across the room by the Shield Throne. Diagrams surrounded each of the Thrones, illuminated by the green glow emanating from the marble seats. The light swirled and spiraled up like an upside-down whirlpool, spearing toward the distant ceiling. There the light gathered into one massive funnel, which streamed out the skylight above.

Kellan stared upward, green light reflecting from his face. "They're siphoning it all away," he whispered. "The very power of the Thrones is being stolen. I almost hoped he was lying about being able to do that."

"Xavier," Lillie called across the space, and Vola wondered if she'd done something special to make it boom like that. "Innis."

Xavier didn't even look up right away. He sighed and put down his chalk. Then he brushed his hands off and stood. Only then did he finally deign to look at them. Innis, at least, stood behind him, looking wary.

"I see you found a way out of the prison," Xavier said. He tilted his head. "And you got Kellan free of his leash. I suppose I should say well done, but this is getting old, Lillie. I know you're supposed to be the annoying baby of the family, but you could learn when to step aside and let your brothers do their work."

Lillie flushed, but her voice came out strong. "Work? You mean play, don't you? You've never had to work a day in your life, Xavier. You've always had everything handed to you. At least I knew enough to know how helpless I was when I left Glenhaven."

Red crept up Xavier's elegant cheekbones, staining his scowl with shame. "I am a knight of the realm. Of course I've had to work. I've trained and I've sacrificed to earn my position."

Vola let them talk and gave Sorrel and Talon a hand gesture low enough to hide it from the brothers, sending them along the walls to flank their enemy.

Lillie snorted and rolled her eyes. "Father begged the princesses to give you your knighthood. You were so bad at your training, there wasn't a knight that would take you on as a squire."

"You wouldn't have any idea what a knight has to go through to earn his way."

"Actually, I do because I've traveled with a real knight. Not one who betrays his vows the moment he gets the brilliant idea he wants to be king. Not one who is so weak he doesn't even recognize strength when he sees it."

"So says the girl who ran away."

Flames snapped into being around Lillie's hands, and she lowered her chin. "Do you see me running now?"

Xavier rolled his eyes toward the ceiling. "We've been over this once already today, Lillie. You won't strike me —"

A fireball cut him off, striking dead center of the Thrones and engulfing Xavier and Innis in flames.

Xavier screamed and threw himself to the side. Innis beat at the fire licking up his breastplate.

Xavier rolled to his feet, breathing heavily, and glared at them. His hair smoldered on his shoulders. "Very well, sister. If that's the way you want this to—"

Sorrel sailed through the air, striking him feet first in the face. "Less talk, more fight, big bro."

Xavier roared and swiped at her with his bare hand, but she ducked out of the way.

"Oops. Missed me." She punched him in the thigh and rolled away.

The blood surged in Vola's veins, and she pulled her sword from its sheathe. Finally, she'd get the chance to wipe that smirk from Xavier's face. Or watch Lillie do it. Either way was fine with her.

Talon shot straight into the air, her arrow arching up over the brothers. At the peak of its flight, lightning flashed from its tip, striking Innis as he raised his sword.

Vola charged him, bringing her blade down to slice him from neck to knee as the sparks zinged through is armor, distracting him.

But Innis dove aside at the last second and spun on his knees to block her blow. He moved much more gracefully than Xavier.

Note to self, don't underestimate the middle brother.

Lillie appeared beside Innis, the air cracking with the force of her spell. She reached for him with hands wreathed in flames, but Innis jerked back. He turned to slice Lillie, but she was gone again in a split second.

Vola used his movement and knelt to sweep his legs out from under him. His shin guards kept her from doing much damage, but he crashed to the ground, fumbling his sword.

Sorrel rolled past Vola. "Incoming," she said. "I'll trade ya."

Vola spun to find Xavier charging at her. She kept spinning, letting the heavy knight sail past her. He stumbled to a halt and turned to find her, but she'd already closed the distance between them and brought her blade down. It sliced into the metal at his shoulder, and he cried out.

He wrenched himself free, his left arm hanging limp. He brought his sword up one handed to point the blade at her throat. "You…you'll pay for that," he gasped.

She shrugged, a fierce grin settling on her lips. "Maybe. But you won't be the one collecting."

Vola pressed forward.

Ice appeared on the floor behind Xavier, and he backed straight into it, slipping along the slick surface. His feet went out from under him.

"Kellan," he bellowed.

"Oh, don't even start," Kellan called from the other side of the room. "You took away my mind. I hope they carve you to bits."

Vola pressed forward and the ice obligingly cleared before each of her steps. Her fingers creaked on the hilt of her sword, the blade a strong extension of her arm.

Xavier scrambled back on all fours, sword scraping along the marble floor, sending up sparks. He ran into Innis's legs and his brother crashed down on top of him. Innis had three more arrows sprouting from the joints in his armor, and he gasped in pain.

Xavier blew the hair from his sweaty face and stared up at them. Innis grimaced but didn't try to stand either.

Vola lowered her sword and stepped back. "Lillie," she said.

The wizard appeared directly next to her in a whoosh of air. "Stop this now," she told her brothers.

"Or what?" Xavier spat on the ground at their feet. "Or you'll have your ape execute us?"

Vola sighed and shook her head. "Or she'll kill you herself, you dumbass."

Lightning struck the marble at her feet, leaving a black mark.

Vola glared at the ceiling. "Well, he is."

Xavier scoffed while Innis just concentrated on breathing. "You don't get it," he told Vola. "She won't do anything to hurt her family. Not directly. She never has and she never will."

"You're not the family I choose," Lillie said, her voice low and venomous. "I'm done protecting you. You weren't worth protecting in the first place."

Xavier's mouth fell open as Lillie straightened her spine.

"Xavier and Innis Ephyra. I place you under arrest for treason and acts of traitorous intent against the Thrones of Southglen."

Xavier started to speak, but Lillie spoke right over top of him.

"And with the authority given to me by the Dagger Throne, I sentence you to exile in the Outer Plane. From which there is no return."

She raised her arms and dark purple light gathered behind the two traitorous brothers, turning the air dark and jagged. A low hum built beneath Vola's feet and in her ears. The hair on her arms and the back of her neck raised.

Xavier's eyes went so wide they could see the white around the edges. Finally recognizing his danger. He scrambled forward, grabbing up his sword.

Innis remained still, hanging his head.

The purple coalesced into a swirling disc of dark color hanging in the air. The misty edges reached for Innis and Xavier, snatching at their forms and wrapping their figures in ropes of purple and black before yanking them back into the void.

Vola's ears popped as the portal snapped back out of existence.

A different sort of hum made Vola rub the side of her head, trying to get rid of the ringing. It didn't work, and she glanced around, trying to find the source. Finally she looked up.

"Uh oh," she said.

"It's still going," Sorrel said, eyes wide with horror.

The green swirl above them hadn't dissipated. Light was still being sucked out of the Thrones and into the vortex. But now it was getting faster and faster.

"How do we stop the siphon?" Talon asked, stepping up next to them, bow still in hand.

Lillie had already slid to her knees beside the Thrones, squinting at the chalk circles her brothers had made.

"Lillie?" Vola said. "Please tell me we can fix this."

Lillie glanced up, lips pressed thin. "Not with normal magic," she said. "The spell—whatever they got from the slaver—is using the divine power of the Thrones itself to keep the siphon going. Regular old magic just won't work."

"Bet you never thought you'd say that," Sorrel said with a chuckle. Then she realized the rest of them were looking at her, and not like they wanted to laugh at her joke. "What?" She glanced at the staff in her hand. "Oh…"

"Maxim's power is divine," Lillie said, climbing to her feet with a wince. "It should be able to stop the siphon and return the power to the Thrones."

"What about Cleavah?" Sorrel turned desperate eyes on Vola. "She's a goddess. Let's just ask her."

Vola glanced up at the swirling cloud with a wince. "I'm not going to underestimate my lady again," she said. "But she's a Lesser Virtue. The Thrones were imbued by the Greater Virtues. I don't think she'll be able to stop this. But Maxim's Warhammer might."

"That would be so much more helpful if this thing came with an instruction manual," Sorrel snapped, holding the staff out in both hands. "I've been trying to use it all week, and all I've done is electrocute some people."

"You say that like it wasn't highly entertaining," Talon muttered.

"Just use it like a monk would," Vola said, casting a glare at Talon. "Maxim gave it to a monk, so Maxim must have thought a monk would be able to use its power."

"A monk would bash people on the head, but there's no one to bash," Sorrel cried, gesturing around the empty Throne room.

Vola rolled her eyes. "And what do you do when there aren't any enemies and you want to keep in practice?"

"Forms!" Sorrel yelled. "Lots and lots of forms." She glared for a second. "Well, maybe I should do that."

Vola cast her gaze to the ceiling as Sorrel took a deep breath and planted both feet apart on the marble floor. She held the staff out in front of her and closed her eyes.

Then she drew one hand back and began a slow spin on the balls of her feet, staff tucked at her side. Her hands moved gracefully from a pseudo block into a closed fisted strike. She tilted and balanced on one foot to thrust her heel into the air.

All throughout, she moved with deliberate grace at half-speed.

Vola watched, her brow furrowed with worry, glancing between Sorrel and the green siphon above them. The staff moved like it was an extension of Sorrel herself, flowing from one form to the next. But nothing around them seemed to change with the movements.

Then, as Sorrel swept the staff around inches from the ground, bits of green sparked near the end. Tendrils of light broke from the power siphoning off the Thrones and followed the tip of the staff.

Vola drew in a sip of breath but kept her lips clamped tight on any comments. Sorrel still moved with her eyes closed, feet confident in the wide circle.

More tendrils broke free of the siphon and flowed toward Sorrel, disappearing into the staff as she moved. Each form seemed to beckon more power, limning Sorrel's limbs with light so it almost seemed like she blurred as she moved.

Sorrel's movements picked up speed. Her fist shot out, and she flowed seamlessly into a kick which morphed into a spin. Faster and faster.

Now the swirling mass above them slowed, the light winding to a stop before reversing the direction it flowed. The siphon flowed back the way it came, picking up speed even as Sorrel did. The green flowed down and back through the Thrones into Sorrel's staff through her movements.

Lillie held up her hand to shield her eyes. Sorrel glowed now, the light gathering along her limbs.

"How much more do you think she can take in?" Lillie said.

Vola squinted up at the vortex, which spun the opposite direction now, sucking down toward Sorrel. "Hopefully all of it. Why?"

"Oh, no reason," Lillie said faintly. She glanced around the room. "Perhaps we should take cover. Just in case she explodes."

"Explodes?" Vola glanced at Lillie sharply.

But the last of the light swirled overhead, spearing down toward Sorrel and her staff where they danced in time to some inner cadence only Sorrel could hear.

The light grew, making Vola's eyes water, and she flung up her hand to protect her sight.

Sorrel's blazing after image continued to move behind her eyelids before spinning in one more slow movement and coming to rest back in her original position.

Air whoomphed past them, knocking Vola and Lillie and Talon off their feet as power rushed from the staff back into the Thrones.

Vola rubbed her eyes and scrambled back to her feet, blinking.

Sorrel stood in the center of the Throne Room, her staff held horizontal before her, her eyes still closed.

Around them, the Thrones pulsed lightly and then subsided, the symbols of each princess the only thing about them that still glowed. Somewhere out in the city, down in Ephyra's manor, Vola could imagine the princesses sitting up and blinking, discovering that their power had returned.

Lillie and Talon both pushed to their feet as well. Gruff slunk forward from behind one of the pillars where he'd taken shelter and bumped Talon's hand. She absently petted his head.

Sorrel finally opened her eyes and brought the staff down to her side. She blinked up at the clear air and the skylight where the sky was just turning pink with the dawn.

Then she grinned. "Well, that wasn't so bad. Maybe I could be a wizard after all."

TWENTY-THREE

I**T ONLY TOOK** a couple days for the city to return to its normal bustle. Vendors crowded the markets, rushing to fill the void left by Virvalim's defunct enterprises. The princesses took the chance to breathe and steady themselves after nearly losing their power.

Together they mopped up the last of the noble rebellion. Lillie braced her father, before telling him what had befallen her brothers. And Vola tended Finn, who spent most of the days asleep.

But less than a week later, the team Rilla had dubbed Mishap's Heroes gathered outside the Throne room again.

Vola glanced over at Talon. The ranger wore her hood pushed back for once and her cloak pinned over her shoulders, revealing a bright pink tunic under her leather cuirass.

The effect was striking and fit the ranger better than Vola would have thought.

"I like it," she said, gesturing.

Talon didn't even flush as she glanced down. "So do I. It's… comfortable. And practical. I've decided I'm practical."

Sorrel tilted her head. "Pink, though? It doesn't really lend itself to hiding in the shadows, does it?"

"I'm not hiding right now," Talon said.

"Did you do something to your eyes?" Vola asked.

Talon glanced toward Lillie. "Just a little kohl."

Lillie flushed and touched her own face, which showed some subtle highlights. "Rilla showed me how to use the rouge. Xavier was the one who had a problem with it, and I'm not listening to him anymore. Is it really noticeable?"

Vola cleared her throat. "It's nice."

"I kept the black underwear," Sorrel said. "It makes me feel very daring. See, look." She yanked her shirt up.

Vola reached to stop her. "We believe you."

"Well, it's about as exciting as the racy book you're still hiding in your bag."

Vola rolled her eyes. "It's not hiding if everyone knows it's there. Besides, Lillie promised to read the rest out loud. I want to know how it ends."

Lillie beamed at her.

"Aw, so you found something new that you like, too. We all did." Sorrel threw her arms around Talon's waist.

Talon stiffened. Then patted the halfling on the head.

The doors opened, and Rilla stood framed in the archway, eyebrows raised. "Am I interrupting?"

"Not at all," Vola said as the princess gestured them inside. "You look much better."

"Justice will do that to you." She gestured to the Justice Throne as they passed. "Not that Justice. She's a bit of a stickler at best and a micro-manager at worst."

Justice frowned behind Rilla's back.

Today, every Throne was occupied, its princess sitting firm in her place. Rilla stepped to the Dagger Throne and took her seat, leaving them standing in the middle alone. Scorch marks marred the marble under their feet, evidence of their fight which hadn't been mopped away yet. And one of the pillars had a crack as wide as Sorrel's staff.

"We wanted to thank you personally," Justice said. "The four of you saved the Thrones and quite probably our lives."

"We also wanted to let you know that the last of the traitors have been rounded up," Law said. "Everyone who has moved against us is either exiled or dead."

"And Lillie's brothers?" Vola asked, seeing the way the wizard wrung her hands.

"Her judgment stands," Justice said. "Xavier and Innis Ephyra will remain in exile indefinitely. However, due to their actions over the last few days, Lord Ephyra and Kellan are exonerated of all guilt."

"In fact," the princess of the Magic Throne said as Lillie's shoulders relaxed. "Lord Ephyra is helping us develop new ways to keep the Thrones safe from tampering. Our adversary won't be able to drain their power and use it again. Nor anyone else."

"Oh, father will love that," Lillie said.

"As for you, we would love to reward you for your work," Justice said. "But Dagger says you're on retainer for her and therefore that's her job and privilege. I've learned not to argue with her." She raised an eyebrow in Rilla's direction.

Rilla waved an airy hand. "Fame isn't really on the table while you're working for me; it defeats the purpose. But you'll always get the recognition from us you deserve. This time a combat bonus is in order, of course. But that's kind of boring." She leaned back to sling her leg over the arm of her Throne. "The best reward for a job well done is another job."

The princess of Sewage Management cleared her throat, and Rilla's lip twitched in anticipation.

"I'm afraid we have a bit of a situation," Costa said, pushing up her glasses. "Traitors aside, shit still runs downstream. Or at least it's supposed to."

"Uh oh," Sorrel said under her breath.

Rilla didn't bother hiding her grin this time.

"We've had rumors throughout the city of some sort of sewer monster rampaging through the pipes and terrorizing people in all tiers of Glenhaven."

Vola smacked her forehead with an open palm.

"Yeah, that sounds about right," Talon said behind her. "The damn thing couldn't have just died down there?"

"Of course not," Lillie said. "I'm beginning to believe it's some sort of immortal."

"I take it you'd like us to hunt the thing down," Vola said, lowering her hand. "Since we're kind of sort of responsible for setting it loose."

"To be fair," Costa said with a wrinkle of her forehead. "I didn't believe anything would be able to survive down there for long, either. The thing is much tougher than I was expecting. Maybe once you've fished it out, I could study it to see if it has any useful properties our maintenance crew could take advantage of."

"Done," Vola said. "We'll fish it out and you can cut it open and find out what makes it go."

"Or swim," Sorrel said.

Rilla thrust herself off her Throne and gestured them out. Vola felt a little odd turning her back on a room full of grateful princesses, but they didn't seem to require any sort of bows or curtsies from the team that saved their asses. They just nodded respectfully, and the party slipped out.

Lillie, Talon, and Sorrel started down the passage, complaining about the swamp beast and passing around ideas to track the thing down, but Rilla stopped Vola with a hand on her arm.

"Before you go…"

Vola looked at her expectantly.

"How's Finn?"

Vola took a bracing breath. "He's all right physically. But he's a bit confused. He doesn't remember anything that happened after we got into the palace."

Rilla blew out her breath. "Probably won't be able to help track down the perpetrator, then," she said. "Damn. We need to talk about the fact that we have an enemy who can get in someone's head and control them."

"Kellan did say it was a lot harder for him once people were aware and on guard against it."

"And were you on guard once you were aware?" Rilla said, casting a hard glance at Vola.

Vola's lips thinned.

Her employer scowled. "You knew Kellan was controlled before entering the palace. But you did nothing to protect yourselves against it. And one of my people died for that mistake."

Vola drew herself up. "That was my mistake," she said quietly. "I'm sorry. I can't make up for that girl's death. But I take full responsibility. Finn is blameless in this."

Rilla sighed and rubbed the back of her neck. "I know. And I know you'll handle it. But this isn't something that I can just let go. Action must be taken."

Vola froze.

Rilla shook her head. "But not now. You have a trainee to see to. Take care of him and we'll address this after."

"Yes, ma'am," Vola said. This time she did bow before she joined the others leaving the palace.

Vola sent the others to get geared up for the hunt for the Terror of Glenhaven while she returned to the inn.

Finn sat up in Vola's bed, swinging his legs over the side.

"You must feel better," Vola said as he tried standing.

"I can't figure out why I'm just lying around. Sure, I'm tired, but that's not a good excuse."

"It's fine as an excuse," Vola said, pushing him back down onto the rumpled covers.

"But…" Finn said, rubbing his forehead. "It doesn't make any sense. We got to the palace, and I just passed out? And now I'm tired all the time? I don't understand why I feel this way. Did… did I do something wrong?"

His eyes were so wide and open, waiting for a blow or for encouragement.

"No," Vola said quickly. "No, you didn't do anything wrong."

"Then what happened?"

Vola chewed her lip. He didn't remember, and maybe that was a good thing. She herself couldn't sleep at night with the echo of her mistake playing behind her eyelids. She couldn't imagine the damage it would do to him to watch the serving girl he'd tried to protect fall to his blade over and over again.

Finn had spent so much of his life believing he was as low and wicked as everyone told him he was. Vola knew from experience how hard it was to believe something else about yourself with the world's rhetoric constantly ringing in your ears. But Finn had done it. In the last few days, Finn had gone from someone who'd seen stealing as his only option to someone willing to risk himself to protect a stranger. When he'd paused to haul that girl out of the noxious gas, he'd proved he'd been listening to everything Vola had been saying about choice.

Then he'd had that ability to choose ripped away from him in the next second. Right when he was beginning to really believe.

No. She was not going to take that belief away from him.

But she didn't have much time left to protect him.

As his knight trainer, she was responsible for him and every decision and action he made while under her care and protection. She hadn't been exaggerating when she'd said she took full responsibility for what had happened.

She could have stepped away. She could have disavowed him and left him to face the consequences of his inadvertent actions alone. She could throw herself free of the explosion and avoid any damage to herself. There were knights who did that. Knights who didn't deserve their shields, in Vola's opinion.

But once the paladin council learned of what went on here, they would take action against both of them.

At best, they'd take Finn away from her. They'd set him up at the academy, and he'd experience the same mocking and ridicule she had. So many of the trainees there were nobles like Xavier, privileged brats who felt like the world owed them something because of their rank.

At worst, the paladin council would throw Finn out entirely. Kick him back onto the streets where she found him, except this time he'd have proof he wasn't good enough.

She could prevent both of those possibilities, but only if she acted fast.

"You were hurt," Vola said and tapped his forehead. "Up here. We fixed the problem, but you're still recovering. Give yourself time. A warrior has to take his lumps along with his heroism." She took a deep breath. "And you're going to need your rest before you start the next part of your training."

His brow scrunched. "The next part?"

"I'm sending you to study with someone new. Someone who is a lot better at turning out paladins than me. And he's not going to let you lie around in bed."

His eyes widened and his mouth dropped open. "What? You're sending me away? Oh, gods, I did do something wrong. I'm sorry, okay? Please, please, don't send me away. This is what

I want to do. I want to be you when I get old enough. I want to fight bad guys and protect people. No one else will understand that the way you do."

She grabbed his hands to still them and spoke before he could keep begging and tearing at her heart. "It's Henri, Finn. I'm sending you to Henri."

He froze, mouth wide as he blinked. "Henri?"

"Yes."

"Your trainer, Henri?"

Her lips quirked. "That's what I said. Yes."

"But he…he's the best there is. He trained you."

Vola raised an eyebrow. "Exactly. So he will understand. Because he taught me how to protect."

Finn drew himself up and snapped his mouth closed. "You… you think he'd take me? Doesn't he choose who he trains?"

"I know he will," she said quietly. Especially if she asked him to.

"Then, you aren't…aren't ashamed of me?" he said, his voice very small.

She hoped his doubts were just as small and easily shattered by her next words.

"Never. I'm so very, very proud of you and what you're becoming." And that's why she was sacrificing herself like this. The paladin council would need someone to blame, and it couldn't be Finn. He needed someone to protect him. And that's what she did. She protected the people she loved.

That was the only thought that bolstered her two days later when she had to say goodbye. She wrapped him in her arms there on the docks and tried not to think about how he'd inserted himself into every bit of her life. How long would it take before she wasn't checking over her shoulder to make sure he was there and safe?

She only sniffled a little as she pulled back. Finn for his part had been talking nonstop about Henri since she'd told him. Lillie had used some fancy little spell to message Astrid and Henri back in Water's Edge, and the old trainer had already agreed to take on Finn as his new pupil. His first since he'd left the paladin academy.

Sorrel and Lillie each gave him a hug while Talon gave him a slap on the back that staggered him.

And when he climbed on board the barge and waved until Vola couldn't see him anymore, he was grinning ear to ear, completely oblivious to the nuance of her actions.

"You're doing the right thing," Lillie said quietly.

Sorrel had climbed up onto one of the pylons and was still waving even though they couldn't actually see the barge anymore.

"I know," Vola said after she managed to clear her throat.

"He's going to be fine," Talon said. "And so are you."

"Maybe," Vola said. "It might have been his blade, but it was my fault. We knew the enemy had mind control, and I didn't protect him from it. I was supposed to protect him."

"So you made a mistake," Sorrel said, spinning around to sit on the pylon, feet swinging. "Best thing you can do is learn from it and not make the same one twice."

"We're going to miss him," Lillie said. "But just imagine him with Henri."

Vola couldn't help smiling at that. Even if it was a watery smile. "Henri's always been great with kids."

"Even big ones," Sorrel said.

"I always thought of Finn more like a wolf pup anyway," Talon said, turning from the waterfront.

"And Henri is also wonderful with dogs," Lillie said, following. "So this is perfect."

"And we've got our own work to do, now," Sorrel said. "Smelly, evil work with more teeth and scales at the end."

"Why do you sound so excited to go after the swamp beast?" Lillie said.

"I'm not excited about the beast," Sorrel said with a shrug. "I'm just that glad it's not me on the boat this time."

Thank you so much for reading!

The misadventures continue in *Illusions and Infamy* where Vola pays the price for her mistakes and seeks refuge in the worst place she can think of. Her parents' house.

Ever wondered what happened to Vola, Talon, Lillie, and Sorrel before they met? Sign up here to get the Mishap's Heroes prequel, Creation and Calamity, and read their origin stories!

And finally, if you loved spending time with Vola, Lillie, Sorrel and Talon, consider leaving a review so other readers can find more stories about heroes who don't look like heroes but save the day anyway.

THANK YOU FOR READING

Keep reading for a preview of the next book, *Illusions and Infamy*!

ONE

Vola was hip deep in shit. Again. When all this was done, she'd be able to navigate Glenhaven's sewer system in her sleep. Although hopefully the nightmares full of tight tunnels and muck-smeared tile walls would eventually fade.

"Vola," Lillie's lyrical voice said in Vola's ear even though she knew the wizard was several pipes over and well out of ear shot. "It's headed your way."

"Thanks," Vola said and resisted the urge to rub her ear to get rid of the tingle the magic always left. Not a good idea, considering what her hands were covered in.

"You're welcome," Lillie said, perpetually polite, even in the middle of a sewer.

"You know we could just let it stay here," Sorrel's voice chimed in. "It couldn't have picked a better home for itself."

Lillie had managed to connect them all through the spell, making Vola feel pleasantly crowded even though she stood alone.

"It's terrorizing the people of Glenhaven," Talon grated from her place at the end of the trap. "And it's sort of our fault it's down here in the first place."

"Yeah," Vola added. "Only leave out the *sort of* and you've got it right. Besides, Rilla wants this done."

And when your employer said get it done, you got it done. Especially when said employer was the princess of the Dagger Throne.

Vola ducked so she had enough room to draw her sword and shield in the tight space of the tunnel, and she planted her feet. She braced herself, head cocked, listening for the scrape of broad, blunt claws on tile. That was another sound she was likely to hear in her dreams for months to come.

There. A swish and a scrape. Then a blast echoed down the tunnel as the monster encountered Lillie's trap and a wash of hot air made Vola hold her breath. Shit didn't smell good in the first place. Lighting it on fire didn't make anything better.

The creature they hunted squealed in anger and frustration and suddenly the sound of splashing came toward Vola.

Her grip tightened on the hilt of her sword, her sweaty palms creaking against the wrapped leather.

At the end of the tunnel, a screaming, rushing whirlwind of scales and spit and spite appeared and careened down the tile. The creature's evil eyes narrowed when it saw Vola.

"Not this way, beast," Vola muttered and swung her sword to deter the swamp monster from charging through her into the rest of the sewer system where it would disappear like soap in water. It had done it multiple times in the last two weeks.

The swamp monster had learned some new tricks in its time underground, though, and instead of trying to charge through a fully armed and armored paladin, it sped up the side of the tunnel and used its speed and claws to scrabble along the ceiling.

"Uh oh," Vola muttered. "I didn't know it could do that."

"What? What can it do?" Sorrel's voice asked anxiously in her ear. Apparently the spell connecting them all was still active.

Vola swung at the monster as it sped past her but it spat

viscous mucus at her, making her duck. The wad of spit hissed where it landed.

"Vola?" Lillie's voice asked. "Vola, please check in. What's going on?"

Vola growled and stepped back to sling her shield toward the monster, who squealed with glee as it escaped down the wrong tunnel.

Her shield flew true down the pipe and struck the beast hard enough to knock it from the ceiling.

Vola leaped on it, arms splayed and wrestled the creature around, twisting to avoid the razored teeth that tried to snatch at her limbs. Its slimy crest trembled in rage and it snapped its jaw just inches from Vola's face.

Red crept into the edges of Vola's vision and she felt the surge of heat rise in her chest.

No. No, she refused to lose control here in a sewer. She was more likely to beat this foul creature into a nasty red paste than actually capture it that way. And they needed to get this done right. If only to earn Rilla's goodwill again. The princess of the Dagger Throne was still unhappy about certain things that had happened during the palace coup three weeks before. And Vola didn't blame her. One of the princess's people had died and Vola was indirectly responsible.

But the only thing she could do about that was prove to Rilla that they were still competent. Still the best at their jobs. And that Vola wasn't going to be caught unprepared again.

With a mental shrug, she thrust away the rage swelling inside her and yanked the swamp beast around, then released it back down the tunnel the way it had come.

It scrambled away from Vola, but before it could escape back into the sewers, a figure appeared and wove a net of green light across the main tunnel.

The swamp beast hissed and ducked down the only way left to

it, the side passage Vola had been stationed to herd it into in the first place.

"Great timing," Vola said as Rilla strode down the tunnel. The muck didn't dare cling to the princess's dark clothes and she was short enough, she didn't have to duck to keep her curly hair from brushing the ceiling. She managed to look sleek and perfect even in the bowels of the city.

The princess didn't answer, only extended a hand with a frown.

Vola winced and used the hand to help herself up out of the shit. "Talon," Vola said, knowing the others were still listening. "The plan's working. It's headed your way. Costa, we're ready."

"Ready for a shit storm?" a gleeful voice rang in Vola's ear. "No one's ever ready for a shit storm. Hold on for your lives."

Vola and Rilla stepped back from the opening as a foul-smelling whoosh rushed down the passage where the swamp monster had disappeared. A wave of sewage blasted past their opening carrying an angry scaled creature with it.

Vola and Rilla pressed themselves against the wall and turned their faces away, waiting for a count of twenty before the roar gradually decreased to a rush and then a trickle.

As the unholy flood subsided Vola ducked to retrieve her sword and double checked her shield for damage. The round buckler was as dented and scarred as always but she was pretty sure those had all been there before. The angry slash mark where Henri had defended them against an acid-throwing swamp flower had faded some but the metal around it was still bright.

"Let's move," Rilla said. "Make sure it ended up where it was supposed to be."

Vola settled her sword and shield on her back again as Rilla took point, slinking down the tunnel, her knives drawn. There wasn't anything to though, though. Costa's sewage tidal wave had swept everything downstream.

They'd picked this particular pipe for a reason. It wasn't very long and it ended abruptly in an opening that dumped out into Costa's home turf.

Rilla and Vola stepped out into the light at the edge of the pipe and squinted at the scene. The afternoon sun glinted from three large tanks angled directly underneath them. The closest was filled to the brim with a greenish brownish sludge that surged and lapped against the edges. Magic swirled across the surface, making the liquid ripple and glint.

Costa's sewage treatment facility tucked into a cove at the bottom of the city, just out of sight from its gleaming walls. This was where her power removed disease and debris from the city's water and recirculated it back up through the tiers in clean pipes.

The swamp monster thrashed in the center of the tank, Costa's power holding it trapped in the liquid. Across the way, Talon slipped into the sludge to wade across to the beast. She'd left her enveloping hood at the edge of the tank, guarded by Gruff, the big black wolf. It meant Vola could see her grimace from here.

"Hah hah," a voice called. "It worked."

Costa stood at the edge of the tank, hands on her hips. The princess of sewer management wore a pair of thick gaiters and goggles. Vola glanced down at her soaked and smeared armor. Gaiters probably wouldn't have worked anyway, even if she'd asked for them this morning. They'd been climbing around in the sewers for weeks hunting down the swamp monster.

At first it had seemed like a simple job. The creature couldn't possibly have wanted to stay in the sewers. But after days and days of filth and close calls, Vola and the others had finally settled in for the long haul.

Hopefully it paid well enough to buy them all new clothes. They'd grown inured to the smell, but even after multiple baths Vola still noticed people hurrying to the other side of the street as they passed.

There was a pop and Lillie appeared beside them.

"Would you like a ride out of this pipe?" she said. And before they could answer, she'd tucked her hand in Rilla's arm and the two disappeared only to reappear beside Costa. Sorrel danced around the edge of the tank, small feet sure on the narrow surface. The halfling sang a little ditty at the top of her lungs.

"There once was a swamp beast from Water's Edge,
Who had some very sharp teeth in its head.
It evaded the law,
Arrogance was its flaw,
And now its evil butt will be put to bed."

"That was terrible," Talon said, halfway across the tank with the swamp beast.

"Thanks," Sorrel said and did a little spin before bowing.

Vola jumped as Lillie appeared beside her in the pipe again.

Lillie cocked her head and smiled. She tucked her hand in Vola's elbow. "You didn't think I'd forget you, did you?"

The spell pulled them into the air and for a second it felt to Vola as if every piece of her had been scattered to the four corners of the world. It only lasted a moment and then the two of them were standing with the others at the edge of the tank, watching Talon drag the swamp beast back to dry land.

"I guess that teleportation spell is really coming in handy," Vola said, taking some deep breaths. She hated that method of travel already, but she didn't have the heart to tell Lillie that.

Sorrel gave Talon a hand up out of the tank and Vola moved to take the lead rope and tug the swamp monster up, too.

It scrambled up onto the ledge and pulled its lips back to bare its teeth at Vola.

"Careful," Talon said, shaking out her arms. "I think it's more ill-tempered than usual."

"Well, it did just spend three weeks as the god of Glenhaven's sewer system," Sorrel said, cocking her head to study the creature. It looked like a cross between a crocodile and a donkey with a head cold. "It's probably not ready to live among mere mortals again, yet."

"You'd think it would appreciate the fresh air," Lillie said. "I know I do."

"Yay, no more sewers," Sorrel said, throwing her hands in the air. "I'll be happy if I never have to see another toilet again."

Talon made a face. "I don't think that means what you think it means. You seem to like plumbing well enough."

"From the outside, yes," Sorrel said. "I'd rather leave the insides to the experts." She waved a hand toward Costa, who examined the pipes where they'd reappeared.

"I think that's why the Sewage Management Throne chose me," she said without looking up. "I really like the insides of things. Well, most things. Not people. I'll leave that one to the Health Throne." She straightened and pushed her goggles up until they perched on her head, leaving red rings around her eyes. "We managed not to break anything in this whole mess. Well done. Well done indeed. What do you intend to do with it now?" She squinted at the swamp monster.

Sorrel sighed. "What we always do. Drag it along with us until hopefully one of our adventures finally kills it for real."

Vola kicked her.

"Ouch," Sorrel said. "What was that for? I know you're all thinking it."

"Yes, but none of us were so uncouth as to say it," Lillie pointed out. "It is a living, feeling creature…I think. And it deserves some modicum of respect—"

The swamp monster reached out and tried to take a bite out of the wizard.

Lillie yelped and teleported behind Vola. She leaned out to

glare at the creature. "Although, Costa, you did mention wanting to dissect it. Are you still interested in some research?"

"I'm always interested in some research. I'd especially like to know how it survived down there for so long. I'll take it off your hands. You guys deserve a celebration. Dinner. At the nicest restaurant in the city. I'll pay." She wrinkled her nose. "After we've all changed, of course."

She turned with a raised eyebrow to Rilla who had stood uncharacteristically silent since they'd emerged into the fresh air.

Vola raised her chin and met their employer's eyes hopefully.

"Good work," Rilla said almost as if it pained her. Then the princess of the Dagger Throne spun to follow Costa back into the city.

Vola's shoulders slumped. Apparently they'd need to work harder to make up for their mistakes.

ACKNOWLEDGMENTS

I started out thinking I was writing something fun and light and hopefully hilarious. But it turns out I can't just write fluff. Meaning creeps in from the sides and makes its home between the lines. And then someone likes it, and I have to write more, and more meaning forces its way in, and suddenly it's a whole "thing." I blame these people:

First, the Kickstarter backers, for making all this possible. And for believing in the series before I'd ever sold a copy.

Mom and Dad, for reading every book ever. And always asking where the next one is.

Arielle, Betsy, and Alison, for being the first inspiration for a group of inept heroes who have no idea what they're doing and manage to save the day anyway.

Miranda and Lacey, for sisterhood which looks a lot like party dynamics sometimes.

Kevin and Andrew, for inviting me to play this little game called Dungeons & Dragons.

Kyle, Mary, Amy, Clark, Tim, Greg, Lauren, and Dave, and a host of other party members, for providing endless opportunities for inspiration. These books are all your fault.

Lucy Lin, for all the amazing cover art. I don't think anyone else could have brought Vola and the others to life the same way you did.

Fiona McLaren, for copy edits and flexibility. And for

enjoying my humorous fantasy as much as my slightly more serious stuff.

And Josh and Abby, for endless support. Especially when I decided to launch a series the same month I was supposed to have a baby.

ABOUT THE AUTHOR

Books have been Kendra's escape for as long as she can remember. She used to hide fantasy novels behind her government textbook in high school, and she wrote most of her first novel during a semester of college algebra.

Kendra writes familiar stories from unfamiliar points of view, highlighting heroes with disabilities. Her own experience with partial paraplegia has shown her you don't have to be able to swing a sword to save the day.

When she's not writing she's reading, and when she's not reading she's playing video games.

She lives in Denver with her very tall husband, their book loving progeny, and a lazy black monster masquerading as a service dog.

Visit Kendra at
www.kendramerritt.com

facebook.com/kendramerrittauthor

goodreads.com/kendramerritt

instagram.com/kendramerrittauthor

tiktok.com/@kendramerrittauthor